THE TIME LIZARD'S ARCHAEOLOGIST

THE TIME LIZARD'S ARCHAEOLOGIST

Trisha Hanifin

A catalogue record of this book is available from the National Library of New Zealand.

First published in 2021
Published by Cloud Ink Press Ltd, Auckland
P.O. Box 8988, Symonds Street, Auckland, 1150
www.cloudink.co.nz

ISBN 978-0-473-57891-6

The novel is a work of fiction; all characters and all dialogue are the product of the writer's imagination.

Cover design: Amandine Riera
(Sandra Morris Illustration Agency — illustration.co.nz)

Internal design and typesetting: Craig Violich — cvdgraphics.nz

Printed by Ligare, Auckland

For Jillian Green, Anne Lester and Claudia Goerke.
Three friends who each in their own way supported
and encouraged my writing.

Part One: Blue Marble

Jason – Helene – Jenny

Everyone has three mothers: archetypal mother – cultural ideas and patterns of mothering we inherit, including our concepts and intuitions of mother earth, female gods, saints or holy women; our actual physical, human mother with all her positive and negative qualities, her strengths, her flaws; and the mother we as a particular individual need or long for.

(Doctor Jason Winston, Lecture to psychology students on Jungian archetypes, Auckland 2010.)

JASON

Auckland 2036

Sometimes I think I've spent my life learning how to change gear, to shift from one state of consciousness to another. And sometimes I think I've fallen into a no-man's land, and I've spent my life wandering, ghost-like and grieving, unable to find my way home.

Every morning when I wake I search for anchors: an image, a sound, a smell, a touch remembered from the intensity of the sensual world. I reach for my slice of obsidian on the bedside table and hear again the imperious command of my mother's voice, see the sunlit halo of my baby sister Helene's auburn curls, feel the seal of my father's warmth as he stands behind me and puts his hand on my shoulder. I recall the smell of bull kelp left behind on the rocks as the tide recedes and feel the slap of hot black sand against the soles of my bare feet. I conjure up these fragments of the past and then, for pleasure, gather more: the shimmer of blue silk sliding like water across my wife Jenny's skin, the hearth-feel of my nephew Liam's small body tucked against my own, the humming sound he makes as he falls asleep; the wraith-mist rising from the surf, and the tawny fronds of toetoe clumped together and rustling in front of the sand dunes. I sink, I rise, I excavate memories, I gather myself in.

Every morning, I blink and blink again, catching myself in reflection in time's reptilian eye, delving into and out of the layers of my mind.

I close my eyes. I'm ten years old. In my mother's study is a poster of 'Blue Marble', that famous photo of the blue and white water-filled globe taken by the Apollo 17 crew in 1972 as they left the Earth's orbit on their way to the moon. It's the first colour photo of the Earth seen in full view. Underneath the image my mother, Anastasia, a scholar of ancient Greece, has written the words of Anaximenes, one of the Milesian philosophers she loved: *Just as our soul, being air, holds us together, so do breath and air encompass the whole world.* It's the first time I've seen that photo of the Earth and it's the most beautiful thing I've ever seen.

I blink. I shift again: I'm timeless, formless, neither awake nor asleep. I discard the present like an overcoat, allow myself to sink into memories and images bigger and greater than myself. I'm the time lizard's archaeologist: there's a valley with a river winding through it – the riverbed's wide and stony and full of water from melted snow; small settlements are scattered across the land; high up in the valley, close to the bottom of a mountain range, the most distant village glistens in the early morning sun – seventy round huts with thatched roofs, a wooden bridge over the narrowest part of the river, black and white goats grazing on scrubby foothills, the rounded humps of twenty or so beehives clustered in a sloping field rich with clover; a woman, her dark hair in a single braid down her back, stands outside one of the huts, a blue shawl draped across her shoulders; although the sun's out and the sky's clear, it's very cold; steam rises from the ground, from the goats as they move across the hills, and from the woman as she stamps her goatskin boots on the ground to keep warm.

I blink. I open my eyes. I re-enter the present. I breathe. I close my eyes again. In my mind I see my mother – she lies adrift in a rowing boat, like a pre-Raphaelite painting of the Lady of Shallott, her thick white hair unravelling on her shoulders, her pale-green dress wet and clinging to her still powerful body. She has drowned, in spite of her prowess as a swimmer.

Finally, there's enough of me assembled to recognise myself. I'm Jason Philip Winston, born 1962, psychoanalyst and dream therapist. I work with images from the unconscious and the feelings and sensations that accompany them. My parents, Anastasia and Samuel, are both dead. My sister, Helene has passed too; she married my best friend, David. They had two boys, Sam and Liam. I married Jenny, a respected environmental architect. I say these things to lay bare my connections, to piece together who I am.

This is how we wake every morning: we throw out the net and go fishing, we draw ourselves up, we draw ourselves in. Layer by layer, we drag a sense of ourselves out of the ocean of the unconscious, out of memory, out of our dreaming selves. Out of our collective psychic inheritance.

And the older I get the longer it takes to arrive at the necessary level of the present. I'm not sure whether more of me is now submerged, or that, after so many years of delving and digging and sifting, the depths have risen closer to the surface.

I've heard it said that in the past Jewish Rabbis used to say a dream that's not recalled won't come to pass. But is the opposite true? What if too much is recalled, and too much comes to pass? And is that recollection of the dreaming world the path to insight and wisdom, or is it the problem – the road to madness, the road to hell? That great god western science tells us we dream three or four times a night, that there are changes in brain physiology when we dream, that there's a shift in how the brain works. The dreaming brain is different from the conscious one.

There's a shift.

When I was growing up, Anastasia liked to explain that the Milesians were interested in first principles, the origins of all things. After dinner she would place her knife and fork together on her plate, wipe her lips with the corner of her napkin, and say in the same authoritative voice she used to teach at university: What could be more important than first principles? What could be more important than the origins of all things?

As soon as Anastasia started asking rhetorical questions, Helene would shrink in her chair and ask to be excused. I stayed until the end, my legs pressed against the wooden rungs of the dining table chair. I watched the expressions on my mother's face, her finger stabbing the air as she made a point, her neck flushing beneath her tan when she became animated. As a small boy I'd imagined her riding in a golden chariot, like the one Zeus drove in my illustrated book on the gods of Olympus.

My favourite story of hers as a child was about Thales – the most famous Milesian philosopher and one of the founders of western science – using his own shadow to measure height and distance. Apparently, he was asked by the Pharaoh of Egypt to calculate the height of one of the great pyramids. He did so by measuring the pyramid's shadow at the exact moment when his own shadow was the same height as himself. As I got older I always wondered at what point did Thales realise his shadow was an instrument of such accuracy.

First principles, the origins of all things – that's a hell of a thing to be interested in. Whenever I think about Anastasia and the Milesians I return to Blue Marble and to my ten-year-old self, standing in my mother's study while she was away somewhere else. I was overwhelmed by that image and the space it created in me; understanding, even at that age, I could never go back and not know what it was like to see the Earth from the outside. Realising, although I've never been able to put it into words adequately, that what I perceived through my physical senses was flawed. Unreliable. The real world was this extraordinary thing, hanging in space like a jewel.

One evening in 1979 when I was seventeen, I came home late from the library. My parents sat side by side at the kitchen table. Samuel had his dark glasses on and Anastasia was reading to him from her latest article on Anaximander in *The Classic Quarterly*. One of her hands was stretched out towards him and Samuel's long, thin fingers lay over hers. It wasn't until she turned her head as I entered the kitchen that I saw her eyes were red and swollen from crying. She nodded at me and continued reading.

I listened for a while. Her article was about Anaximander's use of the principle of sufficient reason – a principle to explain why the world floated free in space and didn't fall. It was a scholarly article, referring to all the preceding commentaries, highlighting obscure philosophical points. My attention floated above and around what she was saying. I'd begun reading psychology and was now more interested in Freud, Adler and Jung.

I looked at my father – really looked at him. In the past year he'd lost weight and suffered from increasingly frequent and severe migraines. His cheeks were pale, his skin stretched tightly across his cheekbones. His hair was thin and grey. Wraparound sunglasses swamped his face. Beside him on the table lay a large brown envelope and the stiff dark plastic of X-rays. His hand on Anastasia's was gentle, softly stroking a small section of skin as she read.

I left the kitchen and walked quietly upstairs. Helene's door was closed and I guessed she was already asleep.

My bedroom felt small, airless. I opened the window, leaned against the sill and gazed out over the garden. It was spring and the streetlight beside the fence lit up the cherry tree, heavy with pink blossom.

Inside me there was a shift. As if I'd fallen down a lift shaft, or been shot into outer space way beyond Blue Marble, and some other being had taken my place by the window. I watched from a thousand miles away, as everything in the world changed gear: the cherry tree, the garden, the house, sleeping Helene, Samuel and Anastasia holding hands at the kitchen table, all of them spinning in empty space. And I couldn't remember how everything didn't fall apart.

I shut the window, closed the curtains and lay down. I curled up and pulled the covers over my legs. In the darkness I clutched a pillow to my chest.

One night, not long before my father died in December 1980, I came upon my parents as they danced together in the kitchen to his favourite piece of music, 'Moonlight Serenade'.

My father's cheek rested against my mother's. He was as delicate as a leaf and she held him, allowing him to rest in her arms. Her hair was loose; it lay on her shoulders and shone pale gold in the lamplight. She wore a knee-length green dress with a row of sunflowers around the hem. They danced in slow motion in the centre of the kitchen.

I went upstairs and knocked on Helene's bedroom door. She lay on top of her bedspread in her dressing gown, reading. I leaned against her desk.

'What's up Sis?'

She stared at me then returned to her book.

I sat on the desk and counted to ten.

She threw the book across the room.

'I hate her,' she said.

I blink, I open my eyes. I close them. Does it make a difference? Am I awake or dreaming? The net is flung out across the tide and the catch hauled in. I'm awash with memories, and with visions, only some of which seem to have anything to do with me. All my life I've felt I was either losing my grip or having a breakthrough. I've watched all those grainy black and white films about Jung and listened to interviews with him, followed his explanations of dreams and the unconscious, heard what others said about his ability to access images, his belief that images are sovereign in the mind, that the only way you can deal with the unconscious is through image. But words are all I've ever had and they're a poor substitute.

It's one thing to work with other people's dreams and visions, to help them understand them, and yet keep a distance, maintain a barrier, make distinctions between the conscious and unconscious mind, and quite another to be plunged into that vast ocean on your own, to be drowning instead of swimming, to know you control nothing: your mind is just a conduit for something much greater. But it's all I've ever had, except for that one extraordinary image: Blue Marble. That blue and white jewel hanging in space. In the end, almost everything goes back to the moment when I first saw it in my mother's study – she wasn't there and my mind imploded.

JASON

Auckland 2016

On Monday afternoon after I'd said goodbye to my last patient, I felt breathless, dizzy. I sat on the floor of my office with my back against the wall. My eyes were itchy, my mouth dry. Paralysis crept up my body like a noxious vine. It started in my feet, moved up my calves and thighs to my hips, into my belly and up to my chest, wrapping itself around me, preventing me from moving. I tried to wriggle my toes, stretch out my legs, but the only movement I could make was to raise my hand to my face. My skin felt thick. Damp. I slid sideways across the floor.

I saw Anastasia's large, capable hands. They were wet. Light reflected off her gold wedding ring. In the distance there was a rhythmic banging. Triangles of light hovered in the air and a patch of green and yellow light patterned the floor by my feet. It hurt to breathe. There was no feeling in my arms or fingers. The banging grew louder, so loud it sounded like helicopter blades beating directly above me, beating the air into a whirlwind that lifted me like a twig then dropped me into open space.

Thoughts that didn't seem to belong to me danced past, memories darted in and out. I caught hold of a late summer afternoon in 1970. Helene and I lay face down on the riverbank, watching the quick flicker of trout dart across the shallow water of the riverbed, seeking safety in deeper pools of shaded water. The fish were elegant and shadowy as dreams. The two of us spent hours watching but were never fast enough to catch one.

The memory vanished. A rumbling sound, like thunder, filled the room. The image of an old man in a monk's brown robe came to me then, as it often did when panic and paralysis threatened. The monk was solid, stocky, with large hands and bunches of dried herbs tied to the rope around his waist. He sprinkled a circle of ash on the ground, raised his right hand as if to bestow a blessing then turned and walked towards a grove of cork-oak trees. I'd named him Anselmo and whispered, 'Protect me.'

I stayed curled on the floor waiting for my heart to slow and my breath to steady, for feeling to return to my arms and legs. Waiting to come back … but from where?

That night I dreamed I was in a boat, whale watching. Helene stood in the centre of the boat with her back to the whales. Her eyes were closed as if she was sleeping or in a trance. Once the boat was out in open water, I went over and put my arm around her shoulders. We saw the whales surfacing, pushing themselves up from the seabed, coming up for air then diving back down, full of grace and ease in the water. Helene and I stood together and waited for the moment the whales slapped their tails on the surface of the sea.

I left Helene to get my waterproof camera. When I came back she'd gone. She was sinking, her auburn hair loose about her face, her orange shirt billowing above the narrow legs of her brown trousers. Seconds later she'd disappeared and all I could see were her clothes, floating between the whales like strangely shaped autumn leaves. I lowered myself into the water, searched for her, but all I captured on film were the huge dark sides of the whales and tiny, brightly striped fish.

Then I was on dry land, watching a swarm of bees. More and more bees joined the swarm, darkening the skyline behind my house. They flew closer, and the air filled with a sound like thunder. The bees were the colour and shape of bumblebees; they began to grow until each insect was the size of my hand. For the split second before they bashed into my face and neck, I thought how magnificent they were. I raised my hands to protect my face, dropped to the ground and curled into foetal position. I could hear them above me, gaining strength – thousands of hives must have emptied and their bees were now a few inches above me, a mass of sting-infested rage.

When I woke I wrote this in my journal:

These are the things I know, even though many of them make no sense: my mother's spirit still dominates me; whales dive and surface; bees are out there somewhere, gathering; Helene's in danger but I can't reach her; and I'm falling, sliding out of control, my conscious mind taken over by my dreaming mind – I'm swirling in a pool of images and dreams, hallucinations and fears. In the past I've been able to distance myself, work with them as if they belonged to someone else, but that's slipping away; most of the time now I'm just swimming in a sea of panic. I cling to Jenny, and to my own work. I've told no one about these incidents of panic and paralysis. I know I too am in danger, not just Helene. Yet I remain silent, unable to explain, even to myself, why.

The following Tuesday and Wednesday nights I slid between sleep and dreams and wakefulness, but mainly inhabited another state I didn't know how to define or name except to call it 'the shift'. I had a constant sense of vertigo. Sometimes it felt like I was being pushed in one direction, then I lurched backwards or sideways in another.

A vision kept occurring: I was circling the once beautiful blue and white globe in a spaceship that looked like a silver spider. But now the Earth had lost its cover of blue and white, its oceans and clouds. It was wrapped in brown and black smoke, as if fire had consumed everything – the forests and oceans, the snow-tipped mountains and the lakes and rivers that lay beneath them.

I was protected in the spacecraft: there was oxygen, water, and aluminium tubes of concentrated protein; vegetables fresh from the hydroponic garden; vitamins, and tonics full of iron, if I needed them. Each night I slept for exactly eight hours strapped in a narrow bunk. When I woke, I was alert and ready to work.

Every few hours, updates flashed on screens embedded in the walls on each deck: how many kilometres travelled; how much fuel was needed for the next hundred cycles and how much was left; the amount of water being used and recycled; the signals coming back from the surface. I read the incoming data and recorded notes in the ship's log three times a day.

I was absorbed in my work, searching the surface for signs of life, watching for a sudden flare of light or fire; waiting for clouds of toxic smoke to part so I could track the progress of the thin trail of water that snaked across the planet.

After each episode of this vision I went into my study to write it down but the more I tried to capture the details the more mysterious they became. The central thread of narrative that had seemed so obvious was now hidden by flickering shadows. Something was happening just out of sight: a murmur of conversations above or below my level of hearing; a flash of light or colour slipping past me as quickly as the movement of a young trout. There was the background humming of worker bees doing search-and-return forays into the manuka bushes at the edge of the neighbour's garden and an unfamiliar exotic vine growing wild over our shared wooden fence. When I finally gave up and stopped trying to record and understand the details, I realised that while I was on the spacecraft I felt nothing – I was entirely absorbed in my tasks – and I had to ask myself why I felt so numb circling the once so vibrant and fertile, and now so damaged, Earth.

Thursday was my half-day and after morning sessions were over, instead of writing up my notes, going out for coffee and a walk as I usually did, I sat on the office couch and stared out the window onto the street. I drifted and dozed, fell into deeper sleep then woke with a start. I was floating in a terrain of images that spoke to me, but in language I couldn't interpret. I observed myself on the spaceship, sitting by the viewing window. The heavy layers of toxic smoke had parted, exposing sections of the surface. Powerful cameras were operating, relaying images to the screen on the wall opposite me. I looked at the almost waterless landmass of Australia and then, as the ship moved on, at sections of seabed, areas of dried out, low-lying land that had once been covered by the ocean. Just before smoke covered everything again, I saw a patch of muddy blue. It was the size of a large lake and I realized it was all that was left of the Pacific Ocean. I recorded the data, adding it to the intricate water map I was making. I was completely caught up in this task of recording and mapping the water on the planet. Once it was done I watched myself lie down on my bunk and close my eyes. And then, in a state of confusion and exhaustion, I stretched out on the couch in the office and finally went to sleep.

On Friday, I woke in the pre-dawn greyness thinking about my patients and the dreams they'd told me over the years, many of them about water. The lucky ones came to the end of their therapy and surfed or swam through its many forms with ease. They played with dolphins, floated on their backs down rivers with sunlight playing on their closed eyelids; they paddled in the shallows with grandparents or children. The not so lucky ones stood on cliffs and shorelines overwhelmed by the size of the waves coming in, wondering when the next one would rise up and destroy them, or they sank into the murky depths of seas so vast they feared they'd never find their way back to the surface.

It's the sea they returned to. Always the sea.

I thought about my own love affair with the ocean: the heat of the sand on the soles of my feet, sunlight bouncing on my shoulders as I dived, the world hissing and singing when I resurfaced, the ripe, fishy smell of seaweed, the smooth, warm surface of driftwood against the palm of my hand.

All those millennia as sea creatures before we crawled onto dry land.

I turned on my side and, like a child, imagined my arms turned into fins and my legs merged into something resembling a mermaid's tail.

I slid out of bed, tucked the duvet around Jenny's back so she wouldn't get cold, pulled on a sweatshirt and socks and went to my study.

All that history in the ocean: the call of the ancestors and the weight of the past.

Wave after wave carrying us back.

In 2006 a woman came to see me. She'd been recovering from a dreadful car accident. Her legs had been smashed and she was facing the prospect of spending the rest of her life in a wheelchair. Since her accident she'd dreamed she was a dolphin. She described in great detail the barnacle encrusted bottoms of boats gliding above her, the sleek grace of her body, the feel of water against her skin as she played in the surf or swam in deep water.

Three years later her husband died of cancer and she'd come to share one last dream: she and her husband swam together in clear blue water, she said, rolling and diving through shoals of angel fish. During his treatment her husband had lost all his hair and in the dream his head was as smooth and waterproof as her own dolphin skin and his skin was the fresh lime-green of new oak leaves. I asked if she'd grown up on the coast. No, she'd said, inland – her childhood had been spent on a farm in Central Otago.

Jenny appeared in the doorway of the study, her eyes still puffy from sleep. Her blue silk robe covered matching pyjamas. In the early morning light, the fabric shimmered like water. She rubbed her forehead, ran her fingers through her short dark hair exposing streaks of grey I hadn't noticed before.

'Sorry, did I wake you?'

She yawned and rolled her shoulders. 'You were talking in your sleep again.'

I put my pen down and closed my journal. 'Gobbledygook or something interesting?'

She came over to the desk and touched my cheek with the back of her hand. A trace of orange and vanilla perfume lingered on her skin from the hand cream she used every night.

'Maybe you should take a break,' she said. 'I could get a few days off work. We could take the dogs and go up north for a long weekend.'

I held her hand against the base of my throat. 'I'm fine, just a bit tired that's all.'

She kissed the top of my head. 'Okay, but any more broken sleep and I'm sending you to the doctor for a check-up.'

HELENE

Auckland 2016

Helene pulled the curtains across the three oblong windows that looked out over the garden. All morning the light had been so bright it seemed to burn her unprotected face and stab at her eyes. Even with the curtains drawn, sticky blotches of red and green disrupted her vision, silent but painful explosions of colour that stopped her working. She sat at the piano and spread her fingers above the keys. Her hands and wrists felt swollen, her fingertips numb. She closed her eyes and let her hands fall, producing a series of minor chords, unable to pick out the melody that lay behind the swirling colours jangling in her head.

She closed the piano and rested her head on the lid. Words danced in her mind: Cassandra, Casablanca, castanet; elephant, oligarchy, oleander; diamante, diaphanous, discord...

The phone in the kitchen rang. She stood up too quickly and felt dizzy. She stepped towards the door. Just as the answering service clicked on she collapsed on the floor.

'Hey, Sis, it's me, Jason. Haven't seen you for a while. Be good to catch up soon. Say hi to David and the boys. Will try again later. Ciao.'

She lay on the back seat of the car. Her red and green rug had fallen onto the floor. She tried to lift it but it slipped from her fingers and slid under the seat.

The doors were locked. Rain burst against the windows. It sounded like someone throwing stones at her. She curled into a tight ball and sucked her thumb. She was cold but soon fell asleep. When she woke again her mother, Anastasia, was back, carrying two large, wet bags of groceries.

Anastasia picked her rug up from the floor; flicked it like a tea towel then put it back over Helene's lap. The wet grocery bags dripped rainwater onto the seat and floor. Icy trickles seeped under her legs and soaked the side of her tartan skirt.

'I'm cold, Mama.'

Anastasia sighed. She got into the driver's seat and ran her fingers through her wet hair.

Helene watched drops of water fall from her mother's hair onto the shoulders of her orange coat as she turned on the heater then wound the window down a couple of inches.

A tail of wind crept around Helene's neck and arms.

Anastasia lit a cigarette.

'Mama, it's cold.' Helene started to cry.

Anastasia didn't turn her head. She took a deep drag on her cigarette. 'Stop that,' she said. 'Just you stop that.'

Helene opened her eyes. She was lying on the living room floor a few feet away from the piano, curled on her side, her head cushioned on her arm and elbow. Her mouth was sticky, her lips bruised. She sat up and looked at the mother-of-pearl clock on the mantelpiece. Three o'clock. How long has she been on the floor? The pain in her eyes had gone and her head was curiously light and blank. Her mind was like a breakfast table someone had come in and cleared while she'd been away, the crumbs gone, the surface wiped, the dishes removed and stacked somewhere out of sight in a room close by. A room she didn't need to worry about, one she could enter later when she had more focus, more energy.

When she stood up she realised her skirt was damp. Her hand flew to her mouth and she bit hard on her index finger. Not again, she whispered. No. Not again.

She turned and crouched down. A stain of urine was still on the polished wooden floor. Thank heaven Sam and Liam hadn't come home from school and found her there.

What had she had been doing? The curtains were drawn and the piano lid closed – why had she been in here if not to sit at the piano and work? What came back to her was the headache she'd woken up with, the stabbing pain in her eyes and temples, the nausea that came when she went downstairs to make breakfast for David, Sam and Liam and the agony of the bright morning light flooding through the windows.

Her headaches were increasingly severe, her vision disturbed by lights and shadows, but Doctor Mercer said they were just migraines, all too common in women her age.

'But I've had migraines all my life,' Helene had said at her last consultation two weeks ago. 'These are – these are different.'

Doctor Mercer had patted her hand. 'I'll increase your medication. Give it three months. If it doesn't help we'll send you for tests.'

Upstairs she showered and changed into clean clothes. She blow-dried her faded auburn hair and pulled it into a ponytail. Her face in the bathroom mirror was pale, her hazel eyes staring back as if she was a stranger. Behind her she saw a shadowed outline. It swooped and settled, morphing into her mother. Anastasia leant against Helene's bedroom door, smoking a cigarette. Her disappointed voice echoed in Helene's head: Toughen up. Don't be such a bloody baby.

After Anastasia had dropped her at the school gate Helene walked up the concrete path to the playground. Some of the bigger girls were playing on the monkey bars, swinging from rung to rung, their maroon kilts swishing around their thighs and knees. The bell rang. One by one they let go and jumped onto the grass. No one fell over or got hurt. They walked smoothly although their bare legs were flushed with red blotches.

During sport Mrs Thoady would haul Helene up and tell her to hold onto the bars.

'Now, Helene,' she'd say, 'don't be a baby. Let go one hand and reach out for the next rung. Then just repeat that and swing along to the end, just like Marcia.'

Marcia was bigger and had stronger arms. She could do forward and backward rolls, handstands, jump on the springboard and leap over the wooden horse in the gymnasium. Helene sought out the library and the music room and avoided the playground. Miss Livingstone let her curl up on the cushions in the corner and read or practise her recorder.

Before she followed the other girls into class, Helene went to the toilet block at the end of the corridor. Instead of being wedged open with a small piece of wood as it usually was, the outer door was closed. She put her satchel down on the floor and tried to push it open. The door was shiny and heavy and wouldn't move. She crossed her legs and pushed again, trying to hold on. She hit the door with the palm of her hand.

The hotness ran down her legs and splashed her white socks and polished black shoes.

She heard a door open and close.

She took off her wet knickers and used them to wipe at the puddle on the floor, then rolled them into a soggy ball and put them at the bottom of her bag. Her socks squelched in her shoes as she walked back along the corridor, holding her skirt down with her hand.

When she refused to take her turn on the monkey bars after lunch Mrs Thoady marched towards her. Helene ran across the asphalt and hid in the long grass at the far edge of the playground. She kicked off her shoes and spread her socks out beside them. They'd been clean this morning and now they were stained and smelly. Anastasia would be cross.

She made a nest in the prickly grass, lay on her back and looked at the sky. In the distance she could hear the shrieks and shouts of the other girls playing on the bars. She heard the bell and then it was quiet except for birds chirping and the occasional car driving up the road.

She closed her eyes.

She and Miss Livingstone were playing chopsticks on the piano together. Then they were playing their recorders in the music room while the other children played outside, pretending to be airplanes that swooped and dived. She and Miss Livingstone finished playing and ate cake made from oranges with hundreds and thousands sprinkled on the top. They drank from special cups made from magnolia petals. Miss Livingstone held her hand and, unlike Anastasia, spoke encouragingly to her in a warm, quiet voice.

The following morning Helene woke with a clear head. David was still asleep. He lay on his back with one arm flung behind his head, his dark hair crumpled against the white pillowcase. She moved her head carefully from side to side. No pain. No nausea. Even though David was due to fly to Hong Kong at 11am it was going to be a good day.

She stretched, enjoying the release of tension in her arms and legs. Her hands were a little stiff but, thankfully, yesterday's numbness had gone. Once she'd dropped the boys at school and David at the airport, she'd do the grocery shopping and go to the plant barn for potting mix. By midday she'd be back home and then have all afternoon to work.

In the darkened bedroom with the heavy curtains still drawn so David could sleep for another half hour, she walked across the thick carpet rubbing the pale skin on her arms and shoulders with the palms of her hands, her ankle-length white cotton nightdress swishing against her legs. She moved carefully in the dark, reaching for her dressing gown, brushing her hair back into her usual ponytail.

Downstairs, she made breakfast for David, Sam and Liam in the pre-dawn greyness. The freshness of the early morning was soothing. The sky was overcast, the light gentle on her eyes. She hummed a new melody to herself, letting her mind explore its contours and trajectories as she scrambled eggs and put bread in the toaster. She prepared coffee for David, tea for herself and hot chocolate for the boys.

'Hurry up,' she called up the stairs, 'I have to get your father to the airport by nine o'clock.'

At the airport drop off, David gave her a hug and kissed her on the forehead. 'I'll ring as soon as I've checked into the hotel,' he said.

'Once you're back we should have Jason and Jenny round.'

David grabbed his bag from the boot. He leant in the passenger window. 'I'm very fond of Jason but give me a few days to recover first.'

'Godspeed,' she said, and watched until the automatic doors opened and he stepped inside.

Back home she made coffee and a sandwich and sat at the kitchen table reading the newspaper. Even though it was late April, the weather was still mild and she had the back door open. When she looked up she could see the branches of the birch and poplar trees at the end of the garden moving in the breeze, some of the leaves still green, some beginning to turn brown or gold. She let her mind drift, hoping that, without conscious effort, the melody that had come to her this morning would return and defeat the swarm of images and memories that so often overtook her these days.

Unwanted images flashed in her mind, draining her energy: her father riding a bicycle and carrying a parcel of fresh fish wrapped in newspaper under one arm; her mother wearing a pleated blue skirt and white sleeveless blouse, teaching the tango to their next door neighbours, first taking the woman's part then the man's so the couple could practise the dance properly; she and Jason lying on the dusty warm earth overlooking the river, hoping to spot a brown trout, rather than eels that moved lazily between tree roots; sitting at the piano, playing 'Moonlight Serenade' for her father, his eyes hidden behind dark glasses, his left foot tapping in time to the music; lying on the bathroom floor with a towel wrapped around her wrist to stop the blood seeping onto the white tiled floor.

Now she saw fish, floating belly up in the stream that ran from the back of their current property into the river that had bordered her first home in Nelson. She began to count them. Soon an avalanche of dead fish flowed past her and she started to panic. Then Jason was beside her, collecting the fish, organising them into piles according to type – see, he was saying to her, these are snapper and these are cod, and those ones are hāpuka; all along the riverbank he walked, absorbed in organising and categorising fish. But why are they here, she shouted after him, they don't belong in the river, they should be in the sea.

Her body jerked; her eyes flew open. She was in the kitchen and the phone was ringing. She waited for the answering machine to pick up. If it was Jason, she'd ring him straight back.

'Hi, Mrs Campbell, this is Celia, the School administrator – just a reminder about the parent-teachers meeting tomorrow at 4.30. Thanks.'

In the afternoon she tried to work on her new composition but her hands kept returning to 'Moonlight Serenade' and the arrangement she'd played at her father's memorial service. He taught her to play a simplified version on the piano when she was eleven and she'd been developing arrangements ever since, returning to the sensuous, dreamy sadness of the music again and again. They both preferred it as an instrumental although sometimes her father sang the lyrics to her mother as they danced together in the living room.

Her father had played it on the stereo the night her mother returned home from her Churchill Scholarship. It was the only time she remembered seeing them dance in the kitchen. His cheek was resting against hers, his dark glasses protecting his eyes from the glare of the electric lights as they swayed together on the linoleum. Later, when they thought Helene was upstairs getting ready for bed, he told Anastasia what the doctor had said the day before and showed her the sheets of X-rays. A year at most, he'd said in a matter-of-fact tone, and she'd heard her mother's response: Goodness, darling, as long as that?

The last time he'd visited the specialist there had been no other patients in the waiting room and the receptionist had come and sat beside her and chatted about her studies. She asked her what she wanted to do when she left school.

'I'm going to study music,' Helene said.

'Well, good for you.' The receptionist patted her hand. She stood up, smoothed her skirt and returned to her desk. 'You know', she said, 'I can tell your father's very proud of you.' She straightened some files, sharpened a pencil and wound fresh paper into her typewriter. Without looking at Helene, she said, 'And your mother, when does she return?'

Helene put her finger in the magazine to mark her place. 'Tomorrow night.'

'Well that's good now, isn't it?' the receptionist said. 'She'll be able to look after things from now on.'

The door opened and her father and the specialist came out. When they said goodbye, the specialist gripped her father's hand and, instead of shaking it firmly the way men usually did, he held it for a few moments in both of his own as if he didn't want to let go. A large brown envelope was tucked under her father's arm.

'Call me any time,' the specialist said.

David rang just after midnight. She'd been standing in the dark with her back to the piano looking out the living room windows, listening to Chopin's Etude in A Minor on the concert programme. The music and the darkness calmed her and slowed her thoughts. If the music was powerful enough she got a few hours' respite, and the tightness round her temples eased a little.

She turned the radio off. 'How was the flight?'

'Better than usual,' David said, 'there were empty seats so I was able to stretch out and get some sleep. How was your day?'

'I worked a little, then some gardening.'

'How's the head?'

Helene kicked off her shoes and lay on the couch. 'A headache-free zone today.'

'All the same,' David said, 'when I get back next week I think we should see a specialist.'

Helene smiled. 'What would Dr Mercer say to that? Indulging your wife's hypochondria?'

'He should have referred you months ago, Hel. He's an old fool.'

'He's looked after me since I was seven.'

'Exactly – he treats you like a child.'

Helene rubbed the faint scars on her wrist against her cheek and changed the subject. 'So, you have meetings all day tomorrow then?'

The next afternoon she put on track pants and one of David's old shirts, took her hat and gardening gloves and went to the back of the garden to pull weeds and sort the last of the bulbs for next spring. It had rained during the night and underneath the trees near the stream the ground was still damp. A mulch of fallen leaves was beginning to form around the base of the trees. A cool, spicy smell rose from the soil.

She wondered how full the stream was after the rain and climbed down the slope to check. Even though she hadn't woken with a headache – the second day in a row without one, and surely that was a good sign – she moved carefully, aware her peripheral vision was limited.

On her right a shadow moved. It was the shape of a large cat. She took off her hat and turned to see if it was Molly, the neighbour's large tabby. The shadow flew at her face. She cried out. Her foot slipped. She tumbled backwards, raising her arms up and out to cushion her fall. The creature clung to her face. She tried to pull it off her eyes and mouth. The back of her head hit a rock. Pain exploded in the base of her skull.

She curled over in the shallow water: 'Moonlight Serenade' was playing in the bedroom; she crouched in the corner of the bathroom clutching a dark green towel, trying to ride her nausea: her father's face floated above her, his thin grey hair stuck to his forehead; Jason stood beside him, his face white and doughy as flour.

There was blood in the water, the warm metallic taste of it in her mouth. It was impossible to turn over now, her arms and legs were weighted, too heavy to move. She called out to her father but he floated away from her, his eyes closed, his hands folded across his chest. Her lungs filled with water. A final image filled her mind. She was small, three or four years old, sitting on the black sand at Muriwai looking up at her mother's back. Anastasia was standing in front of the waves; she was a large, dark shadow blocking the sunlight. The sea was a sheet of blue water, its edges embroidered with white foam.

JASON

Two weeks later

Light rain dampened the shoulders of the two gravediggers shovelling soil back into the opened earth. I zipped up my jacket and put my hands in my pockets. Anastasia's turquoise and silver ring rolled against my fingers. David had given it to me just before the service. 'Helene never wore it, you know,' he said.

David's eyes were red-rimmed; his mouth collapsed in on itself as if, overnight, he'd lost all his teeth. 'It was too big for her,' he said. 'Your mother had hands like a man's.'

The chunky triangle of turquoise encased in silver dug into the palm of my hand. Everyone else had gone. Jenny had taken David, Sam, Liam and the others back to the house for afternoon tea. She'd organised everything yesterday, leaving me with nothing to do but to stand with a glass of chardonnay in one hand and a mushroom savoury in the other, listening, as aunts and cousins, friends and neighbours discussed their theories about the cause of Helene's death.

At the inquest the coroner stated accidental drowning, although he questioned David, and Helene's doctor, at length. Had she complained to them of severe headaches or hallucinations? The autopsy had discovered a tumour on her brain.

Doctor Mercer's suit and manners had been formal, his voice calm. The symptoms she'd presented were classic migraine, he said. He'd been treating her for that. Nothing Mrs Campbell said at her last appointment indicated anything was out of the usual.

David sat with his head in his hands. 'I should have been there,' he kept saying, 'I should have been there.'

I listened to what little evidence there was of Helene's state of mind in the weeks before her death. I took notes out of habit, a semblance of detachment and focus, but, in reality, I was holding my breath behind clamped teeth, trying to rein in rising panic. As Doctor Mercer finished his summary of Helene's medical history I saw a ginger cat curled up in the corner of the room. I dropped my pen and bent to pick it up. My hand was shaking.

Jenny squeezed my arm. 'Are you okay?'

I watched the gravediggers pat down the mound of raised earth with the backs of their shovels. I was trained to listen, especially to what was never said, but all I could hear now was the dull thud of shovels and one of the gravediggers saying to the other, 'Glad there wasn't a bloody downpour.'

In my memory, when I went to identify Helene in the morgue, her eyes were wide and staring, although, if I were to go back and check the facts, her lids must have been closed. But that's how I remembered her. She'd smelt faintly of riverbed and dried mud in spite of being cleaned up by the pathologist's assistant. Her face and shoulders were sickly white, leached of her usual freckles; her lips thin and pressed together. And on her left hand her delicate gold and ruby wedding ring still glowed.

It was true she never wore Anastasia's jewellery, not the turquoise and silver ring, nor the heavy lapis lazuli necklace that was a birthday present from Samuel, just before he died. She hadn't taken any of Anastasia's possessions, not even her collection of silk scarves and shawls. All she'd wanted was a photo of her and Samuel, taken when they were on holiday in Crete when she was fourteen, just before he became ill.

The drizzle finally turned to rain and I drove home. I stood at the kitchen window and imagined it sheeting down on top of the raw soil of Helene's grave, turning everything into a muddy river. In my mind her bleached body transformed itself into a carp; she was a flash of gold swimming through reeds and tree roots.

Jenny offered me a glass of wine but I made a pot of tea instead. She placed the palm of her hand on my shoulder for a moment then went back to their guests. David came in from the living room and sat at the table. He moved a chair beside me and began a hoarse dissection of the last phone conversation he'd had with Helene while he'd been away on business in Hong Kong. I tried to listen but kept losing track. I touched David's arm. 'In those last two weeks, did she mention having any dreams?'

David smoothed the edge of the tablecloth between his fingers, bunched it, smoothed it again. He looked at me through bloodshot eyes. 'Should I have asked her?'

'No. Of course not – I just wondered...'

Later, when the other guests had left, David slumped on the couch with his eyes closed, his head resting against a cushion. Sam was asleep on one side, and wee Liam snuggled into him on the other. Jenny sorted through the photos of Helene they'd displayed on a notice board in the foyer of the funeral parlour. She passed one to me. 'Here's that one of you all in Kaikōura,' she said.

In the photo Anastasia and I stood in the centre of the boat with our arms around each other's shoulders, the huge raised tail of a whale captured in the background; Helene stood to one side, a few inches away from Anastasia. She looked pale and tense. Yet it had been her idea to go on the chartered boat trip out of the harbour to watch the whales. She'd even shouted us our tickets.

I gave the photo back to Jenny. 'I'm never sure why she insisted we go – she didn't like boats; she always got seasick.'

Jenny poured some pinot gris into a glass and handed it to me.

'Anastasia loved seeing the whales,' I said.

I sipped the wine and put the glass on a coaster on the coffee table;

straightened a pile of magazines; moved a vase of pink and white roses a few centimetres to the left; felt every nerve in my body twitch. 'Helene never said a single word the whole time we were on the boat.'

After breakfast the following Saturday Jenny put our two labradors in the back of her station wagon and we drove over to David's. She stayed to help David decide what to do with Helene's clothes while I took Sam and Liam and the dogs out to Muriwai beach.

I drove past the shop selling ice cream, hot chips and coffee, past the almost deserted camping grounds and parked in front of the sand dunes. 'This was your grandmother's favourite beach,' I said. 'She loved the black sand and the wildness of the waves.' I turned to the boys sitting silent in the back seat. 'She body-surfed right into her seventies.'

The dogs squirmed and barked in the back of the car, excited at being at the beach. We let them out and walked through the sand dunes onto the long, wide stretch of dark sand. It was Sam's ninth birthday. He hadn't spoken all morning and now he marched ahead, throwing tennis balls for the dogs.

Liam, three years younger, reached up and took my hand. 'Why was Mummy in the creek, Uncle Jason? She didn't like swimming. She liked being in the garden and playing the piano.' The boy stopped walking and looked up at me, his eyes screwed up against the sunlight. 'Did they dry her hair afterwards? She wouldn't like it dripping down her back onto her clothes.'

The next day I drove out west again, this time bypassing Muriwai. I stopped on the main street in Helensville for a take-out coffee and a newspaper then carried on to Shelly Beach. The tide was high, and, for once, the autumn winds had dropped and the water was smooth and calm. I sat in the car with the windows down looking out at the water, listening to the concert programme on the car radio. I tried to keep my mind as blank and unruffled as the surface of the water but images of

Helene rose like gulls lifting and tipping on a thermal. At first it was her auburn hair, her loose curls swirling around her shoulders as she danced barefoot on the grass in Albert Park that summer afternoon she first met David – I had introduced them. They'd liked each other instantly, and ignored me for the rest of the afternoon. More painful was an earlier memory, two weeks after our father's funeral, just before her sixteenth birthday. She was lying on the floor in the bathroom, a shock of blood oozing from the paleness of her right wrist onto a green towel, an old razor blade still in her hand. Afterwards, in hospital, she'd told him she meant to cut both wrists but it was so painful and she felt so weak she couldn't manage it. When Anastasia arrived, she'd been furious: How dare you, she'd shouted at Helene from the doorway, how dare you be so selfish!

On the drive home I saw a hawk circling effortlessly above empty paddocks, its serrated wings etched against the setting sun. I slowed down and pulled over to the grass verge to watch the hawk, my breath catching in my throat as it soared and then dived. The light transformed it into a flash of tawny-gold. A stand of poplar trees shimmered like melted butter on the side of the road. Beehives clustered cairn-like in the far edges of the paddocks. I turned the engine off and sat until the light faded from the sky and the hawk flew away with its prey in its claws. Driving home in the dark with the front windows down so I could smell the cooling autumn air as it spread and settled on the still-warm soil, another memory surfaced: I was sitting in my office twenty-two years ago listening to a patient, Stephen, talk about his recurring dream of being a hawk.

The next morning, an hour before my first appointment, I opened the bottom drawer of my old filing cabinet. My hand trembled as I pulled out Stephen's file and I could hear Anastasia's voice admonishing me the way it did when I was a child and wanted to tell her the details of a dream. Concentrate on the important things, things you can prove, she'd say. Don't waste your time in dreamland.

I reminded myself I'd spent most of my life, and all of my career, steadily ignoring her advice and put Stephen's file on my desk. I went to the water dispenser and filled a glass with cold water. Stephen did the same thing at the beginning of each appointment. During our sessions he often picked up his glass and held it to the light as if seeking inspiration in it.

Stephen had been suffering from recurring nightmares that were beginning to affect his work and marriage. At our first appointment he told me his grandfather had suffered from mental illness and spent time in an asylum. He was worried his dreams were the first signs of a congenital madness.

He usually sat on the two-seater leather couch I had then, his jacket folded beside him, his tie loosened, his hands sometimes running through his dark hair. He was a lawyer, an old-fashioned man who worked hard and looked after his family. Nothing in his life had prepared him for the strangeness and intensity of those dreams.

In the beginning, I sat in an armchair beside my desk taking notes, a model of objectivity and professional distance, although, after our first session, I'd asked Stephen's permission to tape the sessions so I could go back and listen to them.

Now, my glass of water within easy reach, I pushed my chair back a little. Breathed in and raised my arms above my head. Breathed out and let my arms fall. My chest and shoulders were tight from too much holding: holding in; holding down; holding on; holding back. My hands were slightly numb. I opened the file and read notes from the first transcript.

I'm in another land, a land so ancient and familiar it has no
name. I dream I'm a hawk – a totem of the village, protector of
the valley, companion to the village witch. An old crone broke
my shell a day early, took me wet and squashed from the egg

*and put me in a human nest. She trained me in the fields above
the valley, by the banks of the river and on the cliffs high above
the caves. She bound me to the village for life. Just before she
died she gave me to the young woman who became her succes-
sor and who feeds me from her own hand. I kill for her, bring
my hunt and drop it at her feet.*

*At dawn, while the villagers sleep in their round thatched
huts and their goats graze out on the hills, I fly above the valley,
checking for intruders and searching for prey. I see the shadow-
men as they stumble out of the caves.*

*I've seen these men before, smelt their scent on the wind. I've
watched them moving in and out of the caves on the other side
of the valley, shovelling coal into wooden carts, hauling them
down to the river. They load it onto flat wooden rafts and carry
it away. I've followed the movement of the rafts on the river,
tracking their journey out of the valley.*

*This morning the shadow-men run like hares, screaming
and wailing. Above their heads they hold flaming torches, dried
rushes bound together and dipped in oil. Water gushes from the
mouth of the cave. The shadow-men shout and fight, chopping
at the water with their shovels. The water's sluggish, full of mud,
but as it rolls out of the cave it flashes with streaks of brown and
gold. Some of the men jump into the river and drown. Some of
them turn and run towards the village. They throw their picks
and shovels in front of them and hurl blazing torches into the
huts.*

*At this point I wake. I lie in bed, shaking, damp with sweat.
It's impossible to go back to sleep. I creep out of bed and walk
through the darkened house, checking the doors and windows,
watching my son sleeping in the small bedroom next to ours.*

I crossed to the window and looked out into the oak leaves. Stephen had come twice a month for three years. Then one day he disappeared. His distressed wife said he went to work as usual one morning and never came home. During the police investigation, and with her consent, I handed his files over to the police. They'd asked if I thought it was normal for a man to have these sorts of dreams and whether Stephen was in sound mind. I'd signed a statement saying Stephen was sane but troubled by recurring nightmares. It was certainly possible Stephen had committed suicide but, if that was so, why had his body never been found?

I went back to my desk and read another dream.

I'm no longer a hawk. Now I'm the witch-woman from the village.

It's dark and I can hear the sound of a river. Cypress trees move in the breeze. I lie on large river stones, still warm from the afternoon sun, their heat seeping into my back. My hawk circles high above.

In the distance, pinpricks of light shimmer. A streak of gold rises into a passageway between sandstone cliffs. It flows into a channel carved into the rock floor by the constant movement of a stream of water. There had been gardens here once, fruit and flowers, and palm trees providing shade from the sun.

On either side of the stream the ground is covered with sand and broken rocks. A snake appears. It advances along the steep slopes of sandstone. Its skin is mottled, a patchwork of brown and gold, its head so large it looks deformed. Sunlight strikes the rocks. The snake's eyes are yellow. It rustles closer; I can hear its skin scraping over sand. A dry, sweet smell is in the air, like baked cinnamon.

The sun disappears behind the cliffs. The snake curls and twists, taking the shape of a burial urn. The sky darkens; the wind returns. The snake's head appears in the rock. It clicks its tongue.

In the distance the hawk calls out a warning. The snake speaks:
Aretis, it says, and the sound of the word echoes in the air.

Smoke fills the sky, casting a shadow across the valley. The
huts in the village are on fire.

This dream disturbs me even more than the first one. I'm
trapped in the woman's body and long to be the hawk again, cir-
cling high above the village watching everything from on high.
In her body there's no distance or detachment, and every sense
is magnified a thousand times.

In the last session we'd had together I abandoned objectivity and told Stephen about an experience I'd had when I was ten years old.

It was summer and we'd been on a camping holiday. One night I couldn't sleep. Everyone else was wrapped in blankets, stretched out on the ground sheet beside me fast asleep. I unzipped the tent and went outside. Above me I saw a trail of shooting stars. When I looked away from the sky and the glitter of stars I felt myself falling in an arc across the surface of the earth. I saw the curve of the hill against the sky. I sank through soil and rock, down to a river that ran like a giant snake through the valley below. In the morning, Anastasia and Samuel found me a few metres from the tent, curled around a rock, my blanket wrapped across my shoulders and head. The soles of my feet were cut and bruised as if I'd walked barefoot across sharp stones.

Stephen had listened, his dark eyes never leaving my face, his pupils dilating when I mentioned the river. We sat in silence for a few minutes then Stephen stood up and walked to the window, resting his forehead against the glass.

I waited, pen poised above my notepad. Stephen eventually turned back to face me but seemed surprised I was still there. He blinked as if he'd just come in from the dark and the light dazzled him.

Over the three years I'd worked with Stephen, I suggested sedatives and sleeping pills, a referral to a hypnotherapist or a neurosurgeon, but

Stephen refused them all. It was enough, he said, to have his dreams discussed and recorded. Perhaps, later, many years later, he said, he would read his notes and discover a logic that was currently invisible to him. A pattern might emerge or something might unfold that would make sense of it all. In the meantime, he said, he just had to ride it out.

The buzzer sounded to announce my first appointment of the day. I closed Stephen's file and slid it into the top drawer of the desk. Rubbing my fingers across my cheek, I checked pen and paper, took a breath, recognised a flutter of panic beneath my ribcage, reminded myself to go back over Stephen's notes, and tried to focus on the day ahead.

In the late afternoon, after I said goodbye to my last patient, I closed and locked the front door and returned to the office. On the wall above my desk there was a photograph of the four of us – Anastasia, Samuel, Helene and myself in Crete. The silver frame and glass were dusty. I took it down to clean it.

It was 1978, the last time we were photographed together. I was sixteen; Helene had just turned fourteen and we were celebrating her birthday in a small restaurant. Anastasia had asked the waiter to take the photo. She was in the foreground, raising her glass of wine, smiling at the camera. Samuel was sitting to the right and slightly behind her, smoking a cigarette, his face shadowed by a straw hat. Helene was beside Samuel, her hand resting on his arm. I stood behind the three of them at the outdoor table, hair bleached by two weeks in the sea, wearing sunglasses to protect my eyes from the glare. I'd always thought everyone had been happy that summer: Anastasia less imperious than usual, Samuel quiet but content, Helene satiated from swimming, reading and sightseeing. But when I rubbed my handkerchief across the glass to clean it, Samuel's mouth was a tired line, Helene's hand clung to his arm and, in spite of her smile, Anastasia's face looked bruised around the eyes.

The leaves on the oak trees outside the office window were beginning to fall. The air was sharp; the damp-earth smell of autumn came through the partly opened window and curled around me. I wondered whether Jenny had come home early and cooked something comforting for supper – pumpkin soup or maybe venison stew. For fifteen minutes I meditated, clearing my mind of the day's sessions, a discipline I'd engaged in for many years. When my mind and body started to relax and I was focused on slowing down my breathing, I realised I'd experienced 'the shift', but in a new and even more disorientating way. My consciousness had split – instead of being in one state or another, I was in two places at once: equally aware of the couch in the office and the viewing seat on the spaceship. My body started to shake. I attempted to stretch my arms and legs, roll my shoulders, to stay calm. But no matter how hard I tried I didn't have the energy or the willpower to remain aware of being in two places at once for more than a few seconds.

I blinked: below the hum of machines on the spaceship, incoming images from the surface, and the constant update of data, a sound crept through the speakers on the wall above my head. At first it was like a lump of metal being drawn across a rock. Then it turned to faint rumblings. It rattled and echoed.

A voice.

The hair on my arms and the back of my neck bristled. It sounded as if it belonged to someone trapped in a cave in the centre of the earth. I listened as best I could but the static coming through the computer speakers made it difficult. The voice stopped and started. There was a booming sound then an attack of coughing. I held my breath; my jaw tightened; it was hard to swallow.

A minute or so passed before the voice came back through the speakers. It was thinner, weaker than before, but for a few moments it was clear: the trembling voice of someone old or ill and it repeated a word he'd never heard before. 'Vellen,' the voice said, 'Vellen.'

On the couch in my office I reached for the jug of water on the coffee table and poured the clear, clean liquid into my favourite blue glass and held it out to catch the last of the afternoon sunlight.

On the viewing deck I plugged the microphone into the computer. I asked who and where the speaker was, and whether they were close to water, so I could identify them and plot their location on my map of the planet. Nobody answered.

There was another fit of coughing. I sat like a relative at a deathbed vigil, unable to move for fear of missing the dying person's last words. In a whisper the voice began again and my hand flew across the page, making notes of everything I heard.

When the voice finally stopped, I returned my focus to the couch in the office. I was reflected in the window, sitting upright, staring back at myself. Outside the window the sky had darkened. The creamy outline of the rising moon was visible through the branches of the oak trees. People were walking home from work, buses rumbled past, car lights shone on the un-curtained glass. And the image of Blue Marble, the photo of the blue and white Earth seen from outer space, illuminated my mind.

I blinked and shifted back to the spaceship. Data from the planet below filled the screens. On the viewing deck, I stood with my hands raised above my head in a gesture of surrender, my wet cheek pressed against the speaker. All I wanted was to circle the Earth and wait for a break in the smoke-laden clouds so I could see what was happening below.

I blinked again. On the couch a wave of vertigo gripped me and I had to lie down. A long-ago memory of a tramping holiday with Anastasia surfaced. We were in the high country in Central Otago and I was standing in the middle of one of those swing bridges that crossed a ravine – a rickety wooden and rope artifice that stretched from cliff to cliff. Below me water gushed over rocks. The exhilaration of walking through the air on something so flimsy was almost too much to bear. I stopped, looked down and froze. Anastasia walked calmly across the bridge before me, strolling as if she was on a suburban street.

'Hurry up Jason,' she shouted from the other side, 'we need to get to the hut before it gets dark.'

There was no choice. If I wanted to keep up with her, I had to grip the rope and go.

The memory shared with Stephen from my childhood pushed at me again: I was running, falling across the surface of the Earth, plunging beneath the grass and soil and rock to an underground river that twisted and shimmered like a snake.

I sat back up and put my head in my hands. The shifting had sped up. I was switching and sliding between one place, one landscape, and another. It was out of control. These visions, these hallucinations, had to stop. I was losing my ability to focus, to remain detached; losing my grip on reality. More and more, when I was working with patients my concentration wandered; I was thinking about what was happening to me, not listening to them. They weren't being given the attention they deserved. Right now, I needed to focus on the ordinary, the tangible, material world. From the coffee table I picked up the piece of polished obsidian I'd had since childhood. It was a present from Anastasia and when I was a boy it had filled the palm of my hand. She'd explained that pre-historic people used obsidian as a cutting tool. Now it sat small and shiny black in the centre of my hand. I curled my fingers into a fist around it. It was once my lucky stone and there was still something comforting about it. I slid it into my pocket.

With both hands flat on the dark brown leather of the couch I pushed myself up; forced myself to walk out of the office to the bathroom to wash my face and hands. Maybe I had a fever or was coming down with a virus. Ever since Helene's death Jenny had wanted me to take some time off, but I preferred to keep busy; it was no good to David and the boys to have me moping about.

I ran the cold tap, splashed handfuls of water on my face then reached for the navy-blue towel hanging on the chrome handrail by the basin. My hand seemed thinner than usual, elongated, carved into planes of shadow and light, mesmerising as a cubist painting. The towel slipped through my fingers, fluttered through the air in slow motion like a giant butterfly. It landed on the grey tiles in front of my feet. I bent down to pick it up. Pain rippled behind my eyes. I stretched my hand towards the towel rail but it was too thin and the rail too far away to grasp. There was a clap of thunder and the buzzing of a thousand bees. Away in the distance I saw the shadowy figure of Anselmo, the medieval monk. The bathroom darkened. I slid to the floor.

—*Aretis (first visit)* —

He was lying on the dirt floor of a round hut with a thatched roof, clutching his piece of obsidian in his left hand. There was a strong smell of goat meat. A young woman with a braid of heavy dark hair and a blue woollen shawl across her shoulders lit an oil lamp. She gave him a blanket and helped him sit up. His head was pounding. His eyelids and lips were swollen; his hands and feet ached with the cold. She passed him a bowl of stew then sat opposite him on a low stool by the fire. He slipped the obsidian back into his pocket and scooped up a spoonful of stew. Warmth flooded his mouth. His bottom lip throbbed.

'What were you doing in the snow by the bridge?' she said.

She untied her shawl and folded it across her lap, unwound her braid and combed out her hair with her fingers, two dark wings on either side of her face. Behind her a hawk perched on a wooden shelf, its eyes closed as if asleep.

He looked at the woman's face. His vision blurred. There was darkness and pinpricks of light. For a moment he saw the faint outline of Stephen standing in the shadows behind her.

'Stephen?'

'Aja,' she said. 'My name is Aja. Where have you come from?'

Outside the hut green and orange lights flared across the sky. Beyond the hills the earth rumbled and shook. He lay on the dirt floor by the fire wrapped in the blanket. His eyes were closed to protect them from the flashes of bright light. His head still throbbed. Whenever he tried to stand up a wave of vertigo pushed him back down.

Aja stood by the door watching the lights. 'Yesterday the largest of the cypress trees in the clearing behind the bridge cracked open,' she said, 'and the caves where we collect coal and firelighters are full of noise and shadows. Southerners crawl through our ancestors' burial tunnels, taking more than their ten per cent share of our coal, tearing up bones with their pickaxes. When I'm out on the hills herding the goats, I've seen strange lights sweep across the entrance to the caves.'

She closed the door, returned to the stool by the hearth and took off her shawl. 'This morning the two youngest goats broke from the herd, ran to the edge of the top meadow and climbed straight down the rock face. They tumbled and fell into the river, smashing their heads on the stones.'

As she spoke she pleated the edges of the blue shawl folded in her lap. The hut was warm. Her voice was low-pitched, soothing. He drifted in and out of consciousness. When he opened his eyes, he saw the hawk fan its wings and land on her shoulder. Behind her, in the flickering firelight, he glimpsed Stephen's face again, softer, thinner, the outline of his nose and jaw less pronounced. Aja's hands and feet were bare and patterned with blue tattoos. He wanted to sit up and write down what she was saying but his head hurt too much and his body was so heavy he couldn't move.

'The winter snows will start soon,' she said. 'Because the Southerners have taken more than their allotted share of coal, what we have in store won't last the winter. We'll need to go deeper into the caves to get more.'

She unfolded her shawl and draped it across her shoulders even though the hut was now so warm he was beginning to sweat.

'The village council will allow one more journey to the market in Rozza before snow blocks the pass through the valley. Only the strongest can go. We need more oil for lamps, molasses, honey and dried fruit for the children and old people, and as many blankets as we can buy or trade.'

He fell asleep listening to the murmur of Aja's voice and dreamed of his parents: Samuel standing on the dark sand of Muriwai beach, his trousers rolled up to his knees, holding towels and clothes, watching Anastasia bodysurf. Further out, wet-suited surfers paddled in the water, their sleek dark bodies hovering in the distance like birds of prey.

When he woke Aja was standing by the open door of the hut again, watching lights flare across the sky, her shawl wrapped around her head and shoulders.

Without turning she said, 'I was chosen when I was ten years old. They tattooed coiled snakes on my hands and feet. It took three nights and the pain made my head ring. The old women held my arms and legs steady while the men worked. I looked up at the stars tattooed across the sky. Each time they tapped the chisel I left my body and joined another star until I was dancing across the heavens in time to that tap, tap, tap. I didn't cry or scream or faint. I just lay still and followed the map of stars.'

He slept again, this time in a warm, dark place with no dreams.

—*Auckland*—

I was face down on the bathroom floor next to my office, my forehead bruised and cut. A smear of dried blood stained the floor by my head. In the distance, the monk sprinkled a trail of ash around the base of a cluster of cork-oak trees. My obsidian rolled out of my pocket across the grey tiles and clattered against the door.

Jenny stood in the kitchen holding a mug of coffee. She was dressed in a woollen shirt, khaki shorts and tramping boots. Her daypack was on the floor by the door.

'Not even a phone call,' she said, 'and you come home and act like nothing's wrong.'

She slapped her mug down on the white bench, slopping black coffee on the surface. 'After Helene's accident, I was beside myself.' She crossed her arms over her chest. 'I thought…'

I reached out to hug her but she pushed me away. 'I slipped on the tiles in the bathroom and knocked my head,' I said. 'When I woke up I was disoriented; I thought I was only out for a few minutes.'

She swiped at the puddle of coffee on the bench with the dishcloth. 'I'm tramping in the Hunua ranges with Merle and Celia today – it's been organised for weeks and I'm not cancelling.' A tear rolled down her cheek. 'You're not yourself, Jason. You haven't been for months. You pretend there's nothing wrong but I know you. It's like you're somewhere else, you're not really here. I want you to go to Doctor Robertson and have a check-up.' She bent down and picked up her pack. 'I want you to do that today.'

After she left I went upstairs and had a shower. I stood in front of the mirror to shave. My face looked different, unfamiliar – my cheekbones and the lines of my jaw chiselled into a dozen different angles, as if I'd been reassembled into a collage. I put the razor down. I didn't understand what was happening to me, but what could I possibly say to a doctor that wouldn't make things worse? In spite of years of study, training and clinical experience, nothing had prepared me for this.

I dressed and went to my study looking for something on the bookshelves that could help me. I pulled out Jung's book, *Memories, Dreams and Reflections,* from the top shelf. I hadn't read it in years. It opened at a page I'd bookmarked, where Jung talked about his spirit guide, Philemon, a figure generated by his psyche. A figure that made him realise there were things inside him he didn't understand or control but that had some kind of objective, psychological reality.

I stood behind my desk holding on to the book. It seemed as good an explanation as any for what was happening, and, right now, better than a diagnosis of mental illness by a well-meaning GP. For reasons I didn't begin to understand, I decided to keep going, no matter how irrational the experience. It was too important to walk away from; but to appease Jenny, and give me time to think, I spent the rest of the day cancelling appointments for the next month, apologising to patients for the short notice, and referring them to other therapists.

Later in the week I went for a check-up. I didn't mention the incident in my office, just said I'd tripped and fallen, hitting my head. Dr Robertson tracked my eye movements, tested my balance, checked my pulse and blood pressure. It was a little high but other than that, he said, things seemed fine. Robertson coughed and mentioned my recent bereavement, recommending having a break. Perhaps you and Jenny could have a little holiday? If that wasn't possible, he said, then plenty of exercise and rest.

I stayed away from the office and my patients but sat in my study at home and read and re-read Stephen's file. I wrote down what I remembered of my encounter with Aja, making notes of how I'd felt beforehand and afterwards, trying not to over-analyse or judge, just explore it as if it were a series of images, as if it were the narrative of someone else's dream.

Each morning and evening I walked the dogs through the park at the end of the street, down past the mangroves and over the bridge to the water; let them off their leads and watched them chase each other through the mud. When the wind rippled across the water they bristled and barked, and when they met unknown dogs they sniffed and chased them across the rough paddock behind the mud flats, an area set aside by the local council for unleashed dogs. When they hauled broken branches back to me, I threw them as far as I could and watched as they raced after them.

On a wooden bench facing the harbour I sat and watched the shadows of fast-moving clouds on the water – light and shadow moving across the surface of the sea. Shadows moved inside my mind, writing in an ancient calligraphy I couldn't grasp. The more I tried the more they slipped through my fingers, my logical mind unravelling as if it were a skein of silk.

When alone and in my study, I retreated to the spacecraft. I searched for glimpses of the sea, any sea, northern or southern, and for valleys and rivers, but sulphuric clouds covered the surface of the planet. It was hard to imagine sunlight penetrating them.

The silence of being in space and the quiet pursuit of observation lessened my anxiety. I performed my duties, made charts and maps, recorded and reported information. On the ground, I was weighted by gravity; distress pinched and bit, and intense attacks of vertigo unnerved me.

If the breeze was strong on the harbour, I watched windsurfers skim sideways across the incoming tide and listened as they shouted encouragement to each other. It was late autumn and the water was grey-green and choppy. The sounds of wind and barking dogs should have been in my ears, and the muddy smell of the mangroves in my nostrils. Instead, I was overtaken by images of a valley with steep hills on either side, a village of round huts with heavily thatched roofs, smoke from cooking fires rising on the breeze, a fast-flowing river running beneath a wooden bridge and the hum of bees gathering nectar from clover-covered fields.

Each day it was harder to distinguish being awake from dreaming. I wasn't even sure I slept; I just seemed to go somewhere else. When I lay down for an afternoon nap I was either on the spacecraft in a place of peaceful observation, waiting for the voice to return, or trying to find a way back to Aja. When panic threatened to overwhelm me, I called up the image of the medieval monk and watched while he sprinkled ash on the ground. I saw him in my peripheral vision dressed in his brown robe, standing beside a cluster of trees, the skin on his tonsured head as brown as a walnut. The monk raised his hand in blessing then beckoned me forward, but I was too afraid to follow. All I wanted was to be that boy again, standing in my mother's study, knowing she was away but would safely return, seeing the miracle of Blue Marble for the first time, feeling that implosion of knowledge, the sensation of space expanding inside me.

Jenny watched me out of the corner of her eye. She left fruit, bread, cheese and a thermos of coffee on the kitchen table when she went to work or to meet friends. She was worried and I didn't blame her. Yesterday she reminded me she'd be away in Sydney for a few days next week for an urban planning conference and I had to swallow a lump of panic. She stood behind me as I sat at my desk, her hand massaging a tight spot at the base of my neck. 'I really need to know you're going to be okay,' she said.

On our walks the dogs guided me back home along the path, nudging me when I stopped too long on the bridge that spanned a section of the mangrove swamp. Images flashed, but I was too slow and too fearful to catch more than a few. I heard flutes; got glimpses of a skinny boy swimming in a river; his grandfather, watching him from the bank, called out, Uzra, it's time to come back. Sometimes there were darting shadows of snakes moving through water and, sometimes, dark, child-like creatures crouched at the entrance of caves when the full moon was rising and chanted in high-pitched, ethereal voices.

The ability to write notes or contemplate what to do with them was slipping away from me. Time rippled and merged, reality buckled. I was everywhere and nowhere. And my ability to distance myself, to analyse and organise, was almost exhausted. I held onto two things, both of them maternal: the faded poster of Blue Marble now pinned on the wall of my own study and my cutting tool, my lucky piece of obsidian. Everything else was raw, unreliable and unmediated, occurring in the places between living and dreaming, memory and death.

—Two weeks later—

Jenny stood beside Doctor Robertson as he examined me. He checked my pulse, put the cold metal of his stethoscope on my chest, shone a beam of light from his miniature torch into my eyes. I was lying on the day bed in my study, unable to move or speak.

'His vital signs are fine,' Doctor Robinson said. 'There's no outward sign of stroke.' He placed the stethoscope on my chest again.

Jenny picked up my right hand and held it between her own, as if to warm it. 'It's all come on since Helene died,' she said. 'Sometimes when I come home from work I find him sitting here staring blankly out the window. I speak but he doesn't answer. These last few weeks he just sits for hours doing nothing or lies on the day bed like this.'

The spacecraft circumnavigated the globe. Occasionally, the clouds parted and when they did, I took photographs and studied the surface, looking for traces of water. When the cloud cover was too dense I moved away from the viewing deck to collect computer transcripts of all the messages sent to the spacecraft from the planet below. I put them in chronological order so I could read them. In the background monks chanted and sang plainsong.

When I came back to myself in the study, I was washed and shaved, dressed in fresh clothes and stretched out on the bed with a rug over me. Jenny slept in an armchair at the foot of the bed, her head on one side, her reading glasses dangling on a chain around her neck. When she exhaled it sounded like she was sighing in a slightly annoyed way, as if she was too tired to move even though the chair was uncomfortable and she'd wake with a crick in her neck and an ache in her lower back.

It was late. The room pulsated with hidden energy, the way it did when I was a child and woke in the middle of the night and felt the air glowing around me, covering me with mysterious particles that stuck to my skin. In that childhood dark my hearing had been more acute, my sense of smell heightened, the pores of my skin opened to minute changes of temperature. When I was very young – three or four – and woke in the night and felt the darkness moving around me, I'd call out for Anastasia but, more often than not, it was my father who came. Samuel would turn on the night light in the hallway, pull up a chair and sit beside me till I fell asleep again. At boarding school in the dormitories, it was never completely dark and the sounds of a dozen boys breathing and coughing and turning over disrupted any sense of mystery or fear.

While Jenny slept the night-air touched me. For the first time since childhood my skin opened to the particles, and a coil that lay hidden deep inside my body compressed and expanded like an extra lung, helping me absorb essential elements. The particles had a faint glow and, as they passed through the pores of my skin into my muscles and veins and entered my bloodstream, a new energy filled me.

The paralysis was easing. I was able to turn my head a little, move the fingers of one hand, stretch my calf muscles, and wriggle my toes.

Jenny stirred in the armchair and tried to turn over. I called out her name and the sound vibrated in the space between us. Had I really said her name out loud or just thought it, or was the air too moist and thick for the sound to carry across the bed?

She woke, sat up, leaned over and squeezed my foot. I gathered energy and practised moving my fingers and toes. I didn't want to leave her but felt driven to find a way back to Aja. I managed to turn on my side and curl into foetal position. My obsidian was lying on the bed beside the pillow. The coil inside my body compressed until it was as tiny as a newly formed embryo. I counted to a hundred and took a deep breath. The coil sprang open. I catapulted into the air, flew through the room and out into space. Multi-coloured particles rushed past, snapping and stinging as they contacted the skin on my face. My arms and legs, and the trunk of my body, were elongated, fluid. I turned to liquid and poured out and down through the funnel that lay between the layers of the world.

—Aretis (second visit)—

The winter snows had melted. Outside Aja's hut rain clouds were massing. Thunder rumbled behind the hills. Aja squinted at the sky and whistled for her hawk. Her clothes and hair were scorched and smelt of smoke. Ash smudged her face and the skin on her hands was cut and blistered.

When the hawk didn't come she went back inside her hut. A few minutes later she reappeared with an old tunic in her hands. She walked to the river, ripped the tunic into strips and soaked the material in the water.

He called out: 'Aja!'

She smeared honey on the burns and cuts on her arms and wound sections of wet cloth from her wrists to her elbows. Mint grew wild along the riverbank and he watched as she plucked a handful of leaves and crushed them between her fingertips. She made a small ball of leaves and pushed it between her teeth and gum at the back of her mouth.

He held his obsidian tight in his hand and called out again. 'Aja.'

She turned around. He waved his arms but she stared past him. Black smoke from the bonfires in the centre of the village billowed beneath the clouds. She hauled herself to her feet and walked back towards her hut. It was one of only two still standing.

For the rest of the day he followed Aja and another woman from the village, Lilly, as they piled the dead together in family groups. They worked with wet cloths tied over their faces and balls of mint leaves wedged in their mouths. They lifted bodies, one supporting the head, the other holding the feet, and threw them into the flames. They stood side by side watching while fire claimed their friends and relatives.

In the afternoon the rain came, turning the funeral fires into mounds of steaming ash and mud. He walked through the village, unseen, moving between doused bonfires, unable to offer help or comfort, unable to communicate. Aja and Lilly searched for survivors, moving from the centre of the village near the communal oven to the outer circle where vegetable gardens and sunflower plantations grew on the terraced hills.

A man lay in front of a burnt-out hut. His face was bubbled with blisters; his legs twisted beneath him. Aja crouched in the dirt and cradled his head in her lap. He whimpered as her fingers brushed against the raw skin on the back of his neck.

Jason crouched down in the dirt beside Aja. In a soft, clear voice she spoke to the dying man, reminding him of the times they were children together, high up in the hills above the valley, watching goats climb ridges, goats so sweet and nimble they could walk straight across the sky.

The man's eyes rolled back. He cried out. She wet his lips and tongue with a few drops of water.

Jason heard his own breath rasping in his chest and throat. He remembered: he was nine years old and in the waves at Muriwai beside his mother. The water was cool on his sunburnt shoulders, and he held his breath until his whole body ached for air. When she went further out to play amongst the breakers he retreated to the shallows and knelt in the coarse black sand, letting the spent waves wash over his stomach and chest. In the distance he watched Anastasia's head appear and disappear as she bobbed among swells waiting for a big wave so she could body surf back to the shore.

When the man was dead Aja and Lilly chanted a prayer then placed his body on a new pyre. Aja put a small brown pellet that looked like dried animal droppings among the wood and coal. She soaked a rag in kerosene, lit it and threw it on the pyre. Flames exploded in the air.

Just before sunset the hawk returned, a field mouse hanging limp in his beak.

That night he slept on the dirt floor of Aja's hut close to the door. He woke early, well before sunrise. Lilly and Aja lay side by side, still asleep. He left the hut and picked his way through the burnt-out village to the river; took off his shirt and trousers, sank into the water and lay with his back to the stones. Cold water rippled across his legs and belly. He turned over, put his face in the water and opened his mouth. Water filled his lungs. They were transformed into gills. He floated downstream, under the bridge. It was cool and shadowed. Brown trout flicked their tails past his feet.

Beyond the shelter of the bridge he emerged from the river, his body sleek as a fish and streaming with water. He walked across wet grass up into the hills. The remains of a campsite were still there although the fire hadn't been lit for many days. Goats grazed on the sloping pasture.

A velvet wedding dress was spread on the ground. He picked it up, held it against his body and thought of Jenny. He ran his fingers across the fur-lined collar and cuffs. Helene walked across the grass towards him. He gave her the dress. As soon as she put it over her head she began to shrink, until she was wizened and old, a witch from a Grimm's fairy tale. He snatched the dress back and she became herself again.

He laid the dress back down on the grass, sat down beside it and waited.

Sunlight struck the top of the ridge, turning the earth to a rough golden-brown. Down in the valley the early morning mist began to dissipate. The village glowed like Eden, like Anastasia's rich blonde hair in the lamplight. In the distance Aja and Lilly stood side by side on the riverbank in front of the bridge. The wind was sharp and blew coldly through his lungs.

The bridge was on fire.

He left the hills above the village and returned to the women.

Lumps of blackened wood fell into the river, hissing as they hit the water. Lilly soaked another rag in oil and hurled it onto the bridge. There was a burst of orange light. Flames shot across the wooden planks.

Lilly and Aja collected ash from each of the doused bonfires and poured it into a clean pottery urn. They carried the urn down to the vein of clay that ran along the northern edge of the riverbank.

Under the shelter of willow trees, they cut clay, kneading and shaping it into balls. They scooped handfuls of ash out of the urn and sprinkled it over the clay – salt onto meat. He crouched a few feet away from them while they worked. He listened to the slap of their hands on the clay, the slap of the clay on the stones, the beat of his heart as it slapped against his ribcage. Filtered light shimmered through the willows' new leaves.

As each ball was finished they placed it on a cleaned river stone. With the palms of their hands they pressed them flat. Then they cut the clay into strips, rolling and curving the strips into urns, and left them to dry in the sun. A fresh wind lifted the clouds and stirred the leaves. In the distance, above the tips of the cypress trees, Aja's hawk rose on a thermal and circled the village.

The river was brown and shallow and smelled of mint and mud. He sat by the drying urns, his face opened to the air. Water moved quickly over the river stones and, as he listened to its music, Helene was beside him again. He reached out his hand but she was hunched over, hugging her knees. She refused to look at him.

'You worshipped her,' she said, out of the corner of her mouth, 'no matter what she did.'

He closed his eyes. Light from the sun formed blotches of red beneath his eyelids. A trickle of bright red blood ran from his father's nose onto his upper lip. Anastasia wiped it away with the edge of a damp towel. The front of her dress was stained and wet from leaning over the bath. She smoothed Samuel's wet hair back from his forehead, bent and kissed him on the lips.

'He's peaceful now,' she said.

On the stereo in the adjoining bedroom, the Glenn Miller orchestra was playing 'Moonlight Serenade'. Through the stained glass of the bathroom window sunlight dappled red and green blotches on Helene's hunched back. She was sitting in the corner on the floor, turned away from Anastasia and the bath, refusing to look. Her hands were bunched into fists. She was banging her head on her knees.

JENNY

Jenny sat in the armchair with her feet propped up on the foot of the bed. She watched Jason sleep and remembered the first time she saw him: it was in 1987 at a lecture he was giving at university. She was nineteen, in her second year studying architecture, and as part of the degree they needed to do some general papers. Psychology fitted her timetable. He was a guest lecturer, the newly qualified Doctor Winston, a welcome change from the dry old professor who was responsible for the paper on the history of western psychology and who droned on about Freud's theories and contribution to the twentieth century in a way that made an interesting subject tedious. Jason, on the other hand, lectured enthusiastically about different theorists, and he talked about dreams, how important Freud and Jung thought they were in understanding the unconscious. He gave four lectures that semester and joined some of their tutorials. Even then he had a sense of other-worldliness about him. He was lean, almost bony, and this made him seem taller, and frailer, than he really was. His skin was lightly freckled; his straight, reddish-brown hair flopped over his forehead. He often dressed in shades of green or brown – he was tawny, like one of those harrier hawks you saw circling high above the paddocks when you drove out into open country. He swayed a little when he lectured, moving back and forward from his heels to the balls of his feet, and he kept looking over the top of his reading glasses, glancing away from his notes out across the lecture theatre at them, scanning the room for their reactions, making sure they were following. Something about those quick intense glances from his position above them reinforced that image of a bird of prey. The old professor simply read from his notes in a monotone and never once checked to see if they were still awake.

She was becoming interested in the effects of buildings on people's social and emotional lives, so when he was contracted to deliver a special paper on Jungian archetypes the following year, she enrolled along with her best friend Susie – they both had a little crush on him, although they pretended to each other they didn't. The lectures were interesting, the tutorials even better. She realised he wasn't that much older than them, and only recently qualified as a clinical psychologist. He told them he'd been able to start university while he was still sixteen, and that his mother was an academic too, a philosopher, who lectured on the ancient Greeks. At the end of the course he invited them all to the student bar for a drink and because it was a small class most of them went. Her future brother-in-law, David, was in that class too, slightly older than the rest of them, doing his Master's Degree in Business Management and taking the paper as an elective. He and Jason hit it off straight away and became friends.

There were moments in the middle of the night when her husband stirred, as if he might wake: his eyelids fluttered, his legs or fingers twitched. There were times he muttered words or sounds, none of which made any sense to her. If he seemed agitated or distressed she stroked his forehead or held his feet as if that might ground him. When she needed to sleep or work she let the dogs in to watch over him. They lay at the end of the bed or stretched out on the rug, alert to his moods, attentive to every movement or sound he made. Tonight, he was calm, and distant, only the rising and falling of his chest reassuring her he was alive. Yesterday the nurse had come to change the drip and catheter, to check his pulse and blood pressure, to make sure there were no infections. All this she recorded on the chart beside the bed and in the space underneath the columns of numbers she wrote: no change. Jenny wanted to shout: *No change! Everything's changed!* But she smiled and thanked her and escorted her to the door where they chatted for a few minutes and the nurse said if there was no further change she'd check on him again in two days' time.

It had taken her and Jason a long time to get to know each other: she went on to do a Master's in Social and Environmental Architecture; he continued to lecture part-time and build his private practice. Mostly, they banged into each other at student or staff parties. He would stand or sit quietly in a corner, occasionally talking to someone, but mainly he liked to make himself invisible and watch the crowd.

What she thought most about now was that night in late summer when she was celebrating handing in her master's thesis. He was sitting on the veranda of a run-down villa on an old sofa with his feet resting on a wooden beer crate. His eyes were closed. At first, she thought he was asleep, or maybe just stoned and listening to the music – the owner of the house was a fan of sixties and seventies bands and had put on Pink Floyd's *The Dark Side of the Moon*. The night was overcast and still. It was very humid, and there was that sense of moving through water; of everything, including them, being porous. She studied him for a minute, thinking he was unaware of her but when she went to walk off he opened his eyes and said, 'Hello Jenny, aren't you going to stop and have a chat?'

The party went on inside and the music changed to Led Zeppelin and then to the Rolling Stones. They sat side by side in the dark and talked for a couple of hours, neither of them really drinking, just sipping occasionally from a shared glass of cheap wine. That was the first time she noticed a particular quality he had: being both present and absent at the same time. It was as if part of him was at a distance, watching from a long way off. He talked about the need in his profession for compassionate detachment: he was writing a paper on it for a conference at the end of the year, and she was aware he was using her as a sounding board, testing out his ideas, listening to how they sounded, and watching for her reactions. But, unlike many academics, he was also a good listener, and when he'd finished expounding his theories he asked her about her own work, about what she wanted to do now that her post-graduate degree was finished. She talked about wanting to create self-sufficient houses, heated and cooled from solar and wind power, houses that were organic or built out of recycled materials, easy on the earth, and cheap to build, run and maintain.

As they talked, the warmth and moisture of the late-night air wrapped itself around them; it was as if they were cocooned together. Other people came and went on the veranda but they didn't interrupt or disturb them. They were their own self-contained island, and the others just ebbed and flowed like a tide around them. When she got home she thought about how he'd listened so intently yet, at the same time, had removed himself to a safe distance.

The following week when she was searching through second-hand books outside the university bookshop he tapped her on the shoulder. He was going for a late lunch with his sister, he said, would she like to come too?

They walked through Albert Park together, past brightly coloured flowered beds and equally brightly coloured students lying on the grass and under trees, down past the Art Gallery and into a small café on High Street where they sold cheap vegetarian food – rice dishes, baked potatoes, salads, chickpea curries, lentil loaf, that sort of thing. His younger sister, Helene, was waiting for him there, sitting at a table down the back, drinking fruit juice and reading an art magazine. When she saw Jason her face lit up, and there was only a momentary frown when she realised someone else was with him. Her embroidered peasant blouse and long green skirt complimented the auburn curls that framed her face and fell over her shoulders. Her skin was pale and very fine with tiny freckles scattered across her nose and cheekbones, and when she spoke it was in a slightly breathless way. She was in her third year, studying music and they chatted about the papers she was taking. When Jason teased her about all the young men in her classes asking her out she blushed and rolled her eyes. It was obvious he felt protective towards her and that he was her adored older brother.

It was another two years before she and Jason got married at the registry office with Helene and David as witnesses. His mother, Anastasia, was overseas on a lecture tour. Afterwards they all went out for lunch. For their honeymoon they went camping up north for a week, travelling from beach to beach, swimming, walking, fishing and reading.

They rented an old villa while she worked on the design for their house: something that fitted the landscape, made from recycled rimu or kauri, a place that used natural light and wind and water to create energy. They bought a section in the growing western suburbs, much cheaper than in town. She would have liked more surrounding bush and Jason had wanted to be nearer the sea but they compromised – both the bush and the wild, west coast beaches were close by. There was room enough for a vegetable garden, for flax bushes and cabbage trees, manuka to attract the bees, and plenty of space for the dogs.

They had wanted to build as much of the house as they could themselves, and every weekend for two years they worked on it. The plumbing and wiring were done by professionals, but everything else they managed themselves or with David and Helene's help. It was warm in the winter and cool in the summer and she'd never wanted to live anywhere else. Even Anastasia approved of it once it had been built, although she couldn't resist pointing out things she didn't like or thought were an oversight, such as not having an ensuite in the guest room.

Anastasia. My God, what a powerhouse of a woman! What Jenny remembered most about her was her funeral. It was a public affair, a well-choreographed celebration of her working life and achievements, arranged by Anastasia in advance and it was a master-class in absence. Hers obviously; Jason's usual compassionate detachment was stretched beyond breaking point to a place of almost complete numbness; Helene was mute, the look on her face that of someone stumbling out of captivity, finally released only to find herself standing in a new and confusing world, one without familiar fences or boundaries. David, bless him, had done his best to keep his joy to himself.

After his mother's funeral Jason had spent days in his study, lying on that same daybed looking out the windows into the garden, or simply staring at the ceiling. Sometimes he seemed to fall into a restless sleep, his limbs twitching as he muttered and coughed. At other times, even though his eyes were open, he was like a man gone blind and deaf. He was so closed in on himself, so withdrawn that she grew anxious leaving him on his own. She had an irrational fear that he might just disappear. She kept the house running and went to work, although she did shorter days. In those first few weeks, he roused himself if a patient needed him urgently or when Helene and David came over. She remembered thinking it was the first time Helene had ever felt stronger than her brother, and being able to help him made it easier to find her own feet.

One Sunday afternoon Helene came over alone. She'd brought with her a recording of Glenn Miller playing 'Moonlight Serenade'. She greeted Jenny briefly, went into Jason's study and shut the door. Five minutes later Jenny heard music playing – they played that track over and over. A couple of hours later they both came out of his study and sat at the kitchen table while she made them a cup of tea. Jason wasn't chatty, he was never that, but he was less drained, less absent. Within a few days he went back to work.

But now Helene was gone and what was she to do? She sat here beside him and watched for signs. Would he come back to her? She knew something strange was going on, something she didn't know anything about. Sometimes there was a weird energy in the room, like the jumpy feeling you got just before an electrical storm, when the air pressure was building.

Late last night when she was half-asleep in the armchair by his bed, she thought she heard him call her name. She sat up and saw his legs were twitching; he was trying to move his feet. His eyes were open and although he didn't speak, she could see he was almost present. He seemed to be looking past her, his eyes resting on the poster of the globe on the wall above his desk. It was faded now and a bit frayed round the edges but it was his mother's and, he'd told her once, his favourite image as a child. She reached out and gently squeezed his toes. He blinked, and she heard him sigh, then he closed his eyes and was gone again. It didn't last long but it gave her hope – it was the most present he'd been in weeks.

Earlier that day, in the middle of the afternoon, David had brought Sam and Liam over. Apparently, Liam had insisted they come. When they arrived, he went straight to Jason's study, climbed up on the bed and patted his shoulder. Sam stood in the doorway watching his brother for a few minutes then asked to take the dogs for a walk. She got their leads and tennis balls and said they could go to the park for half an hour. In the kitchen, David told her Liam had woken up that morning and said, Dad, Uncle Jason needs me. He'd collected his mother's teddy bear and his favourite toy truck and put them in the car so he wouldn't forget them. While she and David talked they could hear Liam chatting to Jason and then playing a game with his truck, running it up one side of the bed and down the other. They're good boys, she'd said to David, you must be proud of them. He stood by the window with his back to her so she couldn't see his tears. She'd brushed hers away and emptied and refilled the kettle for something to do. You know, David said, still with his back to her, I never realised until she was gone that it was Helene who held that family together. She wasn't the weak link at all.

Part Two: Energy and Alchemy

Uzra – Ursula – Grandfather Anisth

UZRA

Uzra sat on the treeless western slope overlooking the southern mining camp of Kata. The afternoon sun warmed his shoulders and the strip of exposed skin on the back of his neck. He wiped his face with a damp rag and took a sip of water from the silver flask he kept in his goatskin bag.

A funnel of white smoke rose into a cloudless sky. Below him men shovelled the last of the coal into wheelbarrows. When the wheelbarrows were full they pushed them to the side of a rough dirt track and emptied them into larger wooden carts. Mule drivers attached long poles from the carts to harnesses, cracked whips above the mules' heads and hauled the coal down the track to the shiny black loco.

The engine driver blew the whistle twice and another plume of smoke shot into the still air. Uzra pulled his wide-brimmed canvas hat down low on his forehead. He wanted to lie on the clover-filled grass and sink into a dreamless sleep but every time he closed his eyes he saw, in the sweeping arc created by his swinging kerosene lamp, the outline of bodies lying at the bottom of the mineshaft, their skin sticky with coal dust, their faces resting in puddles of murky water.

By the time he and the other miners had reached them, only

Nathan was still breathing. His head and shoulders were visible, the rest of his body trapped in the rubble. Uzra could do nothing except hold his lamp and wait with him. For the first time in years he'd wished he still carried his grandfather's pistol.

'No warning,' Nathan had whispered before he died.

They carried out as many bodies as they could on blankets strung between wooden poles borrowed from the coal carts, passing their burden from man to man up the slippery steps of the western mineshaft, but half of them were left behind – buried too deep beneath mud and rock and coal.

He'd told his boss, Rohine, they shouldn't be that far down. It was an old seam, well worked over, only stable on the western side of the shaft. But Rohine was the engineer in charge of southern extraction and he insisted they went further down, wanting them to dig out as much as they could before the beginning of the sleet and snow of another winter.

Uzra stayed on the hill and watched the surviving members of his work gang hurry to load the last of the coal onto the train. As soon as they were finished, the loco would leave and he would take news of death back to the families in the village that lay on the outskirts of the great southern lake, Anatusa. Seven men with no family to wash or shroud them, buried away from their kin in unconsecrated ground; the other seven buried deep in the mine beneath the rubble of the explosion. Their relatives had the right to know why. And they would demand compensation, even as they accepted their share of the dwindling coal and complained it wouldn't last them the winter.

He dusted the knees of his trousers with his hat and pushed himself off the grass. The view of the valley encircled by the steep peaks of the southern range was striking but he never wanted to see it again. It was his own region in the centre of the country he longed for, the plains of Otmas, crisscrossed by the river Aretis, the river of snakes. His fingers caressed the indentations of the miniature bone flute he kept tied on a leather cord around his neck. It would have been a comfort to sit by the banks of the river with a real flute and play music again.

Yesterday, at the burial, his hands kept searching for something to do. As he watched the bodies being lowered into shallow graves, he found himself pursing his lips as if he was about to blow into his old flute. His fingers played the notes of a funeral dirge against his thigh. He thought he'd forgotten all that, but it was still there, a perfect memory, not in his mind but in his fingers, waiting for release. He'd had no words to farewell them. They were his work gang but not his own people. He stood to the side, cold and useless, while the surviving men performed the correct rituals and spoke the right words.

The loco breathed out smoke and steam like a living being. He wondered at the sense of the Southerners, inventing something that consumed precious coal even as it carried it at such speed to the villages and towns. They'd travelled further and faster on the locos than ever before, to outer, isolated regions in search of coal, initially returning with full carriages from seams not worked for a hundred years. The new mechanical diggers they transported on the locos extended the width and depth of the old mineshafts but men still had to crawl on their bellies with picks and shovels to get the coal out. The old mines were notorious for collapsing on top of the miners – each trip he returned with fewer men than he set out with.

He walked back down the hill and climbed on board, dropped his bag into the corner of the front carriage and sat by the window. Outside, the remaining members of his crew stood together on the rough wooden platform, their hands sunk into the pockets of their trousers as they waited for the final whistle. They'd scrubbed themselves clean for the return journey but their faces were ingrained with coal dust, and their broad shoulders sagged beneath their best shirts. Uzra turned his head and caught sight of own scarred and lined face reflected in the window.

This load wouldn't make that much difference. Its real purpose was to look good – a train full of shining coal speeding through southern towns and villages – but there wasn't enough coal left in reserve for one more bad winter. And all the winters, especially in the south, were bad now. Snow came down in great drifts and, in some regions, it didn't melt till mid-summer.

The final whistle blew and his men straggled in, their eyes avoiding his. The loco shunted forward and picked up speed. He covered his face with his hat and leaned back on the cushioned seat. The clacking sound of the loco as it rode along the track soothed him. His left hand curled around his miniature flute and he sank, not into the mercy of sleep and forgetfulness, but into the laceration of memory.

It was still dark. He was ten years old following his grandfather across the rock-strewn plain towards the river. His mother had packed his lunch and put his water bottle into the pocket of his new woollen jacket. He was dressed like the other men. This was the first time he'd been allowed to accompany his grandfather to the site. The men walked ahead of him without the aid of torches. He could barely see in the pre-dawn light and kept his eyes focused on his grandfather's back, almost running to keep up.

The men crossed the river, their goatskin moccasins sliding over smooth grey boulders. His feet followed the path of a narrow pipe that ran from the riverbed over the short distance to the mine. He saw the humped shape of the hill and a series of dark tents made of goatskins sewn together and stretched over wooden poles. They called it a hill but it wasn't a proper one, just a gentle rise in an otherwise flat, rocky plain, the result of men over hundreds of years digging among the rocks beside the riverbed, using water from the river to sluice gold from pebbles and soil. He wanted to be one of those men, a man like his grandfather, someone who brought home gold nuggets and exchanged them for sacks of flour, cornmeal, coffee and coal when merchants drove their supply carts into the village at the beginning of each month.

All morning he worked beside his grandfather, watching him, copying his movements, carrying water for him, not stopping until he did. At noon everyone retreated to the shelter of the tents. They shared food then lay with their heads resting on rolled-up goatskins, relaxing for an hour. It was early autumn, there was no wind and it was warm in the tent, almost as warm as a summer's day. The heat, his tired muscles and the reassuring sound of the men's voices lulled him to sleep.

He dreamed he was older, walking along the riverbed in the early morning, following a southern tributary. He saw flashes of gold as he walked beside the water, gold that sparkled like sunlight and poured like paint over rocks and moved like snakes swimming through water. His heart was beating so fast he thought he might faint or fly or explode. He took off his jacket and spread it on the riverbank, weighing it down with stones to make a marker to prove his claim. He ran back to the village, shouting, 'Grandpa, Grandpa, the river's painted with golden snakes.'

He woke to find his grandfather crouched beside him, wiping his face with a wet handkerchief. The other men were standing in a semicircle around him.

'Have I been asleep too long?'

'No, boy,' Grandpa said. He leaned over him and brushed his forehead, pushing his dark hair away from his face.

'Why are they staring at me?'

His grandfather waved his hand at the other men and they left the tent.

'You were talking in your sleep, crying out – did you have a dream?'

'I dreamt of gold. Lots of gold. In the river where it forks and turns to the south.'

Later in the afternoon his grandfather asked him to go to the section of the river he'd dreamed of. As they walked together along the dusty bank he thought about the strange looks the men had given him. He was worried he'd done something wrong even though Grandpa told him he hadn't. He said the men were pleased with him and wanted him to join their gang.

'There it is Grandpa,' he said, pointing to the fork in the river. 'But it was only a dream.'

But the gold was there, hidden beneath surface rocks, enough gold to buy provisions for everyone and to supply coal and kerosene for two winters. He was a man now, able to provide for the whole village.

Grandpa bought him a flute for his eleventh birthday, took him back to the fork in the river and taught him to play. Sometimes they sat together propped up against each other's back and played their flutes. Grandpa told him they were singing to the gold. Mostly he walked the riverbed on his own and explored among the rocks, searching for the tell-tale flash of shiny metal in the sun.

It was when he slept on the earth on hot afternoons with his body protected from the sun by the goatskin tent that he dreamt of snakes – snakes swimming through shallow water, spread out like a mat of glinting hair. In the beginning when he dreamed of them he just stood on the bank watching, following them with his eyes, remembering the places they stopped, memorizing a marker of some sort, a rock, a broken branch, a cluster of small stones. When he woke he told Grandpa and they went together and found the gold. On his twelfth birthday his village named him Uzra, Gold-dreamer.

The spring of his thirteenth birthday he rolled up his tent; packed flour, coffee, his hunting knife and water flask into his bag and walked off across the plains to make his first camp alone. In the mornings he washed in the river, sat naked on the stones to dry himself in the sun and played his flute. The mild breezes tingled his skin and ruffled his wet hair. The Aretis River was full of melting snow from mountain ranges in the north and south. Prisms of light danced on droplets of water caught on his eyelashes.

Snakes came swimming down the river towards him, tangled together, rolling, playful in the early morning. He stood and played his flute and they pooled in a circle at his feet. He dropped his flute on the bank and joined them in the water. They slid over his skin like milk, like another skin, and he glided down the river on his back with them. The river was the same as it always was yet, somehow, it was different: sharper, clearer, deeper.

Snakes brushed past his legs. He touched them with his fingers. He didn't understand what was happening but there were two rivers now, one running on the surface and one running beneath. The surface was the river he had known and played in since he was a small child. Its curves and contours were as familiar to him as his own body. He saw landmarks on the riverbank, places where he and his grandfather had camped and worked, and he saw the cedar trees they sheltered beneath when the summer sunshine was too harsh. He stood up and shook his head. Drops of water fell from his hair.

And the river that ran beneath – what kind of river was that? If he floated on the surface, the river was as it had always been, but once he sank deeper he entered another world; a world in which he was able to see and smell, and hear and think more clearly.

Uzra dived back down into the water and picked up a black stone from the bottom of the riverbed. He curled his palm around it, held onto it as he swam back up stream. He left the river and walked back to his tent, dried himself on his shirt, wrapped a blanket around his wiry body and lay down to sleep. When he woke he was still holding the stone. Part of it had a sharp, shaped edge as though someone had chipped at the surface. He turned it over and saw that, stuck to it, were tiny pieces of gold. He sat up. Something clung to his arm. He brushed it off and it fell to the ground. He picked it up. It was thinner than paper, brown with streaks of pale yellow, almost transparent.

Snake skin.

The loco slowed and shunted into the station. Uzra opened his eyes and pushed his hat back from his face. His men gathered their belongings from seats and overhead racks, opened carriage doors and stepped down onto the platform. The station was newly built, the timber still unpainted. He walked to the open carriage door, stood on the top step and breathed in. Traces of sawdust and linseed oil mixed with the dark wet smell of coal and the hot metal of the engine. Families embraced: wives ran their fingertips over their husbands' faces; children traced the dark lines of engrained coal dust on their fathers' arms and hands. One of the younger men picked up his son and raised him above his head as if to throw him in the air. The little boy laughed and clutched his father's hair while his mother shook her head in mock disapproval. Uzra looked past them and searched for the faces of the other women, the ones standing at the back, saying nothing. He stepped down and walked over to them; took off his hat, turning the brim in a slow circle through his fingers.

The women surrounded him and began to wail. He stayed on the platform, his hat in his hands, looking down at his feet. A woman with the first touches of grey in her long dark hair reached over, grabbed his knife from the leather pouch attached to his belt and scratched her arms and face until blood streaked and dripped. She threw the knife back at him and it landed by his feet.

Another woman picked it up and cut herself. And another.

His left hand crawled up his shirt and grasped his flute. He pressed his lips together. The muscles in his left shoulder began to twitch. He searched for the face of the only woman he knew, Eliza, Nathan's wife. She was sitting on her own behind the others, resting her head against the back of a rough wooden bench, cradling her pregnant belly.

When the women had finished he bent down and rescued his knife. He wiped the tip against his trousers and slid it back into his belt. Later, he'd pass the blade through a candle flame to cleanse it.

'Eliza.'

She stared at him.

'We couldn't bring him back.'

She heaved herself up. 'Who will provide for us?'

She walked away, her body struggling to find its balance and accommodate the weight of the baby.

He sat on the wooden bench. As the platform emptied he stared at the six open carriages stacked full of coal. He'd conscripted thirty men from this village. They'd spent five months away from their families, worked seven days a week in the dark, breathing in coal dust, poisonous gas and dank air. Fourteen were dead, and those who returned looked twenty years older. And barely enough coal to make a difference.

He saw himself as a boy, swimming in the deeper level of the river, playing in the other world, the secret world, with the snakes. He remembered going back and telling his grandfather what he had experienced: two rivers, one on the surface, one underneath. And he remembered his grandfather's response. He'd put his big, rough hands over Uzra's eyes as if he needed to protect them and said, 'You're just like me; just like your father.'

After that Grandpa accompanied him to the river and they camped there all spring and summer. He returned every spring and summer after that until he left the village.

That first summer he'd watched as his grandfather sat on the ground and drew two maps of the Otmas plain and the great river Aretis that wound its way through it – a surface map that matched what anyone could see with their everyday eyes; then the other map, a map of the hidden country that lay beneath, a world only they could see.

Each day they went to a different section of the riverbank and played their flutes. Afterwards they entered the river, swimming on the surface to begin with, lying on their backs, floating with the sun in their eyes and the breeze on their skin. Then they dived into that other river. The snakes came and the world was shot through with gold.

'Tell the others you have dreams or visions,' Grandpa said, 'but don't tell anyone what you really see – not even your mother.'

Uzra sat on the rough wooden seat staring at the loco, his hat in his hands, his knife sheathed. His lungs were heavy with coal dust. He coughed and spat; wiped his mouth with his handkerchief. Spots of blood stained the square of faded cotton. He folded it up and put it back in his pocket. His hand crept to his talisman, the flute around his neck. Sleep was what he wanted, sleep and clean air and the feel of the river against his skin and a few moments when he didn't see Nathan's broken body, his face distorted with pain.

—Three weeks later—

The rich smell of mud and silt washed down from the Otmas valley hit Uzra's nostrils – the sharp sting of the river as it met the sea. He adjusted the shoulder straps of his goatskin bag so it sat more easily against his back and scuffed the toes of his boots in the fine brown dust of the riverbank.

When he was a child his village had trekked to the river mouth twice a year – once in spring and again in early autumn – and set up camp. When the tide was low, they waded across the shallow water to the long stretch of beach on the other side. The men fished with long rods made from birch and the women collected seaweed and cockles. The older children played in the surf and flew kites, and the younger ones, excited by the waves and the sea air, raced along the silver-grey sand chasing gulls and finding shells.

At night, when the moon was at its highest and brightest and the tide at its lowest ebb, they dug in the exposed sand looking for threads of deposited gold. They balanced buckets of sand across wooden poles and carried them back to the river mouth.

Next morning wooden cradles were set out in a row on the bank and men shovelled the sand into them. Water was poured over the sand and they sifted for gold. Later in the day, the women built fires, cleaned and smoked fish, and boiled seaweed and cockles. In the evening everyone sat with their backs against the willow trees further up the river spooning up the rich, fishy soup. Uzra remembered his mother, her skirts hitched up, crouched by the fire cooking flat bread on heated stones.

He lifted his hat, fanned his face and wiped his forehead and thinning hair with his sleeve. He took off his boots, rolled his trousers past his knees and waded across the river mouth, the pull of the outgoing tide strong against his calves. He spread his toes and walked in slow motion enjoying the cool water on his hot feet.

Twenty years ago, he'd packed his goatskin bag and left in search of something different. Now he walked northwest, following the path of the old riverbed – dry boulders and pale grey stones – until he was a couple of miles from the village. He made camp in the dark, knowing the land like his own skin.

After he'd toasted the last of his bread over the flames and fried his ration of bacon, he wiped his hands on his trousers and searched in his bag. He unwrapped the square of dark blue silk his mother had given him before she died and laid his flute on the ground. It shone in the dark beside him. His grandfather had embossed the stem with patterns of swirling snakes. He rubbed the silk cloth over the outside of the flute and blew through it to remove any dust.

Stars arched above him, sharp and clear in a cloudless sky. He stood to play, bowing first to the northwest, to his mother and grandfather, then turning to the southeast, bowing to the men he lost at Kata. In a soft shuffle he walked the eight points of the compass. He raised the flute to his lips. Quiet at first, finding his breath, then louder as he slipped back into harmony with his instrument.

The village was smaller and poorer than he remembered. The twenty cottages in the inner circle closest to the well and the communal oven were still intact. Their walls were whitewashed, their shutters painted pale blue, the roofs freshly thatched, but many of the other houses in the sprawling outer circle had gaping doorways and holes in their walls.

Two women in heavy black dresses and long aprons stood talking at the well. He touched the brim of his hat. They stared at him, a dusty stranger. Their faces were so lined he didn't recognize them. A mangy dog barked at him. He walked across the path that led to the village hall. Four barefoot boys in cut-down men's trousers kicked a ball around on the stubby grass in front of the main door. Twenty years of coal dust coated his tongue.

He walked past the communal vegetable gardens, across the winding dirt path to the windbreak of cypress trees behind which was the graveyard. The ground was dry and the day cold even though it was still autumn. He chose an empty cottage as far from the main hall as possible. With an old straw broom, he brushed huge cobwebs from the ceiling and walls and swept the floor. He checked the doors and shutters closed properly. The only piece of furniture worth salvaging was a small wooden table. Three broken chairs and a set of rickety drawers he broke up for firewood. There was nothing to put his bedroll on but sleeping on the ground didn't bother him. He rescued a dented water bucket and walked back to the well.

The water was clear. He cleaned out the bucket, refilled it and washed his face and hands. In the west, the sky was streaked with thin lines of cloud. Gusts of wind blew dust around his feet and legs. One of the old women he'd seen earlier watched him from her doorway. He thought he remembered her: the matriarch of the Elosa clan who lived in the cottages closest to the well. He walked over, introduced himself and apologized for not recognizing her before. They spoke of his mother and grandfather.

She squinted at his face, shading her eyes from the sunlight behind him. 'People say you took all the luck with you.'

He stood on her doorstep and shuffled his feet on a worn-out straw mat.

'Would you trade with me?' he said. 'I have coffee, sugar and bacon, but no bread, milk or flour.'

She went inside and came back with a loaf of dark rye bread. 'We baked yesterday.'

Next morning, he visited the graveyard. Although the day was clear and fine, he shivered. The wet springs and long, gentle autumns of his childhood had disappeared. Now the winters were long and bitterly cold. Some years the spring rains didn't come at all and the summers were dry. Autumn didn't last long and then the first flurry of snow hit the mountaintops again.

Faint pink and grey clouds started to gather in the east. He bent down and pulled out handfuls of weeds from inside the little wooden fence that bordered his mother's grave. He cleaned the large flecked stone he and his grandfather had dug from the river, removing a thick layer of dirt as he traced the carved letters of his mother's first name: Illa.

'It's been a while,' he said. 'And I guess you wouldn't be that happy if I told you where I've been.' He unsheathed his knife and dug out the root of a stubborn weed. 'I'll come back and tidy this up. Make you a proper garden.'

His mother was buried beside his father who'd drowned a month before he was born. He and his best friend, Brena Joris, were returning home, crossing a section of the Aretis river swollen with melting snow and heavy spring rain. His father had slipped, caught his foot under a rock, fallen and banged his head. By the time Brena realised he wasn't walking behind him it was too late. As a boy he'd loved to hear his grandfather tell the story of how Brena had carried his father's body on his back for two days to bring him home so Illa could have him near her.

His grandfather's grave was next to Brena's, close to the welcome shade of trees. Uzra sat for a while leaning against the trunk of a sprawling oak. His eyes closed and he dozed for a few minutes. Memories of being a child and playing ball with other boys in the village wove themselves between jumbled images of gold and coal dust, shiny black engines as strong as fifty horses and grieving families. His chest ached, and when he coughed there were spots of blood.

In the afternoon he walked out to the section of river being mined by the village. A small dam had been made in order to funnel enough water to sluice the soil and pebbles. A distant flash of lightning lit up gathering clouds. Those villagers old enough to remember him were too worn out to question his sudden return. The others stared openly at his scars and the dark lines that ran the length of his face.

When the rain came an hour later he huddled with the older men under an awning of goatskins strung between willow trees. The younger ones carried on working, enjoying the water on their skin, laughing at each other as their clothes got soaked and clung to their bodies. As the rain increased they put down their shovels and pans and stood upright in the river and flexed their backs. Some of them unbraided their long hair and washed the dirt and dust out of it. Their faces were brown and lean, their hands thickened from working in soil and water.

Uzra waited under the awning with his arms folded like the other men and listened as they talked of shifting camp further north. This part of the river, once full of rich deposits, had yielded nothing in all the months they'd been working here. He said nothing but as soon as he'd arrived and stood beside the river he knew there was nothing left. His skin had felt flat and heavy and the water dull.

The rain clouds passed and the clothes and hair of the younger ones steamed in the returning sun. No one seemed to feel the cold. Three of the women sat on smooth, round boulders, men's trousers rolled up past their knees. They dried and combed each other's hair.

Erika, the camp cook, gathered dry kindling from her tent and lit a fire in the ring of stones that served as her oven. She put a heavy iron grate over the flames and lifted a cauldron onto it. The smell of rabbit stew reminded Uzra he was hungry and, for the first time since he'd left the northern mines, he realised his mouth and nose weren't clogged with coal dust.

They ate together sitting in a half circle under the willows. Afterwards, the older ones stretched out under the awning and the younger ones paired off and retired to their tents. He was startled by the easy acceptance of women in the camp. Erika saw the look on his face and laughed. She wiped her hands on her trousers and sat down beside him.

'The men no longer like to leave their wives and sweethearts,' she said. 'And the women work as hard as the men. They'd rather be out here than stuck in the village with nothing to do.'

'When was the last find?' he said.

He watched her short, strong fingers pick at the fabric of her heavy trousers, the ends of which were rolled up to accommodate her small frame.

Erika wrapped her arms around her legs and hugged her knees. Her long dark plait slipped down her calf. He noticed streaks of grey running through it, water running over black stone.

'There've been no major finds since you left.'

'You're joking?'

She wrinkled her nose. 'Nobody jokes about gold round here.'

He had a sudden memory of her as a young girl in high summer: bare feet and pigtails, large brown eyes in a dirty face, carrying her younger brother on her back to the river, sunshine burnishing their skinny legs and arms. He saw her playing in the water, splashing her brother, teaching him to swim in the warm, shallow water.

'It's been twenty years,' he said. 'There must have been some.'

Erika shrugged and looked past his shoulder out to the river.

Uzra studied the network of fine lines on her face, created by working outside in the sun and the wind. 'Do they blame me for the state of the village?'

She leaned towards him, her voice a whisper. 'The chairman and his committee are lazy and stupid.'

He reached over and touched her hand. 'I'll see what I can do.'

Later in the afternoon he walked further up the river, past the dam and the long narrow water pump made from tin cans the blacksmith had melded together. The sun was an orange ball dropping in a faded lavender sky. He breathed in the clean autumn air then bent over and coughed phlegm and coal dust out of his lungs.

The river was deeper here. When he was a boy he'd worked this section, the water almost up to his shoulders as he helped the older men dig out boulders and roll them up planks of wood onto the bank. Once the mud had settled and the water cleared, he'd dived and found rich gold deposits. A few of the old willow trees had survived, their branches still drooping, trailing a few tired leaves on the surface of the water. He looked out across the plain to the east. In the distance there was a cloud of gathering dust: horses, moving down across the open plains, travelling southeast.

It had been a long time since he'd sat silent and still under the shade of a willow and watched wild horses, their manes saturated with dust, drinking their fill from the river. Uzra's breath caught in his throat as the dust cloud moved closer. He remembered being young, longing to capture and tame his own horse and ride across the plains as fast as the wind. Now he thought of the shiny new locos the Southerners had invented, speeding across the countryside carrying men, equipment and supplies north and returning south with coal.

Two things had governed his life: gold and coal. He turned from watching the approaching horses and continued moving north along the riverbank. As the last of the light left the sky he made a rough camp next to a clump of grey boulders. The reflection of the new moon sliced the liquid darkness of the river. He listened to the music of water sliding over stones.

He gathered dried branches and made a fire. He drank black coffee from his tin mug and cut two thick slices of rye bread. In the distance he heard the faint whinnying and snorting of the horses. They too had settled by the river for the night. He threw more wood on the fire, leaned back against the smooth surface of a boulder and took out his flute.

At first, he was conscious of the river and the darkness, of the crackling and spitting of the flames and of his breath and fingers as he searched for the notes. As a gust of wind brought the rich smell of the horses to him, he slipped across an old border. He was there on the ground by the river playing a lullaby on his flute, his legs stretched out, his feet warmed by the fire. And, at the same time, he had slid through the folded seam of the river and entered that other place – the world his grandfather had mapped out for him, the world that lay hidden beneath the surface of the river and the land.

The river peeled back, its rocky skeleton running like a fault line through the plains. The world's geology was exposed, layer upon layer, thread by thread. He saw a seam of gold nestled beneath heavy grey stones – he would tell them where to dig tomorrow. And then, with the deaths of Nathan and the other miners anchoring and guiding him, he extended his search far beyond his village and the Otmas plains. He travelled the length of the Aretis River, back to its origins in the north, and began to look not for gold but for shiny black deposits of coal.

— *Six months later* —

Pickaxes struck against coal and rock. Uzra heard the voice of his foreman, Aliz, shouting commands. Other men cajoled and whistled commands to the pit ponies.

He turned in the underground tunnel and light from the lantern strapped to his leather helmet exposed sections of the cave walls. Trickles of black water ran down the glossy darkness of a rich coal seam. His lantern accentuated the dull glow of the sticky pellets that littered the cave floor. As he turned his head he saw the movement of his shadow in the narrow throw of light. A gap in the tunnel opened like a mouth into the vaulted chamber where his men were working. He bent down and crawled through it, wincing when he banged his knee against solid rock.

The bones in his hands ached through his leather gloves. Water puddled in the dips and hollows of the walls and floor. He was light-headed and nauseous after a few minutes exploring the coal seam. Marsh gas was building up again. They needed to burn off the tunnel.

After manoeuvring his way out of the tunnel, he relaxed in the more open space of the chamber. He gulped in the cleaner air and brushed at the sticky brown pellets that clung to the bottom of his trousers. Like everyone else working in the caves, he was covered with them. They were the width of his thumb and about half its length and had an oily feel. When he touched them, they smudged his skin like charcoal. He assumed they were the droppings of some creature that used to inhabit the caves, perhaps hundreds of years ago. He flicked them from his trousers with the dull edge of his knife. Some of them broke into smaller pieces about the size of his thumbnail. He ground his boot over a few of them but they didn't disintegrate. They glowed a faint orange. He kicked at them with the toe of his boot. Green and orange sparks leapt out. He picked up a handful, wiped them against the leg of his dirty trousers and slid them into his jacket pocket.

The rest of the shift he helped load coal into wooden carts strapped to small ponies. He and his foreman guided the ponies out through a wider tunnel that ran off the west side of the chamber. They handed the carts over to the men operating the winches that lifted two iron cages to the top of the mineshaft. The cages carried the coal to the surface where another gang of men unloaded it into bigger, horse-drawn carts.

Uzra led a team of forty men: twenty worked the seam, ten loaded and emptied the coal and ten more drove it out of the valley at night so it could be transported south. It was the richest seam he'd ever seen.

Men and supplies were transported in barges and canoes along the river until it forked a couple of miles below the last village in the valley. They walked in from there, guiding packhorses up to the caves. Uzra didn't want to disturb the villagers more than necessary, nor did he want them to discover they were taking more coal than they were entitled to. The village was small and the coal supplies more than it would ever need. He moved men, animals and supplies at night, guiding them up from the river to the caves. He warned the men to keep them away from the villages in the valley. They were paid to get coal for the Southerners, not to interfere with the locals.

The men worked in shifts, twelve hours on, twelve hours off, six days a week. When it was time for each shift to sleep, Uzra did as he was ordered and doctored their double ration of rum with a sleeping draft. So far, there had been no accidents. So far, he'd been lucky. The coal was transported down the hill to the river by horse-drawn carts where barges waited to carry it a hundred miles further south to the newly expanded railway tracks. It was backbreaking work but worth it. The Southerners supplied everything, except the miners.

When the shift had a break in the afternoon Uzra got the winchman to lift him to the surface. He sat on the ground at the mouth of the cave with his hat pulled down low until his eyes adjusted to the wide band of pale afternoon sky. The early winter air smelt of wood and coal fires burning in the valley below. He took the pellets out of his pocket and held them up to the light. In the daylight they were almost indistinguishable from lumps of dirt. But when he rubbed the surface briskly he uncovered a core that glowed green and orange.

He put the pellets back in his pocket and walked over to the cooking hut. It was warm inside from the fire burning in the coal range. Steam from a large cauldron of soup misted the windows. He opened the door of the oven and saw it needed another shovel of coal. He remembered the pellets in his pocket and threw a couple in and shut the door. The fire crackled and hissed behind him. He took off his jacket and stared out the steamy window.

Six months earlier, when he'd left his own village in the Otmas valley the only person he'd said goodbye to had been Erika. She'd touched the sleeve of his jacket then the scars on his cheeks. 'Will it be another twenty years before we see you again?' she said.

He took her hand away from his face and held it, feeling her calloused palm against his own rough skin. 'I've one more job to do for the Southerners,' he said, 'then I can come home.'

'I thought you'd had enough of coal.'

He bent down and kissed her forehead.

She stood leaning against the trunk of an oak tree and watched as he walked away.

Behind him the fire roared as if someone had opened the vents at the back of the stove and let in a rush of air. He turned around. Flames shot out the oven door into the hut. Tongues of orange and green pushed the cast-iron rings off the top of the stove. The cauldron of soup bounced in the air then crashed, pouring boiling liquid onto the floor.

He grabbed the sacking oven cloth from the table and wrapped it around his right hand; snatched the long-handled poker hanging from the hook on the wall beside the stove and tried to close the oven door. The metal poker conducted a wave of heat up into his arm. He leapt back and dropped the poker on the floor. He slipped and banged his leg against the corner of the table. The oven door sprang open.

He covered his face and dived through the window.

The cabin exploded. Flames leapt twenty feet into the air.

Aliz, his leading hand, came running from the mouth of the cave. Uzra tried to stand up and move away, but his knees buckled. He sat back in the dirt.

Aliz dragged him further back. 'What the hell was that?'

Uzra ordered the miners to collect all the pellets from the floors of the caves. He stored them in large, tightly woven wicker baskets in the back corner of the entrance cave. When his men asked what he wanted to do with them he shrugged.

'Just leave them there,' he said, 'I don't want them sticking to everything.'

When the next load of coal went down the river he sent a sealed message south to his boss, Rohine. He began to blow out small sections of the narrow tunnel with gunpowder. He made wicks by tearing up long, narrow strips of cotton, trickling gunpowder down their length then rolling them tight. He attached one end of each wick inside an empty food can no bigger than the size of his hand; packed gunpowder tight around the wicks until the can was full, drawing the long tail of the wick far enough out to light the exposed ends once the tins were in position. Now he knew the power of the pellets, he secured the cans high up on the cave walls, checked and rechecked the walls and floor to makes sure everything was clear before he lit the end of each wick.

Three days of blasting and the tunnel was wide enough for the day shift to start digging out coal.

Uzra sat above ground beside Aliz, coal dust and grime etched into the deep scars that lined his face. He rubbed a dirty hand across the stubble on his chin, sucked in a mouthful of fresh air then coughed up a lump of grey phlegm. He spat and rinsed his mouth with the remains of his mug of coffee.

Aliz squinted at him in the sunlight. 'How long since you had a bath and a hot meal?'

Uzra shaded his eyes and looked out over the valley. A few funnels of white smoke drifted across the early morning sky and merged into streaky pink clouds.

His clothes hung off him and his muscles ached. He could barely remember what it felt like to be clean. He closed his eyes and watched the play of light behind his eyelids. He wanted to talk to Erika, to touch her long dark hair, to unplait it and feel it run like warm water through his fingers. He wanted to forget the bones, the broken skulls, the shards of shattered pottery dislodged from the roof of the tunnel by his explosions. The men were spooked, some of them refusing to work the tunnels again until everything was cleared. Thousands more pellets had appeared, falling out of pottery jars that contained skulls.

He rubbed his chin again and a tiny flake of white came away on his finger.

Bone.

He flicked it away and coughed up more phlegm.

Two weeks later, Rohine, Senior Southern Engineer, stood on a barge, his body braced against a couple of large sacks of grain. An oatmeal-coloured woollen cloak was wrapped around his tall, thin frame. His silver hair and clear pale skin shone in the moonlight. He reminded Uzra of a fish. He put both hands in his pockets, touching the pellets he'd brought with him.

Rohine raised a hand in recognition, revealing a gold and ruby ring on his middle finger. They moved away from the barge to let men unload and pack the horses. Rohine placed a bony hand on Uzra's shoulder. 'What's so important I need to come all the way up here?'

Uzra took his hand out of his pocket and opened his palm.

Rohine scratched a silver eyebrow and coughed. 'Animal droppings?'

'Maybe.'

Uzra gathered a few twigs and dried leaves, pushed them together in a pile, added half a dozen strips of paper from his pocket and stuck a match. As the flame took hold of the paper, he dropped a small pellet into the pile. He counted to thirty in his head. Orange and green flames shot into the air, casting a bright circle of fluorescent light over them.

Rohine stepped back and put his hands in front of his face.

An hour later they were still standing in front of the fire. Rohine had removed his woollen cloak. He dabbed sweat from his face with his scarf. He poked at the base of the fire with a long stick. Flames licked around it and heat rushed up his arm. He dropped the stick in the fire. 'How long do they burn for?'

Uzra shrugged. 'Depends what you mix them with. With coal, up to six days.'

'One pellet?'

'I threw two on the coal range in the cooking hut and blew it up. The fire burned for a week.'

'How many do you have?'

Uzra rolled a pellet between his fingers.

'Enough to make a difference.'

URSULA

Before I die I'll tell you how all this came to be. It's a tale told at the end to explain the beginning, a tale told before my bones are broken and returned to the caves of Aretis.

Long, long ago, beneath the mantle of Great Darkness, our Grandfather's ancestor said, I will create the wind, and he sneezed and the wind was formed.

Out of the wind and darkness came the beginning, the dust that formed us all. This dust swirled in the heavens until the sky creatures were formed: the bear, the scorpion, the snake.

Time passed. Our worlds were formed: the land, the mountains and caves, the seas and the rivers, all the waters that sustain us. Water once shimmered like the skin of our ancestors; it reflected the face of our sister the moon. It ran beneath our gardens in the north and flowed out through the opening in the great rock we call the northern gate into the valley below. It twisted and turned, lithe, like the body of Grandfather. It ran between the three worlds. It kept us separate and bound us together.

The starlit realm of our ancestors was part of the Great Darkness, and only Grandfather ever returned to its embrace. The surface world, filled as it was with plants, trees and animals, was equally divided between darkness and light. Our own world lay hidden in the valley, beneath the caves. We harvested the crystals; we mixed our bodies with soil and rock to make gifts for Grandfather.

Aretis, our sacred river, flowed out of the valley, past villages that blossomed, faded and grew again, like flowers returning each spring. Her waters travelled east, west and south. Snow, melting from the great mountain ranges in the north, filled her tributaries, and in the west the rocks in the riverbeds shone with gold when her waters slid over them.

That time of flowering has now passed.

Aretis no longer runs like an artery through the worlds. Soon there will be nothing but a trickle of brackish water no one can drink. The sunlit world will darken; ice and snow will cover the land.

The Gardeners have been destroyed and, without us, Grandfather cannot renew himself or the world.

They took me from the caves. Light penetrated my skin, burnt my muscles, scorched my bones. Against the onslaught of light, I said my name and rank. I am Ursula, senior navigator, keeper of the Northern Gate.

They tied me down. Forced metal down my throat, clamped my glands. My flesh was cut; my blood seeped onto the hard bench they'd bound me to. The pale creatures of the surface world took away what belonged to Grandfather. Their fingers poked and prodded my private places. Their voices so harsh they damaged the air around me; their words flaked into thousands of pieces, flaying my ears, my skin.

Three hours in every twenty-four they took the tube from my mouth and turned off the lights. When their footsteps faded and there was no sound except my own breathing I began the chant. I whispered the words that celebrated the dimming of daylight and the rising of the dark.

There were twenty of us, working deep beneath the eighth level; carving out new tunnels, harvesting for the Festival of Longest Night. Ten pairs: an older navigator teamed with a younger digger. At the beginning of the shift, we navigators gathered round the diggers. We sat side by side, braiding each other's hair, twisting it in coils around their heads so we could work unhindered.

As the most experienced navigator I led the search for the chant. Our voices rose and fell, moving through the air of the caves as we searched for the pitch we needed to guide the diggers. When the air began to warm and the crystals already harvested started to vibrate, I accepted the harmony and set the chant for the shift. Navigators sing to the crystals but the life of a navigator is not easier or better than that of a digger – we are sisters, joined together, each dependent on the other.

The time of the Festival drew close. We ascended to the entrance of the third level and spent a day and a night there, resting, and talking about the preparations we needed to make. My skin was tingling from the power of the waxing moon pulling me towards the surface.

When I first heard the banging, I thought I must have fallen asleep and it was part of a dream, but once I was awake and it continued I wondered if it was a warning of earthquakes or some other upheaval.

I woke my sisters and we listened together, trying to find a pattern in the strange hammering and rumbling. Then the noise stopped. We waited a couple of hours and when nothing more happened we moved through the eastern tunnels to the second level.

I stayed on guard while the others slept. The noise started again. Instead of getting warmer as we approached the surface my skin began to cool. I shivered and wondered if we'd ascended to the second level too fast. I unfolded my cloak, draped it around my shoulders and pulled the hood over my head. Being so close to the surface, I could feel the moon setting. We were still protected by rock walls but I feared the light of the returning sun – it burned and blistered our skin, blinded our eyes, upset the harmony of our blood.

The noise was louder now, a rhythmic hammering. I began to count: twenty beats then a break of ten; thirty beats then a break of twenty. This pattern continued until there was a long, shrill whistle; it hurt my ears and disturbed my sisters. Leal, the youngest and most sensitive of the diggers sat up and put her hands over her ears.

I bent down, refastened my sandals and arranged my cloak so it covered me from shoulder to ankle. I was still shivering.

'It's quiet now,' Leal said. 'Shall we move to the first level?'

I nodded at each of my hooded sisters and they began to walk in single file towards the next row of tunnels.

A powerful vibration shook me. I was thrown against the wall. Rocks fell around my head and shoulders. Water and coal poured through the tunnel. My sandals were torn from my feet. I landed face down with my ears ringing, my mouth full of coal dust and dirty water.

I struggled to stand. Another rush of water pushed me over. I twisted into a crouching position and braced myself against the force of the water. A gash appeared in the wall before me. I fell forward. Two of my sisters floated past, their legs twisted at odd angles, their long black hair spread out like bats' wings. Their faces were submerged in the stream of coal and water filling the tunnel.

I was grabbed from behind and pulled to my feet. Leal dragged me out of the collapsing tunnel into a side alcove.

'We have to go back down,' she said.

I leaned against the damp wall and spat out a mouthful of black water. 'Where are the others?'

Leal wiped her face on her torn sleeve. 'Dead,' she said, 'they're all dead.'

Three more explosions ripped apart the rest of the tunnels on level two. Water flooded the tunnels that led down to level three. We were thrown to the floor of the alcove, knocked down by falling rocks. Leal cried out and clutched my hand.

When I woke, I was still holding Leal's hand. It was stiff and cold. My ears were ringing. I rolled over and vomited then sank back onto the ground. I opened my eyes for a last look at Leal and saw behind her the golden shadow of Grandfather, his huge body undulating through the water, moving through the holes in the tunnel walls. 'Grandfather,' I shouted. 'Warn the others to stay below. My team is dead. The second level has been destroyed.'

He turned towards me. Gold filigree spun out of his mouth and settled over me like a net. It was warm and numbed my skin. I closed my eyes again.

Much later, streaks of blue and yellow light streamed onto my face from the tin helmets the ghost men wore on their heads. I raised my arm to protect my eyes. They stood in a circle around me. One of them prodded me with his boot.

A man smaller than the rest, with scars on his face, made a rumbling sound in the back of his throat. He pushed the rest of the men away. He bent down and picked me up. Tremors ran through his arms as he carried me away from Leal, away from the others, up to the surface world.

I can't remember how long I've been here. Light damages my thinking as much as my organs and skin. My mind lurches and slides, searching for graduations of shade or shadow. I close my eyes but behind my eyelids lights shriek and swirl.

The small man with the scarred face came back. He sat beside me, using his body to shield my face from the light, the tip of one of his fingers touching the back of my hand, drawing small circles on my skin. Tears ran down the scars on his cheeks.

He spoke to some of the other ghost men, low, urgent sounds I didn't understand. There was one word I did understand though, because he pointed to himself and said it many times: Uzra. He told me his name was Uzra.

Even when they turned the lights off, it was never completely dark, or quiet. There was always noise from outside the room – people walking, the sound of their sandals slapping as they walked up and down the corridor. In the background there was a high-pitched humming and beneath that the roaring of a furnace that eats the coal they dig out of our caves and transport here.

'Grandfather,' I whispered whenever they left me alone, 'can you hear me? Can you find your way to the surface? Can you travel faster than their coal-eating machines?'

I rolled onto my back and stretched out my legs. The skin on my feet and ankles was cracked and swollen. Above me the lights on the ceiling blocked out the beauty of the night sky.

'Grandfather, don't let me die here on the surface. Don't let me die among the ghost men. Take me home so I can be washed in the waters of Aretis and buried in the caves with my sisters.'

UZRA

8 months later

Uzra stood on the viewing platform that encircled the lookout tower. The platform rose a thousand steps above the southern town of Javiers into air so sharp and clear it cut holes in his coal-damaged lungs and made him feel lightheaded. In the southwest, mountains covered in heavy snow formed a semi-circle around a serene blue lake. Silver and blue domed buildings fanned out from its edges, spreading back as far as the clover-covered hills that sat at the feet of the mountains. He could just make out the faint humped outlines of thousands of beehives that dotted the hills. Every time he came south he stood here and took his fill of the light, making up for so many months working in the darkness of the underground caves in the north – caves that fed this city and most of the south with coal.

From his jacket pocket he took a couple of the small pellets he carried whenever he travelled now. He rolled them in his hand, working his fingertips against their sticky surface. How insignificant they looked in the bright sunlight. A few bits of hardened dirt mixed with he wasn't quite sure what, yet they'd become an underground currency in the south, as tradable as silver or gold. He put the pellets back into his pocket and wiped his hands with his handkerchief.

He hadn't given all the baskets of pellets to Rohine. He'd hidden small caches in the hills behind the caves and each night he'd been above ground at the camp he'd sewn handfuls of pellets into the lining of his clothes and bedding. Insurance against hard times.

In the biting wind he started to cough. He sat on one of the rough wooden seats and spat a lump of phlegm onto one of the wooden planks of the platform. At least he'd stopped coughing up blood and he wasn't covered in the purple rash that was the beginning of the sickness that now plagued the whole of the south and parts of the north. It was hard to believe just how quickly it had taken hold.

A few months ago, Javiers' harbour had been filled with ships arriving from the north, laden with passengers, food and coal. Now it was almost a ghost town. The only thing moving on the harbour this morning was a coffin ship taking the dead out past the heads to bury them in the open sea. He shuddered at the thought of all those bodies consigned to water. If he couldn't return to Otmas and be buried beside his parents and cousins he would rather be burnt on the bonfires that were lit every evening on the hills outside the city. Bonfires fuelled by coal. Two years ago, there'd been barely enough coal to keep people alive during the worst months of winter. Now bonfires blazed every night.

He'd heard rumours that the poor, unable to pay the price of the passage out to sea, threw the kerosene-soaked bodies of their dead relatives and friends directly into the flames. He wondered, as he always did when he came south, why they didn't bury their dead. No matter that he'd worked for Southerners for years, some things never made any sense.

He sat with the wooden slats digging into the back of his thighs, not wanting to return to ground level and begin the walk back to the laboratory. He looked at his hands, at the split fingernails, the ingrained coal dust, the scars, the broken index finger on his right hand. That morning he'd soaked his hands in hot water and mustard then scrubbed them with lemon juice in preparation for his visit later in the afternoon but nothing he did made his hands feel clean. He stood up, turned his back on the sea and faced the mountains again. The glare from the sun shining on the whiteness of the snow made him shade his eyes. I'm so used to darkness, he thought, it's as though I've never left the northern caves.

For months he had moved between north and south, travelling on the locos, cadging a passage on cargo ships, using some of his precious pellets to persuade southern officials to give him the authority to take her from the laboratory and return her to the caves above Aretis.

The last time he'd come to Javiers to visit her she was so blinded from too much light she hadn't known him. She'd been lying on her side on the narrow wooden gurney in the corner of the laboratory, so motionless and quiet he thought she was dead. When he touched her on the arm, she didn't respond. Her skin was dull and icy cold beneath his fingertips. He searched her wrist until he found a flicker of pulse. He wrapped her in his heavy woollen coat, picked her up and marched out the door. Rohine and two guards met him halfway down the corridor.

'Put her down, Uzra,' Rohine said in that soft southern way he had, smiling at him as if this was a social visit.

Uzra elbowed his way past one of the guards. 'She's barely alive.'

He'd tried to run, to make it to the outer door, but even though she was small and half-starved she was still too heavy and his lungs began to wheeze from the effort.

The guards reached the doors just as he did and blocked his exit. Uzra stood in front of them, his lungs rattling in his chest, the muscles in his shoulders and arms aching from holding her. 'She's no use to you now,' he said. 'Let me take her.'

Rohine put a hand on his shoulder. 'If we'd left her in the mines, she would have died. Just like all the others.'

Uzra shrugged his hand away.

A sigh went through Rohine's long pale body. His tapered fingers smoothed the collar of Uzra's shirt. 'Don't be difficult, Uzra. We needed to find out how she produced the pellets.'

Uzra's arms had begun to shake. He lowered her to the floor and knelt beside her.

Rohine raised his eyebrows and signalled to the guards.

Uzra unwrapped his coat to check her pulse again. It was stronger now; she wasn't so cold. He covered her again, shielding her face from the skylight in the corridor roof. 'Something happened, didn't it Rohine? Something you did created the sickness.'

Rohine touched the finely woven woollen scarf wrapped around his neck. He rolled his shoulders then adjusted the lapels of his jacket. 'You've spent too long underground, Uzra, breathing in noxious gases. Your mind has become addled.'

Uzra bent over her, whispered goodbye. He stood up. 'I'm coming back, Rohine. And she'd better be in a lot better condition than this.'

He watched as one of the guards picked her up and carried her back into the laboratory. His breath caught in his throat and he began to cough. He turned his back on Rohine. He bent down and retrieved his coat from the floor. He tried to put it on but his hands were trembling.

Rohine reached out with his long arms, took Uzra's coat from him and held it open so he could slide his arms in.

'After all this time,' Uzra said, 'we don't even know her name.'

Rohine shook his head. 'Don't be a fool, Uzra. Animals don't call themselves anything.'

Uzra took a last look at the mountains and the lake, wishing he could store light in the pores of his skin. He began to descend the thousand steps to the ground. The sky remained a deep cloudless blue but the sun was beginning to sink behind the mountains.

He walked back through tree-lined streets towards the city centre. The domed blue and silver buildings of the richest citizens seemed deserted. Many of the shops and warehouses were boarded up. Notices were tacked onto doors: *Closed until further notice.* The healthiness of open sky, fresh air and sunshine was at odds with the reality of dying people and empty streets.

As he walked he remembered the white scarf wrapped around Rohine's neck. He wondered if Rohine had already been ill when they'd last met, whether it had been his death that had speeded up her release. Now he finally had permission to take her, he had to find a way to get her back to the northern caves – caves damaged by the explosives he'd used to excavate coal from deep within the underground tunnels that crisscrossed between different levels like elaborate staircases. Tunnels built by her and her people over millennia.

He kicked at a stone lying in front of him on the road. He watched it bounce across the street, heard the ping as it hit the side of an overflowing rubbish bin. A large grey rat scuttled from the open bin dragging something small and bloody into an alley between two shops. His stomach heaved and he covered his mouth and nose with his hand. For a moment he hated the endless sunshine; he wanted heavy, driving rain to wash everything clean.

The door to the warehouse that enclosed the laboratory was unguarded. Uzra stood on the step and wiped his hands on his handkerchief again. He walked down the corridor, glancing into the room that was once Rohine's office. Like so much else it was abandoned, the desk still stacked with piles of papers now gathering dust. The laboratory door was unlocked. He pushed it open with his foot. Inside it was dark. He waited a few moments for his eyes to adjust.

She was alone, lying on her back on the floor in the far corner of the room.

'Hello,' he called, his face hot with shame because he didn't know what to call her.

She turned over and faced him. Her mouth was cracked; her lips caked with dried blood.

'Vellen,' she whispered, pointing to her mouth. 'Vellen.'

'Your name is Vellen?' Then he slapped his thigh. Water – she was dying of thirst.

He cradled her head, gave her small sips of water from a glass he found in Rohine's office; wet a clean corner of his handkerchief and dabbed at her lips, trying to moisten them and wipe away the blood. There were deep cuts on her mouth and tongue.

'Vellen,' he said, touching her forehead gently with his broken index finger. 'Shall I call you Vellen?'

GRANDFATHER ANISTH

Anisth patrolled the north-western section of the border. He stretched, flicked his tail and extended his tongue to test the sharpness of the air. His body slid along the path that led to the northern gate. He was dehydrated and raw from shedding.

A thread of mucus spun out from his tongue as if he was a spider making a web. He rubbed the barbed end of his tail across his body, scraped off a layer of dead skin, flicked it into his mouth to moisten it then spat it out to make a sticky covering. While it was still wet he spread it out, smoothing it across the stretched and thinning fabric of the border. As his patchwork dried he felt the edges of the border move back in and heard the snap as the boundary expanded and then contracted to accommodate its new shape.

The Northern Gate lay folded beneath the valley closest to the base of a mountain range whose snow fed the great river of Aretis. Ancient gardens rambled and decayed. For millennia the remains of the Gardeners had rested here, buried in tunnels deep beneath the surface, their bones preserved between the layers of rock and coal in the caves.

Anisth approached the gate and remembered the past.

He was thousands of years younger. Giant ferns rustled in the breeze and made shadows on the rocks. Gardeners surrounded him as he entered the gate. Dumana emerged from the tunnel that led to the main entrance of the underground gardens. She'd been planting the fibrous black tubers that needed no light to grow. Even though it was dusk, she shaded her eyes from the last of the light.

The Gardeners worked below the surface. They tied the strands of the gate together with the roots of the tuber, forming a knitted mass that captured and contained the current. Once, the frayed edges of the current were dissipated, wasted, but over time the Gardeners had learned to harness the energy.

As the light faded from the sky, children emerged to play a game of hide and seek in the plantations that formed a barrier between their home and the village below. They raced towards the sunflowers, dwarfed beneath the tall stems, brushing past the lowest of the drooping, elongated leaves.

The village was cradled in the valley beneath them, cupped between the plantations, the river and the hills, its centre curled across the surface of the border like another snake. The sky darkened and the moon rose. Fires flared in the village, fuelled by trees and branches swept down the river when it flooded, and by coal the villagers collected in the caves from the seams closest to the surface. Smoke seeped across the sky, filling the evening air with the faint smell of sulphur. The children wrinkled their sensitive noses and moved back to the entrance of the caves. An old woman from the village with the blue tattoo of a snake on her left arm stared into the smoke and stepped her mind across the border, greeting Anisth and Dumana as holy ones – guardians.

Anisth entered the Northern Gate and prepared to sleep. It was his favourite resting place, even though it was also the place that was the most porous. Currents pushed and pulled at its boundaries, creating a shimmering, unstable pulse that needed constant weaving and containing. It was only his vigilance that kept the balance, yet he preferred it to all the other gates.

The surface gardens and giant sunflower plantations camouflaged the entrance to the Gardeners' home but there were times when the most curious of the villagers glimpsed them at their work. Sometimes, when the Gardeners came to the surface for moon ceremonies and to present gifts to him, the oldest women from the village watched from a distance. Then the barriers that kept them separated thinned, and a few were able to cross over.

The boundaries of the border breathed and moved, expanded and shrank. Anisth felt these movements as a tingling in his own skin, as warnings that warmed or chilled his blood. He travelled its intricate loops and folds and spirals, searching for weakness or danger. He pushed himself against the outer edges, feeling the surging of the current as it flashed out. He used his tongue to find the worn, burnt-out places, rubbing his saliva and skin into the cracks and holes.

Once upon a time all the gates remained open and the current ran free. Then any creature who could see, and who wanted to, could take the risk and move across. But that was long ago, before there was need or reason, before the ascent of the surface people.

Anisth sighed, slid between steep walls of pink and gold sandstone and entered the inner passageway of the Northern Gate. Lately, there'd been a dark-haired girl who played on her own by the river, forming balls of clay and drying them on flat stones in the sun. She liked to wander alone over the hills that surrounded the village, herding her goats. She lay on top of the ridge and looked down on the caves and the Gardeners' secret entrance. She kept very still, unaware she'd crossed the border; unaware of him and his endless cycle of weaving and mending, or of the Gardeners as they cultivated their plantations and maintained their underground networks. He didn't know exactly what she did see only that she wasn't afraid. And because she was still young, and had disturbed nothing, he left her alone. Perhaps she thought he and the Gardeners were ghosts, visitations from the world of the dead.

He settled inside the inner cavern on top of the coarse sand that covered the floor. A shaft of light from a hole high up in the ceiling illuminated a small section of the rock wall. It was flecked with the remains of many ages: pieces of broken shell, skeletons of small fish, the fine bones of a bird lodged in the rock along with fragments of larger bones. He sighed again and curled into the warm sand. The wind rose and pushed against the outer walls.

He dreamed of ancient days, of lepidodendron forests long vanished, sunk beneath the earth and transformed into seams of fire-bearing coal. He dreamed of the veins that ran through the earth's layers, of underground streams of gold and silver. And he dreamed of his dead companions, the friends of his youth, the Gardeners who built the first tunnels, who ploughed out a network of caves with their hands and feet, fertilising the soil with milk fresh from their own glands.

Sinking further into sleep he revisited his own beginning, when he was one of a pool of thousands of worker snakes serving the electric mother, the first one to harness the current and create the paths, the passages and gateways – all the things necessary for the creation of the borders. In his dreams he was young and fresh, learning how to ride the waves and surges of the current, basking in its phosphorescence with his brothers and sisters, travelling to the outer edges of the universe.

And later, millennia later, as he grew older and stronger and renewed himself with the help of the Gardeners, as he changed from worker to master to keeper, he travelled beyond what was known, leaving everything behind except the current singing in his veins. He knew then he carried the spark. He could extend the curve at the edge of the universe, make it fold over on itself, create a new seam – a little world, a pocket of space and time stitched out of fragments of his own skin.

He dreamed of all that had been created, the length of his great body curled in rings around his head, the tip of his barbed tail resting high up against the rock face in the cave. He dreamed to remember the past, to surf the current, to travel again. He dreamed and was lithe and free again: his spit a constant stream for weaving, his skin plump and fresh and streaked with gold. In his dreams he was never alone. There were others like him stretching the current, creating new borders. And later, when his kind had vanished to the farthest corners, there were hundreds of Gardeners in the folds and seams he had created, tending gardens above and below ground.

Anisth stirred from his sleep and rubbed his huge head against the gritty sand that littered the floor of the cave. It was no longer safe to rest here and dream and wait for the jewels that allowed him to renew himself. The Northern Gate had been violated. Ursula had been taken to the cold lands of the south and the rest of the Gardeners lay dead in the tunnels. Unless he found her, he would grow old and weak, his skin would dry out and crack, his eyesight fail, his mucus disappear. The gates would collapse; the boundaries fall. The uncontained power of the current would surge and wipe out the worlds he'd created.

He wove his tired body back through the Northern Gate. He didn't have time to mend the breach properly. He travelled down through the valley to the deepest part of the river and lowered himself into the water. His skin was already thinning, soon it would tighten and split. The current was strong and carried him south.

Once he was submerged Anisth closed his eyes and allowed the water to wash over his head. His skin and then the muscles and organs in his body began to cool. His breath and heartbeat slowed. As the current carried him out of the valley he relaxed. Occasionally he flicked his tongue, sending out a current of his own, alerting the river snakes to come and guide him to the great lake in the south.

He found a deep pool and stopped to sleep. A day and a night passed. His mind slowed to match his pulse; it slipped between the comfort of ancient memories and the horror of more recent destruction. Images of the Gardeners assailed him, their hair spread out, their bodies face down, arms outstretched as if in supplication, as they were swept out of the tunnels on a tide of coal and dirty water. As the rocks fell and the water rose, Ursula had cried out to him to save her sisters still working in the deepest tunnels. He'd paused long enough to spray her eyes and face with his spit then turned his massive body around and smashed headfirst through layers of rock. But there were too many explosions. Each time he cleared a passage wide enough to move through, another tunnel was flooded or blocked. The cries of dying Gardeners rang in the air. Raw current, contained for millennia by cultivation, and channelled through the architecture of the tunnels, snapped and surged through the caves. The explosions had damaged the Northern Gate; the boundary had been breached.

On the morning of the second day the river snakes arrived, thousands of them swimming upstream from the Otmas Valley, leaving their favourite resting place to answer his call. Flecks of gold still dusted their skin and they glinted as they glided over his back and around his head, tiny as goldfish as they swam against his bulk. He waited until they formed into two streams and flanked the length of each side of his body. Even though his skin was icy and his eyes almost blind from being submerged in water, he could still feel the hum of their energy against him, enlivening his heart. Each flank was linked head to tail, weaving itself together to support him on the rest of his journey. He waited until the last of the snakes arrived. They surrounded him front and back. Fully encircled, he flicked his tongue again sending out a sharp spurt of electricity. The snakes merged into a shell around him, the movement of their bodies warming the water closest to skin. His heartbeat increased. He twitched the tip of his tail to signal he was ready. The leaders of each flank twitched their tails in response. They turned southeast and moved him out of his resting place in the pool and back into the river.

After travelling all day, they guided him through the tangled roots of ancient willow trees so he could rest again in the deep water close to the riverbank. Although his skin was still warm from their constant movement as they swam less than an inch away from him, and moist from being in the water for so long, it was now so thin it was starting to crack. He lifted his head out of the river and put it on the bank. He needed to be renewed. Ursula was still many days away in the South and even though he sensed she was still alive he knew she was very weak.

He opened his eyes. Above him in the gathering dusk he saw the shadow of a hawk, its wings wide as it glided on a thermal. He watched the hawk circling, waiting for it to plunge earthward to capture its prey but it continued moving in high, slow circles. Anisth sniffed the air. The evening breeze brought him the smell of mud and eels, the spicy dust of the dry earth on either side of the riverbank and the musky scent of the river snakes as they fanned out to stretch their tired bodies and seek food. He moved his head, burrowing it more deeply into the bank and picked up the faint vibration of a creature walking towards the river. It was moving slowly and on two rather than four feet.

As the vibrations grew stronger his skin started to itch, reacting to the electric pull of being close to the Gardeners' jewels. For a moment he hoped Ursula had escaped and come to minister to him so he could shed and renew. He looked at the darkening sky searching for a glimpse of the rising moon but clouds obscured it – it was almost night.

Out of the gloom he saw a woman stop to rest beneath a willow. Behind her a darker shadow lurked, stopping when she stopped, sitting when she sat. But when the woman approached the riverbank to wash her face and hands, the shadow stayed crouched beneath the tree, trembling like a child.

Anisth lifted his head and clicked his tongue.

The woman stepped back and stared at him. 'Holy One,' she said, 'how can I serve you?'

He arched his back and his skin split open.

She crouched close to his head; reached into her tunic and brought out four of the Gardeners' jewels. She rolled them in the centre of her palm then placed them on the ground in front of him.

He pushed himself further out of the water. The shadow leapt from beneath the tree, its edges pulsating. Anisth's tongue darted out. One by one he scooped the jewels into his mouth. He swallowed. At first there was just a familiar oily taste in his throat, then the welcome sensation of spreading warmth. His old heart quivered and began to shut down. He swallowed again and stung the inside of his mouth with the barbed tip of his tongue. His new heart opened. Blood pumped. His veins and arteries expanded. Energy surged through him charging his organs with electric current, renewing every cell in his body. He was strong again, capable of harnessing the boundaries, of mending the breaches in the Northern Gate.

In front of him, the woman bowed her head on the ground. She moved back to the shelter of the trees. The shadow stayed by the riverbank. With his new, sharper vision, Anisth realised the shadow was a wraith: a lost creature wandering between worlds, covered in a cloud of darkness. It bent towards the river, plucked a fragment of snakeskin from the surface of the water, clutched it to its breast. Anisth spat a fine stream of mucus towards it, a wrap of gossamer energy, something to sustain its journey through the borderlands.

The clouds parted. A yellow half-moon climbed in the sky. The river snakes returned, satiated from feeding. Anisth lowered his body back into the water, leaving his head floating on the surface. He called the leaders together. They circled him, creating ripples that spread out and splashed the edges of riverbank.

'Go south,' he said, 'Find Ursula. I need to mend the Northern Gate. Wait for me in the Southern Lake.'

Part 3: Search and Return

*Jason and Aja – Captain Damian
Uzra – Ursula/Vellen – Grandfather Anisth*

JASON AND AJA

Aretis (third visit)

The hills and plains were dry on either side of the river. Jason walked behind Aja. She wound her shawl around her head and face to keep out the dust. As they walked, he watched the wind move over clumps of pale grass, their tips opened to reveal a darker, greener core. The hawk had been following them all day, rising up over the hills then sinking down again to the river. He tracked the shadow of its wings on the ground as it flew above them.

In the afternoon, the sun transformed the brown slopes of the western hills into stripes of red and gold. Aja stopped and spread a blanket between two cypress trees close to the river. He lay down and looked at the sky. Her hawk circled high above, searching for prey. He waited until it dived then curled up and closed his eyes.

In his dreams now, there was always fire. Columns of thick black smoke rose from the earth and spread into the sky where they merged with the clouds, dragging them back to lie, dark and heavy, over the land. But something frightened him more than those dreams of fire. Whether awake or asleep he heard the wail of a creature taken against its will. He didn't know what or where it was, only that it was desperate for water, blinded by light, its body cut and scarred, and on its neck there was an open wound, weeping pus.

When he woke again it was almost dark. A half-moon climbed in the sky. The river smelt of musk. He moved closer to the edge. Eels moved through the water, over stones, under the roots of trees that overhung the bank. He saw the snake then, swimming through the eels, yellow eyes glowing, its skin metallic and scaled like a fish. Its scales caught the moonlight. It glided towards him over the surface of the water. For a moment he thought it had wings: that it would spring from the river and destroy him. But it stopped in front of Aja. It wound itself among the tree roots and put its huge head on the riverbank.

Aja reached for her shawl and wrapped it around her head and shoulders again. She slid her hand inside her tunic, brought out a small urn and placed it on the ground between herself and the snake. A dry, clicking sound filled the air. Jason scratched the side of his face with his fingernails, just to check he was awake.

The snake opened its eyes; uncurled itself from the tree roots and laid its body flat across the water. Its back was thick enough and wide enough to bridge the river. Clouds obscured the moon. In the darkness there was the smell of fire and ash. Jason bent down and searched for a stone from the riverbank, one that filled the palm of his hand. Then he remembered his talisman, his piece of obsidian. He took it out of his pocket and rubbed his thumb against its sharp edge. One shot would be all he got.

The clouds parted and the moon returned. Aja reached out and put her hand on the snake's head. Its tongue darted out. He took a step back and raised his arm, ready to strike. A strange image entered his mind: plantations of giant sunflowers and a tribe of people the size of children tending them under the moonlight.

A rumbling sound came from the snake as if it was clearing a bone from its throat. It rested its head at Aja's feet. Jason lowered his arm, unclenched his hand and dropped his stone back in his pocket. Bile rose in his throat. He crouched and retched.

Aja fed the snake small pellets that looked like animal droppings. Once it had eaten them the snake began to glow as if it was on fire. Its skin burst open. A smaller, younger snake emerged. The old, scaly skin was discarded on the ground, half in, half out of the water.

Aja leaned over the water's edge and washed her hands.

He crawled towards the old snakeskin. His hands were shaking. He reached out, touched a fragment of skin. All the layers of his mind – conscious and unconscious – imploded.

The new snake returned to the river and disappeared among the tree roots but in Jason's mind its yellow eyes shone like flames in the dark. He tried to blink them away, the way he did when he was a child and wanted something to disappear. Then he was looking down on a rocky plain, on the ruins of an ancient city. The kidnapped creature came to him again. She was small with dark skin and hair, crying out in terror, pus weeping from eyes that should have been protected from the light.

He came back to himself lying on the blanket beside Aja. The night sky arched overhead and he dredged it for familiar stars. He whispered the names of his parents and sister. He repeated them many times, hoping they'd anchor him, keep him safe in that strange landscape. The sound of their names rustled in the air like dried leaves.

In the morning an easterly wind covered them with gritty dust. Aja pulled her shawl lower over her head to shield her eyes. They walked on, making their way towards the sea; even at a distance he could smell wet sand and the salty tang of the ocean. The hawk flew down, settled on Aja's right shoulder and brushed its head into the side of her neck. He listened as she spoke to her companion.

'Old friend,' she said as she gently stroked the top of its head, 'yesterday, while you were away hunting, I remembered my eighth birthday and my first kite. It had red outstretched wings, and in the centre of each wing a yellow spiral was painted. My cousin, Nerilly, was holding the kite string and I was laughing and following the kite, watching it climb and dive in the strong breeze. But I wasn't looking where I was going and I tripped and fell, my head just missing a rock. I lay on the ground, the breath knocked out of me. I rolled over onto my back and tried to track the movement of the kite. It was much higher in the sky and, in the distance, I could just see the yellow spirals on the red wings. The sky was very blue and empty except for the kite. I blinked and the yellow spirals were right in front of me, filling up the whole sky. I blinked again and sat up. Nerilly was on top of the hill holding the kite in one hand and waving at me with other.'

Aja walked in silence after that, leaving the hawk to hunt. All afternoon Jason glimpsed it flying high in the sky, tracking them. Towards evening when it returned she spoke again.

'Old friend,' she said, 'I can smell the sea.'

For the first time he saw tears fill her eyes. He wished she could see him and talk to him. He wished he understood what it was she was planning to do.

'I've left behind the brown river and the banks of clay I grew up with,' she said to the hawk and the empty sky, 'and the grey stones of the riverbed warming in the afternoon sun. There's no one left to lie on them now.'

In the distance he caught a glimpse of the sea – it rippled beneath the setting sun.

An hour after sunset they reached the gates of a walled city.

'Stone walls and stone buildings,' Aja muttered. 'Dark, narrow streets.'

Clouds hid the moon. Beneath his ribcage something flicked like a whip. He was desperate to lie down and sleep but whenever he did he dreamed of the small, trapped creature crying out in pain. All around them were the sounds of waves and wind and shrieking seagulls and the strong briny smell of the sea. He followed Aja through a maze of streets and lanes until the smell of burning oil and lights flickering among the trees drew them to a crowd of people gathered in a square.

Five men, unsheathed swords held in front of their chests, stood in front of the crowd. The men all wore the same long, dark brown jackets, three thin lines of gold braid sewn around their hems and cuffs. The curved blades of their swords glinted in the torchlight. The oldest man stepped up to a wooden table that had been placed in front of the crowd. He lowered his sword, drove its sharp point into the ground. The other four men fanned out, one to each corner of the square, their swords still unsheathed. A small woman dressed in red and black joined the man in front of the table.

Jason was so tired he swayed on his feet. He thought of Jenny asleep in the armchair at the end of his bed in the study. He wanted to go home but no longer knew how. He was nebulous, ghostlike, fading away even from himself. Helene's voice hissed in his ear: I won't forgive her; I won't – she only ever did what she wanted.

He looked down. His feet were covered in river mud. Snakes swarmed over the cobblestones. They moved in a wave; they wound themselves around the feet and ankles of the grey-haired man and the woman in red and black. Under the lamplight, drops of water glistened on their skin. Sixteen-year-old Helene sat at a grand piano wearing a pale green evening gown. Long sleeves embroidered with silver and gold sequins covered her wrists and forearms. She was delicate as a lily. The scars on her left wrist were hidden from the audience. She opened the memorial evening for their father with her own arrangement of 'Moonlight Serenade'.

Aja hid in the shadow of the cypress trees at the back of the square. She waited until the crowd dispersed then left the shelter of the trees and walked through the pools of snakes lying on the cobblestones. She stood in front of the man and woman.

'I need to go south,' she said. 'Our village has been destroyed; our coal and firelighters have been stolen.'

He followed Aja through a gap in the cypress trees. They crossed another cobble-stoned square flanked with two-storied wooden warehouses and walked through more narrow streets until they came to a wide road that led to the main quay. The port was deserted. It smelt of tar and wet coal, fish and brine and rotting vegetables. Oily water slapped against wooden posts and jetties and a few small fishing boats swayed in the dark. Further out, larger boats fanned across the mouth of the harbour.

They found a dirt track that led to the southern tip of the harbour. There the land graduated into a series of low sand dunes. In the distance he could just make out the grey outline of a range of hills. Aja wrapped her shawl more firmly around her head and shoulders and knelt on the sand.

The sand was pale brown and so fine it ran through his fingers like water. He sat down beside Aja. In his memory the dark sand of Muriwai glistened in the afternoon sunlight; his mother swam out past the breakers and floated on her back; his father paddled in the shallows, his white cotton trousers rolled up to his knees; five-year-old Helene sat on the wet sand brushing the top of her sandcastle with a seagull feather. He watched Anastasia swim further and further out until the bright yellow of her bathing cap was just a speck in the distance. It's too far! he shouted. Samuel walked over to him and put his hand on his shoulder. She knows what she's doing – she could have gone to the Olympics, you know.

The shrieking of gulls woke him. The sun had risen and the dunes were patterned with shadow and light. His knees were stiff and his feet and calves ached. He stood and stretched his arms above his head. The sand was silky against his bare feet. Below him the sea was calm and silver-blue. The air shimmered. Light penetrated his skin; particles of light entered his bloodstream. He was strung like a curtain between sea and sky. If he stayed too long his skin would dissolve, his bones turn the colour of sand. He was already invisible. What would he become if he couldn't return home?

When Aja woke she uncoiled her body and bowed to the sea. 'I'll buy goats,' she said, 'and sell milk in the marketplace until I have enough for a passage south.'

CAPTAIN DAMIAN

The sky began to lighten. Chief Councillor Saraz threw sprigs of sage and rosemary on the unlit funeral pyre of her parents and only sister, Janise. Captain Damian stood behind her, bareheaded in the rising wind. He watched as his oldest friend knelt and touched her forehead to the damp earth. She placed three red scrolls at the base of the pyre, one for each member of her family. He waited until she stood up again, conscious the soles of his bare feet were getting increasingly cold from the dew on the grass, then opened his tinder box, struck the flint and lit the funeral torch.

He stepped three paces closer to the pyre holding the sputtering flames high above his head. Gusts of wind whipped at the torch. In his left hand he held his family's ceremonial shears. Saraz's face was shadowed by the edges of the finely woven, black hood of her cloak. He touched her shoulder with the tip of the shears. She turned. Her face was pale, her eyes red-rimmed. Three thin horizontal cuts were freshly etched on each cheek. He handed her the torch.

'Throw it high,' he said, 'then stand back. It will take quickly.'

He heard the whoosh of flames as the torch ignited the kerosene splashed wood. Smoke and fumes rose into the cool morning air. He pulled his regimental coat more firmly around him. His bare feet and damaged knee ached. When the cremation was completed and he was no longer needed he would soak for an hour in a hot bath laced with eucalyptus oil.

Damian listened while Saraz's relatives and fellow councillors began the chant to guide the dead on their journey through the spirit world. 'Peace,' they said, 'peace be upon all who travel this path.' In the distance the monastery bells were ringing, an almost continuous pealing announcing the arrival of other families transporting their linen-wrapped dead on the shoulders of pallbearers. Monks in rough-spun brown robes greeted each group and led them to their appointed place. When he'd arrived in the pre-dawn gloom and walked through the grounds he'd counted thirty unlit pyres, each one waiting in chilled silence to receive its allotted offering.

The monks must have been up all night, chopping and carting wood, apportioning supplies of oil and kerosene to make sure each family had enough. At least they didn't have the horror of digging graves. In his youth he'd travelled to other lands and seen many customs. He was glad his own didn't involve interment in the everlasting darkness of the earth; so much better to be released through the cleansing ritual of fire.

As the bodies of her family were engulfed by flames Saraz removed her hood and unwound her long hair. Damian handed her the shears. She gathered a section of hair, pulled it away from her head, and chopped it half-an-inch from her scalp. Damian caught it and threw it on the fire. She gave the shears back and bowed her head.

Other mourners joined him and formed a circle around her. Damian cut a strand of her hair then handed the shears to the oldest woman. As each strand fell he collected it and when all her hair was cut he threw it on the pyre.

The sun rose in the sky; thirty fires burned. Monks hurried from one family group to another, carrying bowls of water to wash their shears, and baskets of white scarves to wrap the shorn heads of the chief mourners. Damian chose the longest scarf in the basket. He wound it three times round Saraz's head and tucked the end beneath her right ear. She leaned her head against his shoulder. He kissed her forehead. 'It's done,' he said.

She pulled her hood over her head, knelt before the pyre for a final moment then stood up and led them away.

The marketplace was crowded with travellers and locals. They gathered round stalls, haggling over salted fish and barley bread, vegetables and fruit. Gulls screeched overhead and fought over food scraps abandoned on the ground. Wind whipped the surface of the harbour; oily waves splashed against the quay. In port were three southern ships, their main cargoes of coal under guard. A scuffle had broken out earlier when word went out none of the coal was available for public auction. By the time Damian arrived the pushing and shoving between the southern guards and the locals was almost over.

'It's not fair, Captain,' one of the local men said, his white headscarf ripped and grubby. He shook his fist in the guard's face. 'Holding back coal when people are desperate for it.'

The guard was young, no more than eighteen or nineteen. His cap had fallen on the ground, his green uniform was splashed with mud and his pale cheeks were blotched with patches of red. A faint purple rash circled his neck, as if his collar was too tight and had rubbed against his skin.

'It's not our fault,' he said. 'The order came from your council, not us.'

Damian bent down and picked up the guard's cap. He slapped it against the side of his leg and handed it to him.

The guard flushed. He rubbed a finger against the rash on his neck. 'We've been told the whole shipment's for reserves.' he said.

Damian watched coal from the ships being loaded into carts, drawn by the same stocky black and white ponies the Southerners used to haul coal from their mines. Extra guards sat up with the drivers, bullwhips laid across their knees. People grumbled as the carts lurched past but no one tried to stop them.

A middle-aged woman approached him, carrying a basket of homemade bread. 'Captain,' she said. 'My youngest – he's only sixteen. I haven't seen him since the last outbreak.'

Damian accepted the basket. He patted the woman on the arm. 'That would be two weeks ago?'

'He was a runner, delivering parcels, letters and receipts all over town.' The wind blew a few strands of grey hair across her check. She smoothed them back with the palm of her hand. Her eyes filled with tears. 'Nobody's seen him – dead or alive.'

He wrote down the woman's details in his notebook, thanked her for the bread and walked through the muddy streets to the children's hostel. Matron took the basket from him and examined the loaves.

'From a local woman,' he said. 'Her son's missing.' He gave the name and age of the boy.

Matron shook her head. 'The oldest we have is fourteen – she was brought in yesterday. One of our wardens found her camped near the port, guarding her father's body.'

He walked two blocks from the hostel to the hospital. The wards were almost as crowded as the market. Most of the patients had a purple rash scattered across their shoulders and necks, and a few had it on their faces. His sister, Elaine, had been covered with livid purple spots, and mysterious dark bruises, just before she'd died.

He recognized one of the porters who'd helped him bind Elaine's body in her linen shroud so he could transport her from the hospital to the monastery. The man raised his hand in an informal salute and walked over.

'Captain,' he said.

'I'm looking for a sixteen-year-old boy,' Damian said. 'Can you check the admission records for the last three weeks?'

'We don't always get their names, Captain.'

'Just show me what you have.'

An hour later he entered the grey stone building on the outskirts of town the Council used as a morgue. Twelve bodies, two of them small enough to be young children, lay wrapped in striped blankets waiting to be claimed.

There was no sixteen-year-old boy.

'Probably got sick one day, wandered down to the port, got confused, and fell in the harbour,' a worn-out physician said. 'The young ones, it takes them fast.' She sighed and rubbed her cheek with her fingertips. Her gaze returned to the row of bodies. 'Never seen the like of it.'

Sergeant Rico arrived at suppertime with a bag of sweet potatoes for Damian and a flyer announcing the Council had called a public meeting for the following evening. He put the vegetables on the kitchen bench. 'How's Challis?'

'Quiet – he spends most of his time in his room drawing pictures of his mother.'

'There's worse ways a boy could grieve,' Rico said. He took a bundle of coloured pencils from his jacket pocket. 'Give him these,' he said. He pulled a wooden chair out from the kitchen table and sat down. 'Will you go to the meeting?'

Damian leaned against the bench. The last rays of the evening sun brightened a patch of wall behind Rico's head. 'I've finished my investigation,' he said. 'I've compiled detailed records of the last sixty ships. Two or three days after a southern ship docks, people start getting sick.'

He opened the cupboard above the bench, drew out a pale-yellow paper scroll, and spread it on the table. Beside the name and date of each of the incoming ships were two columns of numbers: the first for those admitted to hospital, the second for those transferred to the morgue.

He filled two mugs with ginger tea and sat across the table from Rico. 'They're estimates of course – many don't make it to hospital.

No one knows exact numbers.'

Rico stared at the chart, his finger tracing the time lags between the arrival of the ships and the outbreaks of illness.

Damian tapped the paper with one of Challis' pencils. 'We've got no choice,' he said.

An hour after sunset the following evening eight-year-old Challis walked between Damian and Rico, his eyes following the flickering lights of dozens of lanterns. Damian squeezed his hand then let him run on ahead. 'Stay in sight,' he called after him.

They followed the crowd down the tree-lined avenue that led to the council hall and the town square. In the square, council officials were setting up a trestle table and a row of wooden chairs. Damian looked for Saraz, searching for her red and black robes amongst the gathering crowd.

The air was heavy with the smell of burning oil from lanterns and homemade torches. Slow-moving clouds eclipsed a half-moon. Saraz stood on her own at the back of the square watching the crowd assemble, her face hidden by her hood. A light breeze moved across the square carrying with it the sharp tang of the sea. The clouds parted, exposing the neatly sliced moon.

Damian left Challis in Rico's care and walked over to Saraz. He handed her the scroll. 'My investigation is complete,' he said. 'The records show a clear link between the arrival of southern ships and the onset of the sickness.'

He followed Saraz to the front of the square. She turned and faced the crowd; pushed her hood away from her face, exposing her white-scarfed head and the horizontal scars on her cheeks. She raised her arms. An official rang a large brass bell to announce the start the meeting.

'Citizens of Rona,' Saraz said, her voice carrying to the edges of the square. 'As you know, conditions have not improved. Our best efforts to control the spread of the sickness have failed. Many of us have lost family and friends.' Her voice wavered. She bowed her head for a moment then looked out across the crowd. 'The number of orphaned children grows daily.'

A thin woman with bony wrists and the swollen knuckles of a washerwoman stood up. She coughed and cleared her throat. 'Our sympathy for your loss, Chief Councillor,' she said, 'but what else is the Council going to do?'

The woman's neighbours stood to support her.

Damian put his hand on Saraz's arm. He looked at the woman and her friends but raised his voice so everyone in the square could hear. 'Three months ago, the Council asked me to investigate the origin of the sickness,' he said.

A voice from the back of the crowd shouted, 'Tell us what you know, Captain. My son came down with the sickness last night.'

Damian took the scroll from Saraz, unrolled it and held it up. 'I've traced the outbreaks of sickness to the arrival of southern ships. We need to ban southern ships from entering our port.'

A senior councillor rose to his feet, his right hand twisting the braided hem of his short red jacket. 'Don't be ridiculous! Half our food and most of our coal comes from the south.'

He snatched the scroll from Damian and scanned the columns of dates. When he finished reading he threw it away from the table, as if the paper itself carried the sickness. It dropped on the ground. 'It's nothing but coincidence.'

Saraz bent down and rescued the scroll, smoothed it with her hand and rolled it up again. She put it under her arm and leaned across the table her back to the assembly. 'It's a very strong coincidence Councillor.'

She turned and faced the crowd. Torchlight flickered across her white headscarf, her black and red robes and the fresh scars of mourning on her face. 'There's enough information here to warrant banning all ships – and their cargoes – from the south.'

A chorus of voices cried out, 'How will we feed our families? What will we do when winter comes and we have no coal?'

Damian unsheathed his sword and held it in front of his chest.

Saraz rang the brass bell. 'Until further notice, the port is closed to all southern ships. Guards will be posted at each of the four quays. Northern ships will be allowed,' she said, 'but will be checked for Southern passengers, livestock and produce. Nothing from the south is to be brought into the market or sold in Rona.'

Damian stood between Rico and Challis watching the square empty. He estimated a third of the crowd wore the white scarves of mourning. Behind him, Saraz and other council officials were busy giving orders and organizing guards for the first watch at the port.

A woman stepped out of the shadows. The light from the torches still burning in the square outlined her face. She lowered her eyelids and swayed slightly, as if she was exhausted and might fall asleep where she stood. Her knee-length tunic and trousers were streaked with fine brown dust and her heavy leather sandals were covered with dried mud. She opened her eyes and unwound a blue shawl from her head and shoulders.

'I need to go south,' she said. 'My village has been destroyed. Our coal and firelighters have been stolen.'

Her accent was unfamiliar, the vowels flat, drawn out.

'Where are you from?'

She shook dust from her shawl. 'Aretis,' she said.

The skin on her forearms and wrists was burnt and scarred and on the back of each hand was the faded blue tattoo of a snake.

Saraz touched his elbow. 'Good night, Damian. Call on me at noon tomorrow.'

Damian bowed to Saraz and turned back to the woman. 'There's sickness here,' he said. 'We have closed the port to southern ships.'

'I need to go south,' she said.

'Then you will need to find another port. From tonight there is no traffic between Rona and the south.'

Damian tried to push his way to the surface but the dream dragged him back. The more he struggled the more submerged he became. He watched the approach of an enormous shadow. A she-bear emerged from the penumbra and walked in a wide circle around him. In her mouth she carried a large bone. It was polished white, all the meat long gone.

The bear walked towards him and dropped the bone at his feet. She reared up on her hind legs. A sound like wind soughing through the branches of a pine forest swept over his body. Had she spoken? Was she a harbinger of his death?

Light splintered around him then disintegrated. He fell into darkness. There was nothing to guide him.

At the market people pushed forward, straining to see what was for sale. Fishing boats still worked the northern coast from Rona to the Cape of Sol twice a week; at least there was no shortage of salted, smoked or fresh fish.

The wind was strong and cool, blowing crumpled leaves across the square. The woman from Aretis was standing beside one of the empty vegetable stalls holding a wooden tray, her blue shawl wrapped around her neck and shoulders. Two weeks ago, Damian had seen her buying goats at the market; every morning since then she'd sold their milk to women who gathered with their bowls outside the hospital. In the afternoons, when he returned from council meetings or from checking what was happening at the port, he saw her feeding food scraps to her goats. Two days ago, she'd sat on the town hall steps watching a group of children playing. Yesterday, when he'd gone to collect Challis from Rico's, he saw her sleeping beneath the cluster of cypress trees in the western corner of the town square, her goats tethered beside her. On their way home Challis had pointed to her. 'That's the goat lady, Uncle Damian. She gives me milk.'

Today he decided to approach her.

Her face was thin, the skin stretched tight across high cheekbones, her dark hair drawn back in a heavy braid.

'Thank you for giving my nephew milk,' he said.

He looked at her hands. Images flashed through his mind: small round huts with thatched roofs caught fire and burned; two women crouched beside a river and tied wet cloth over their faces leaving only their eyes free; they dragged charred bodies to bonfires; behind the smoke of the fires shadowy figures moved in single file against the grey outline of hills.

'The boy draws well,' she said, her flattened vowels still sounding foreign to his ear, reminding him she came from the one part of the country he'd never had reason to visit.

He stared past her into the cypress trees. A flock of doves flew overhead; their wings exposing delicate white under-feathers as they swooped and then turned back towards the roof of the town hall.

She put down her tray and held out her hand. 'Aja.'

'Captain Damian Pryce,' he said. 'At your service.'

He sat beside her under the cypress trees. Stallholders packed up tables and canvas awnings and stacked wooden boxes on the back of hand-drawn carts. Fallen leaves scattered in the rising wind. Doves perched in a row on the guttering of the town hall. On the air, the smell of approaching rain.

'The shadow men came and stole our firelighters' she said.

He plucked at blades of grass. 'Shadow men?'

'There are caves in the hills above our village,' she said. 'Burial caves. Our ancestors left coal and firelighters in these caves. Enough to last more than a hundred generations.'

She reached out and drew the youngest goat to her and stroked its ears. 'Men from the south have stolen our inheritance. Their skin is pale but their faces and hands are black from the coal dust. They're armed. They move like shadows over the hills. At night they cart coal and baskets of firelighters to the river and load them onto rafts.'

'These firelighters?' he said, 'What are they?'

She reached into the pocket of her tunic and removed a small cylinder of dark, polished wood. It was slightly longer and wider than his thumb. When she held it out he could see the surface of the wood was decorated with carvings of snakes.

'Open it,' she said.

He twisted the lid. Fragments of what looked like dried mud fell into his palm. He looked at Aja.

'I'll show you,' she said.

She took a flake between her thumb and forefinger. 'Gather a few twigs and some dried leaves,' she said.

He collected a dozen twigs from beneath the trees and an armful of leaves. He piled them in front of her. She crumbled the flake between her fingers and sprinkled it over the top of the leaves.

'Strike your flint,' she said.

Flames leapt into the air. The leaves were consumed in seconds. The twigs burned immediately, as if kerosene had been poured over them. He felt the heat of the flames against his hands and arms.

'They work best with coal,' she said. 'You only need a few shavings to have a fire that cooks food all day and keeps your hut warm at night.'

Aja sat on a chair beside Damian's kitchen table. Her long plait of dark hair fell over her right shoulder; her blue shawl was folded in her lap; her eyes were closed as if she was asleep. Challis sat on the other side of the table drawing a picture of her goats in the town square.

Damian walked over and stood behind him, resting his hand on his shoulder. Some of the goats were nibbling on the grass verge, some on the lowest branches of trees. Challis chose a pale blue pencil and began to colour in the sky.

Damian went back to the bench, scrubbed sweet potatoes, cut them into thick slices and arranged them on the bottom of a baking dish. He splashed oil over them and shook the dish to make sure they didn't stick.

'Challis,' he said, 'please get me some more wood from the yard.'

Challis returned with an armful of logs.

Damian opened the heavy cast-iron door.

'I want to put them in the stove,' Challis said.

When Challis had finished Damian opened the oven and slid the dish in. He sliced barley bread, took smoked fish out of the safe and put it on a plate on the bench. He heard the intake of Aja's breath and the collapsing sigh as she released it. She was like a cat, he thought, able to snatch sleep anywhere.

Challis cleared his paper and pencils from the table, washed his hands and stood in front of Aja.

'Goat lady,' he said, 'you want to see my picture?'

Aja opened her eyes and smiled at him.

Damian put knives and forks on the table. 'Five minutes,' he said.

After supper he showed Aja to the small room next to Challis' bedroom. He lit a kerosene lamp and put it on the shelf beside the door. In the room there was a narrow bed covered with a blue and yellow patchwork quilt his sister Elaine had made, an oblong table underneath the sash window and a faded brown armchair. A multi-coloured rag mat brightened the plainness of the wooden floor.

Aja sat on the edge of the bed. 'The shadow men threw torches into the village,' she said. 'Our huts were burned. We made funeral pyres to burn the dead.' She drew from her tunic pocket a small ceramic urn. It fitted into the palm of her hand. She held it out to him.

'This is what remains,' she said.

He cradled the urn in his hand.

A shadow lay across a mottled sky filled with circling birds. The birds were sleek and well fed and rose and fell on the currents. Their raucous squawking filled the air. Beneath them, on ground covered with fresh snow, dark figures moved in procession. As he got closer Damian saw they were carrying the bodies of their dead children. Darkness overtook him, black as a raven's wing.

Damian sat on the veranda beside Challis. 'You like going to Rico's. He'll look after you till Aja and I get back.'

'I want to go with you.'

Damian wrapped an arm around Challis' shoulders. Challis turned his head and hid his face against Damian's jacket.

Damian reached into his pocket and pulled out a small box. 'I've got new pencils.'

Challis ignored the pencils. 'Who will look after the goats?'

'Aja has asked if I would give my permission for you to become her goatherd. It's a big responsibility.'

Challis stood up. He picked up the box of pencils and selected a bright green one. 'I'll make a calendar,' he said, 'for all the things I have to do while you're away.'

Damian rubbed his hands against the rough cloth of his jacket. The numbness in his fingers seemed to be spreading. Yesterday, for a few seconds, he'd lost all sensation in his hand. Then feeling had come back, his blood pulsing so hard through his fingertips they hurt. He had been in Saraz's chambers, explaining the destruction of Aja's village, the theft of the coal and the firelighters. He spoke of his duty to escort her south, in spite of the ban. He needed Saraz's signature on his travel documents and her permission to board one of the northern boats plying the length of the coast.

'Can you trust this woman?' she said.

'She's incapable of lying,' Damian said.

Saraz leaned over and touched his arm. 'That's not what I asked.' She squeezed his hand and held it briefly. 'Anyway, since you've retired, you don't have official duties.' She smiled. 'Unless I give you some.'

'No one able-bodied can be spared,' he said.

'What if you get the sickness?'

'I haven't yet,' he said, and put his papers on her desk to be signed. Blood pumped painfully through his fingers. Shadows danced behind his eyes. 'Neither have you.'

She sighed and turned away. 'You're determined to go.'

'Two or three weeks will be enough,' he said, 'to find out what the Southerners have been doing. Once we get back we can lodge formal proceedings on Aja's behalf.'

He stood on the veranda looking out across his vegetable garden into the gathering dusk. He remembered the she-bear standing on her hind legs, the sound of her voice, and the cleaned bone she had tossed at his feet.

JASON

Rona

The room was small and lit by a kerosene lamp. Aja sat on the end of a narrow bed, her back resting against the wall. Her hand stroked the rough cotton of a blue and yellow quilt. The Captain closed the shutters and moved away from the window; he sat on a wooden chair and rubbed his left hand across the knuckles and fingers of his right one then pressed the pads of his fingers with his thumb and forefinger. The light from the lamp cast their shadows on the wall. It was so quiet he could hear Aja and the Captain breathing. His breath came and went more quickly, on the beat between theirs, the way it had when he was a small child, just out of babyhood, when he sometimes crawled back to sleep in his parents' bed. No matter how hard he tried he could never slow his breath to match Anastasia's.

He moved towards the lamp to be closer to the light and remembered yellow light filtered through layers of white net curtains that covered a sash window. Patterns of light danced on the pale walls and ceiling of his first bedroom; sunlight flickered across a section of the door. Reaching out to touch the light was his first game: his hand curled and uncurled as he tried to capture fistfuls and put it in his mouth – putting his hand into it, gathering it, feeling its warmth on his skin, then pulling his hand back to his mouth, watching the light leave his hand, feeling his skin cool. Then the door opened. The dark shape of his mother appeared, the edges of her lit up, zigzagging as she moved towards him. She bent over him, and blocked out the room. He squeezed his eyes shut to hold on to the light. She carried him down the dimness of the hallway and into her bedroom and laid him against pillows that smelt of his father. His parents' bed was a warm boat and his mother's voice rose and fell against his skin like waves. He floated on her sound, shafts of sunlight hidden safely behind his eyes.

CAPTAIN DAMIAN

Sunlight shone through the porthole above Damian's bunk. He squinted through the dirty glass at the teal-coloured sea. They were no longer in open water; they were skirting the southern coast. If the weather held they would be in the southern-most port of Konos before sunset.

Aja was sitting cross-legged on her bunk, her back supported by the wall, her eyes closed. Damian wondered if she ever slept or if she simply withdrew into herself and her memories.

The old man who'd brought them their food the last two nights had washed and dried his clothes and folded them in a neat pile at the end of his bunk. A coin sat on top of his shirt. Even though he'd made it plain he was retired from active service, the Captain of the boat had still accorded him the privileges of his military rank. Damian picked up the coin and rolled it between his thumb and forefinger – southern currency, silver with a small hole in its centre.

On deck the sky was clear and the breeze cool. He buttoned his jacket and wound his woollen scarf about his neck. On his right the coast twisted and curved into dozens of rocky bays. Scrubby trees with pointed, olive-green leaves and bunches of small pink flowers crawled down the side of the cliffs above the bays.

It had been five years since he'd sailed the southern coast. He and Rico had travelled together on a case, summoned by a wealthy merchant family who had lost their youngest daughter in an accident. One of the new coal-eating machines the Southerners called locos had been shunting on a new section of track near their village. The girl and two of her friends, thinking it a game, had been running in front and behind it. She'd tripped and fallen, catching her shoe underneath one of the sleepers. The driver had blown his whistle twice to clear the track but she'd been absorbed in trying to rescue her new shoe and had been run over, her body crushed.

Rico had interviewed the driver and his family, Damian the girl's parents, older brothers and sisters and friends. It had been a successful case. Reparation had been negotiated with the owners of the loco without the need for a court hearing or punishment.

Leaning against the rail he thought of Challis at home in Rico's care, ticking off the days they were away on his calendar. He was only eight and had already lost both his parents. He trusted Rico with his life, and Saraz had promised to keep an eye on him too, but anything could happen.

The smell of dandelion coffee wafted across the deck. The old man carried a tray with two steaming mugs.

'Your friend, the snake woman from the north,' he said. 'Is she still below?'

'Why do you call her that?'

He handed Damian a mug. 'Those blue tattoos on her hands,' he said. 'I haven't seen anything like that since I was a boy.'

Damian sipped his drink. The old sailor settled beside him.

'I grew up in the north, with my grandparents,' he said. 'It's hard country. People up there keep to the old ways.' He coughed and took a gulp of his coffee. 'Came south when I was a lad of sixteen – wanted to see more of the world than a field full of bad-tempered goats.' He coughed again, cleared phlegm from his throat and spat into a clean handkerchief. 'Well I've seen plenty,' he said, 'maybe too much.' He squinted against the bright light and his eyes disappeared into folds of wrinkled skin. 'Never been back.'

He lapsed into silence and Damian waited, his eyes closed, content to feel the sun and wind on his face and to let the old man rake over his memories. He listened to the creak and slap of the sails above him and the screeching of the gulls as they swooped and dived along the coastline.

After a while the old man said, 'The ones with snake tattoos, they're chosen young; trained from when they turn six or seven years old.'

He coughed some more, his leathery face and neck deepening to crimson as he tried to dislodge more phlegm from his chest and catch his breath at the same time.

Damian listened to him cough, unable to do anything to help, and wondered if he'd been a miner as well as a sailor.

'They believe they carry the old ones inside them, generation after generation, right back to the beginning. Back to the foundation of the Gates.'

Damian took a last sip and handed his mug back.

'What's she doing down here?' the old man said. 'Never heard of one leaving their village.'

Damian looked past him to the coastline. Flocks of black and white shags perched on outlying rocks. 'Her village's been destroyed,' he said.

'The Jar's been broken then.'

'What do you mean?'

'That's what they call them – the villages, in northern dialect they're called Jars, refilled every generation, unbroken through time since the opening of the Northern Gate.'

Damian remembered Aja showing him the small pottery urn she carried in her tunic pocket. 'That's all that remains,' she'd said.

He sat on deck with his back against a fat coil of rope, his legs stretched out in front of him. He knew the signs: the plunging sensation in his gut; the bitter, metallic taste in his throat and on his tongue; flashes of colour interfering with his eyesight. If he didn't sit and steady himself he would fall, or worse, the convulsions in his limbs would start. He'd learnt not to fight the visions; learnt he needed to accommodate them.

He waited for the sense of vertigo to pass, for the moment of nausea and fear to grip tight, and then release him. He was plunged into fiery light. He pulled the hood of his jacket over his forehead to shield his eyes. In the distance he saw three of the Xlanin, the ancient guardians of his brotherhood, his military clan. They were standing by the Northern Gate. They beckoned and he walked barefoot across dry earth to greet them. Their curved swords glinted like crescent moons against the dark brown of their robes.

He saw the remains of the sacred jar that had stood as a sentinel at the northern gate for thousands of years. Its pieces were broken and scattered. A dark stain leaked from it onto the earth. The cloying smell of honeysuckle rose into the air.

The sky flamed orange and red. The surrounding cliffs and rocks burned in the evening light. He was high up, exposed, before an open plain that spread below the gate.

The guardians shimmered as if they'd been set alight. 'Find the one who renews life.'

When they disappeared from sight he looked across the empty plain and then at his bare feet and wondered how he would be able to travel across it. He unsheathed his sword and swept it in the air in front of him, using it like a blind man, searching for obstacles in his path. He began to walk, testing where he placed every step. Bones, bleached clean by the sun, lay in great mounds on the dry ground. He bent down to examine them. The last of the evening light radiated from the sky. His own bones felt as porous as his skin.

As he walked he heard voices in the wind. They whirled around him but the more he listened the fainter they grew. He walked in the gathering twilight until his feet started to ache. When he stopped at last he was standing in the middle of the plain, his sword the only point of light in the darkness. He lay down, sheathed his sword, pulled his jacket over his face and slept.

In his dreams he saw a stone man, standing like a reaper by a black river. He was hooded and cloaked. The wind was sharp and cool. A froth of water churned over grey stones in the riverbed.

The stone man raised heavy eyelids, cornering him. 'Get into the river and swim.'

Damian shivered at the thought of icy water and the chill wind on his skin but knew he must obey. He waded into the water, forcing himself to sink; turned on his back and floated downstream, allowing the current to take him. The water numbed his body and made the back of his head throb. He closed his eyes. The current carried him over the surface of rocks. When he opened his eyes again he saw the riverbank was lined with trees. Birds sang as if it was early morning and the smell of cedar smoke filled the air. The river widened into a large shallow pool. He lay there, suspended, listening to the birds.

An old woman, her back bent with the weight of the bundles of sticks she carried, appeared on the bank. She reached out her hand and called his name.

It was dawn and just as quickly, dusk. Light blossomed and faded in the sky. Days passed in minutes. Night came and settled over him like his mother's coat.

Later he saw a child, a little girl, playing with a hoop in a pool of sunshine.

JASON

Auckland

At night, when the temperature dropped to its lowest point, I came back to myself. I was aware of my surroundings and the constraints on my body. A drip was attached to my arm, and a catheter had been inserted so I didn't wet myself. Sometimes my legs and arms twitched as if to prove my nerves and muscles still worked. Tonight, I was conscious of my triangulation: I was stretched between Aja and the Captain, my study, and memories of the past. In my study I could smell the vanilla edge of Jenny's perfume as she leaned over to kiss my forehead. I felt the weight of Trojan, our seven-year-old cat, curled against my thigh and heard the dogs' paws as they clicked and scratched on the wooden floor. Memories swam like brightly coloured fish across the surface of my mind.

I was six years old and it was my first day at school. The door to the classroom was wide open. I stopped beneath the doorframe. Samuel bent down and put his arm around my shoulder.

'Anastasia will pick you up this afternoon,' he said.

I clutched my leather satchel and searched my pocket for my lucky stone. It was shiny and black and had been polished smooth so its edges wouldn't cut me. It fitted exactly the palm of my hand. Anastasia had said it was called obsidian.

In the classroom there were five rows of single wooden desks. Each row had six desks. I counted down and then across: thirty desks, but only twenty-five boys. Out of the corner of my eye I saw a ginger cat asleep in an old basket at the back of the room.

The teacher, a thin man in brown corduroy trousers and a dark green jersey, had a large desk at the front. On the blackboard behind his desk the alphabet was written across the top twice, once in upper case and once in lower, and the five times table walked down the left side of the board. I knew my five times table, and the sixes. And I'd started learning the sevens and eights. Was this the right class? I didn't want to be in with the babies. Samuel had already taught me how to count to a hundred and Anastasia to write my name, address and telephone number. I could write her name too – Anastasia – because she didn't like being called Mummy.

The teacher picked up a long ruler and pointed it at an empty desk – the middle seat in the middle row. 'You can sit there,' he said.

I put the strap of my leather satchel over the back of the chair and sat down. In my satchel were coloured pencils, my lunch box, two picture books and an empty exercise book covered with pictures of Roman chariots I'd found in a *National Geographic* magazine.

'Stand up, boy. Tell everyone your name.'

At the back of the room the ginger cat woke, stretched and began to lick her front paws.

I stood up straight like a soldier. 'My name is Jason Philip Winston.' I looked around the room at the other boys. 'I can already do my four and five times tables.'

The teacher put his hands in his pockets and leaned against the side of his desk. 'Sit down Winston, no one likes a show-off.'

I stared at the teacher. What had I done wrong? The boys in the front rows turned around to look at me. Some of them began to laugh – a noise like geese made when Samuel and I walked past them in the park. The ginger cat turned in a circle, raised her tail and stepped out of the basket. She walked between the rows of desks towards me.

The teacher came down the aisle and stood in front of my desk. '*My name*, he said, 'is Simms, but you,' he leaned over and poked me in the chest with his finger, 'you call me Sir – understood?'

I studied the top of my desk. It was covered in scratches and stains. The cat rubbed against my feet and ankles. 'Yes, Sir.'

Simms went back to the front of the room and began to write easy numbers on the blackboard.

I sat down. My face was hot. The surface of the desk felt lumpy against my fingers. The cat settled under my chair. When I closed my eyes to shut out Simms's face I could hear her purr.

At lunchtime I took my lunch box and picture book on the Trojan horse and went outside. The other boys had divided into two teams and kicked a ball up and down on the grass outside the classroom. I sat on my own close to the drinking taps, and ate the egg sandwiches Samuel had made for me. I opened my book and turned to my favourite page. Soldiers leapt out of a secret door that opened on the side of a giant wooden horse.

'Hey, Times-tables, can you read as well?' Curtis, the boy who sat on my left in class stood in front of me.

'Do you know about the Trojans?'

Curtis shook his head and sat down. He poked me with his elbow. 'Can I've a look?'

In the afternoon Mrs Winter replaced Simms. She had a red scarf tied in a floppy bow round her neck and curly white hair. She read us a story about King Arthur and the Knights of the Round Table. We were allowed to draw pictures while we listened. I drew two purple dragons and a knight on a black horse that had a trap door on its side. In the left-hand corner of the page I wrote my name in capital letters and in the right corner drew a small ginger cat in a basket.

Curtis leaned over and borrowed a crimson pencil. 'For the blood,' he whispered. His picture was full of knights chopping at each other's arms and legs with their swords.

When we were finished and had put our pencils and crayons

away, Mrs Winter helped us stick our pictures on the wall. She walked around the room looking at our drawings. 'Oh,' she said, 'Jason, what excellent handwriting, and what a lovely cat – even if it wasn't in the story. Is it yours dear?'

I shook my head and went to the back of the classroom to show Mrs Winter the basket but it wasn't there. I searched the room for the cat. She might have gone to sleep under a desk. Mrs Winter's feet followed me as I crawled between the desks.

'What are you doing, Jason?'

When I got to the front of the classroom I turned around and lay on the floor, looking under all the desks. Some of the boys were pointing and honking, flapping their arms like approaching geese.

Mrs Winter put her hand under my arm and helped me up. I tried not to cry.

'She was here this morning,' I said, 'in a basket.'

I was perched beside my father on the stiff leather couch in the headmaster's office. In my blazer pocket my lucky stone was warm. I smoothed my thumb across the surface. The couch was high and my legs and feet dangled above the floor. One long grey sock had slipped down my calf but I couldn't pull it up without sliding off the couch. Samuel held my hand.

Behind an enormous desk the headmaster opened a brown folder. 'It's been an interesting year, Mr Winston,' he said. He took his glasses off and folded them neatly into a leather case. When he closed it, the case snapped shut.

I glanced at my father. His mouth twitched at the corner. 'In what way, sir?' Samuel asked.

'He's a bright boy, no doubt about it.' The headmaster turned his glasses' case over in his hands a couple of times as if it were a cricket ball. 'Well ahead in maths and reading.'

Samuel squeezed my hand. 'We're very proud of him.'

'However, there have been a number of incidences.' The headmaster flicked through the file. 'Five in the past six months, to be exact.' He scratched the side of his nose with the end of a pencil. 'The last one on Tuesday.'

I watched the ginger cat jump down from the windowsill and curl at my father's feet. I closed my eyes: Not now. Go away. I'll get in trouble.

'He's a bit old for imaginary friends, isn't he, Mr Winston?'

Samuel coughed. 'Einstein thought imagination the most important quality, Mr O'Brien.'

The headmaster made an interlocking bridge with his fingers. 'Well, yes. Yes, of course. But it's important to know the difference, isn't it? I mean between what's real and what's just little boys making up tall stories, and then getting upset and hitting other boys when they turn out not to be true.'

The ginger cat stretched and arched her back. She turned in a circle and raised her tail at the headmaster.

Samuel squeezed my hand again. 'Jason,' he said, 'Is there anything you'd like to say to Mr O'Brien?'

The cat hissed as if a stray dog has just entered the room. I gripped my lucky stone in my right hand. 'Sorry Sir,' I said. 'It won't happen again.'

In the car on the way home Samuel said, 'Why did you hit Curtis? I thought he was your friend?'

I said nothing until we stopped at the traffic lights, just stared out the window. 'He took my picture.'

'Of the ginger cat?'

'He held it up in front of everyone.'

'And that made you mad?'

I watched the lights change from red to green. Samuel changed gear. The car surged forward.

'Everyone laughed at me.'

UZRA

Vellen lay on the floor wrapped in two of the blankets Uzra had found in the cupboard in Rohine's office. Behind the stack of blankets, he discovered six handwritten notebooks detailing the experiments Rohine and his assistants had conducted. There were pages of diagrams and graphs tracking input of food and output of waste, the volume of secretions needed to produce a pellet, the quality of the pellets, but nothing on her health, her feelings or her deteriorating condition. Uzra put the notebooks in the bottom of his goatskin bag.

When he'd found her, she'd been so dehydrated it took two days of steady, slow sipping for her wrinkled skin to fill out. The ulcers in her mouth and on her lips blossomed with pus and he guessed her throat was covered in them because she whimpered every time she swallowed. He needed to find nettles or raspberry leaves to make a tea to soothe her throat, and dock leaves to make a salve for the cuts and bruises on her skin. He kept her eyes covered with damp cloth to protect them against the light. Sometimes, as he sat by her holding the cup so she could sip water, she put her hand on her belly and he thought she was telling him she was hungry, but when he offered her dried food from his meagre supplies, she shook her head. The only thing she accepted was a spoonful of honey diluted in warm water twice a day.

On the third day he covered her with another blanket, locked the door and left to search for fresh food and herbs. It was cold and after three days in the semi-darkness of the laboratory the daylight seemed very bright. The surrounding streets were deserted. Many of the houses and shops were abandoned – a place empty of people but full of rats. He turned down a side street lined with boarded-up shops and warehouses and startled two large grey ones dragging rubbish from the gutter. One of them reared on its back legs, something matted and bloody hanging from its mouth. Uzra left them to it and headed towards the port.

At the wharf four thin, dirty men leaned against a brick wall watching the arrival of an incoming ship. He nodded to them as he walked past and one of them had enough energy to mumble a greeting. The others just stared. As the ship came into port Uzra saw the green and yellow flag of the northern regions fluttering from the prow. He wondered why the captain and the crew were taking the risk of coming south, but he was grateful – he would be able to barter for supplies.

Once the ship had docked and the sails were furled a grey-haired man and a dark-haired woman walked down the gangplank. The four men straggled over to the ship and began to unload cargo. They rolled a couple of barrels onto the wharf, heaved a few wooden boxes onto their shoulders and stacked them against the wall of a grubby warehouse. After that they squatted in the dust and spat. Although their faces and necks were as clear of the purple rash as his own, the men looked so worn out Uzra wondered whether they were the only men left in the city still able to work.

The man and woman skirted the cargo and stood scanning their surroundings, their backs to the sea. There wasn't much to see. A few seagulls wheeling past the ship and a few more scavenging for scraps on the dusty road that led away from the port towards the market.

Uzra pushed his hat back on the crown of his head. He put his hand into his trouser pocket and rolled some pellets between his fingertips. He stayed out of sight in the shade of a run-down building. From the smell of it, it had once housed sheep and goats. What were a couple of Northerners doing coming south, exposing themselves to the worst of the sickness?

The woman took off her light-blue shawl, shook it then wrapped it back around her head and shoulders. Uzra shrank further back. There was something familiar about the way she stood there arranging her shawl. Perhaps she was a miner's wife, one he'd met as he travelled through villages conscripting men to work in the mines? What was she: mother, sister, wife or widow? The man escorting her didn't look like a husband or brother. He wore the long brown jacket of a captain and attached to his belt was the curved sword that announced he was on duty. Uzra waited till they walked past then he opened the collar of his shirt so the sailors could see his throat was clear of the rash and went on board to barter food and medicine for Vellen.

Half an hour later he walked back down the gangplank carrying a small sack containing a tin of molasses, two loaves of bread, half a dozen apples, a piece of hard cheese, a slab of dried goat meat and a muslin bag of nettle leaves. He tipped his hat to the two sailors standing guard.

'What time do you sail?' he asked.

'Six hours,' the younger one said, 'on the tide.' His hand kept returning to the base of his neck. 'Not soon enough for me.'

Uzra walked back towards the row of rundown warehouses that lined the road that led into the city. It was still cloudless but the setting sun added a pale orange sheen to the sky. When he emerged from the shadow of the buildings he saw the northern visitors again. They were standing side by side in the middle of the dirt road talking. They appeared unable to decide whether to return to the ship or carry on. He walked towards them.

'Do you need help?' he said.

The woman stared at him. She took a step back. 'Shadow man,' she said.

'I'm sorry,' he said, 'what did you say?'

The Captain drew his sword.

She put her hand on the Captain's shoulder and nudged him gently to one side. He sheathed his sword. She stepped in front of Uzra.

The sun sank behind the mountains. A gull shrieked overhead.

She raised her left hand and held it in front of his face. 'You took our firelighters,' she said.

Uzra's eyes widened. 'Where are you from?'

'I saw your men at night as they moved across our hills carting coal to the river,' she said.

He took a step back.

'You set explosions in our caves. You took more than you were entitled to.' She dropped her hand and moved closer to him, so close he could feel her breath on his face. She smelt of goat's milk and lavender soap. 'Much more,' she said.

Uzra felt the air shrink around him. His hands and feet began to itch.

She looked him straight in the eye. 'Your men tossed our ancestors' bones out of their resting place as if they were rubbish.' Her voice broke and the Captain moved to stand beside her. 'You stole our coal and firelighters and left our village to burn.'

The Captain drew his sword again.

Uzra's shoulders dropped. His lungs sagged with coal dust. He saw his grandfather's back moving in front of him in the pre-dawn morning of his first day of work as a miner and felt the weakness in his legs as he tried to match his stride. He stepped forward and stood in front of the woman. He removed his hat and bowed his head.

'She's dying,' he said. He rubbed his eyes with the back of his hand. 'She's the only one who survived the explosions. They took her from me and brought her here to milk her glands and now they've left her to die.' He lifted his knife from the leather pouch attached to his belt. He gave it to the woman handle first, so the blade pointed directly at his chest.

The tip of the Captain's sword touched his shoulder. 'What's your name?'

Uzra raised his head. His hand crept to the miniature bone flute he wore on a leather string around his neck. His fingers closed around it. 'Uzra,' he said. 'From the goldfields of Otmas.'

When Uzra unlocked it, the front door of the building swung open and squeaked on its hinges. He put the key into his jacket pocket and led them down a narrow corridor with a low ceiling and dark green walls. The soles of their sandals left prints on the dusty wooden floor. He turned left and stopped in front of the laboratory door.

'She can't stand bright light,' he said.

He sat on the floor beside Vellen and unwrapped the blankets.

The woman crouched on her haunches beside him, her shawl pulled over her head. She rocked back and forward, chanting in a language Uzra had never heard before. She reached into the pocket of her tunic and pulled out a handful of firelighters. She laid them on the floor in front of Vellen. Scattered among the small dark pellets were slithers of dried snakeskin.

Vellen raised her head. She reached out a claw-like hand, groping among the pellets for fragments of snakeskin. She gathered them, scooping them into her palm. Her fingers closed over them. A tear rolled down her cheek.

Uzra heard his Grandfather's flute. He was a boy again, swimming in the river, watching snakes pool at his feet. Their brown and gold striped bodies shone in the sunlight as they wove between his legs then glided away from him and moved in a swarm further up river.

His Grandfather sat cross-legged on the bank with his back resting against a tree. His eyes were closed as he played his flute.

Uzra climbed out of the river, shook water from his hair and sat on the bank. His Grandfather put down his flute and handed him one of his old shirts. Uzra pulled it over his head and rolled up the sleeves. It smelt of dust and sunlight and reached past his knees.

'Grandfather,' Uzra whispered, 'I don't know what to do. It's my fault her kin are dead.'

'Brena Joris carried your father's body on his back for two days and nights to bring him home,' his Grandfather said.

JASON

Southern port

The air was dry and very cold, the afternoon sun already low in the sky. Aja and the Captain disembarked at the southern port. They walked along a dirt road that led away from the port. The road was empty and a sticky dust covered its surface and clung to their sandals. Even though they were close to the sea, Jason could smell fresh water in the distance; his nostrils quivered, taking in the smells of this new place.

From the shade of a rundown warehouse a small man emerged, a goatskin hat pushed back on the crown of his head. Deep scars tattooed his face. He carried a small brown sack in one hand.

Aja grabbed the Captain's arm. 'The leader of the shadow men,' she said.

The man turned and stared at Aja. The Captain drew his sword. Aja put her hand on the Captain's shoulder. He stood to one side and held the blade of his sword flat across his chest. She stepped up close to the man.

The air vibrated. The sun sank behind the mountains, leaving a few wisps of orange cloud in the sky. A gull shrieked overhead.

His attention shifted.

He was watching his seventy-five-year-old mother swim out past the surfers at Muriwai. Technically she was swimming between the flags but she was so far out no one would be able to reach her if anything happened. He had spread a rug on the black sand. She'd asked him to come.

'I want to do a test run,' she said when she phoned. 'I want to know what it feels like.'

He knew there was no point trying to dissuade her – he'd never won an argument with her his whole life.

'Why am _I_ here?' he asked as they drove out to the beach.

'Well I could hardly ask Helene, could I?' she said.

'That's not what I meant.'

She looked out the car window while he drove down the hill, past houses set back in the bush. She patted his hand. 'I wanted your company. And a cup of tea when I got out.'

On the wharf Aja raised her left hand and held it in front of the man's scarred face. 'You took our firelighters,' she said.

The man took a step back. A gust of wet air left his lungs. His words were lost as gulls screeched overhead. Jason looked past Aja towards the Captain who still gripped the handle of his sword. The man's head and shoulders dropped. He moved forward, in front of Aja. He unsheathed the knife on his belt and handed it to her. Then he removed his hat and bowed his head. Around his neck he wore a piece of carved bone on a leather string.

They followed him down the wide dirt road to the city. He led them through deserted streets. Everywhere the stench of rubbish left to rot. They passed a house whose windows weren't boarded up and the smell of burning sage and rosemary washed over them. The memory of that last afternoon on Muriwai beach with Anastasia unravelled as Jason walked behind Aja.

He'd waited on the sand for an hour and a half, trying to read the latest addition of _Psychology Today_. When he saw her familiar yellow bathing-cap reappear among the surfers, a rush of anger surged through him so strongly he almost passed out. He crouched in the sand and retched. He rubbed his throat; imagined swallowing ice cubes until a patch of cold settled in his chest. By the time Anastasia got out of the water he was calm enough to light a cigarette.

He handed her a towel.

'Did you bring the thermos?' she said. 'I could murder a cup of tea.'

The front windows of the warehouse were boarded up. When the man unlocked it, the front door swung open and squeaked on its hinges.

They followed him to a room at the back of the building.

'She can't stand the light,' he said.

On the floor in the far corner a bundle of black and grey rags was partially covered by a blanket. The man bent down and said something.

The bundle moved.

Aja folded to the floor. The Captain's hand shook as he reached for his sword. The man supported the body of a shivering, shrunken being with almost no hair. Her shoulders and upper back were poulticed with a paste that resembled green slime. Her eyes were covered with a wet cloth. On the side of her neck a huge weeping sore.

Jason cried out in recognition but no one heard him. It was the creature he'd been dreaming of ever since he'd followed Aja across the hills and plains on her journey south. The air crackled the way it did before a summer storm. Aja crouched on her haunches, her shawl covering her head. She rocked back and forward, chanting a prayer. She reached into the pocket of her tunic and pulled out a handful of firelighters. She placed them on the floor in front of the creature. Scattered among the small dark pellets were slithers of snakeskin. Aja spoke again. The creature raised her head and slowly reached out, groping among the pellets for the skin.

The moment her fingers touched the snakeskin lightning flashed above his head. Thunder barked and growled. He saw the caves above the village; travelled down through a series of tunnels; saw people the size of eight or nine-year-old children with huge blinking eyes and thick black hair that fanned out from their faces like wings.

Explosions tore the tunnels apart. Rocks crashed into them, knocking them down. They staggered to their feet. The floors of the tunnels opened beneath them. Water rose up and flooded the cave.

He floated with their bodies. Silence filled him, a silence so huge and old it seemed to obliterate the stars. It was the sound of death, come to carry them all away. Helene lay among their small twisted bodies, her pale skin and faded auburn hair matted with dirt from the creek and coal dust from the caves. Samuel lay submerged in the bathtub, Anastasia's left hand holding his head beneath the water, the gold band of her wedding ring shining against his wet hair.

Jason lay in darkness until a cold wind began to blow. The wind picked him up and he twirled like a wooden top. As he spun he entered a new place. The entrance was an archway of grey stone. The air smelt of sulphur. He saw a chamber of blackened rock with flames leaping high into the air. In the centre of the orange and yellow flames was the face of a child. He cried out, tried to reach inside the flames but the heat pushed him back. The child's face shimmered through the flames but her soft skin and halo of brown curls remain untouched. He moved away. The child called his name; told him to breathe his way back to the surface. Above him light moved across the surface of the water. Anastasia was swimming ahead of him. Her green linen dress floated around her as she kicked out with her strong legs. 'Hurry up Jason,' she said, 'we need to reach the hut before it gets dark.'

In the darkened room at the back of the laboratory, Aja was crooning. She sat on the floor cradling the creature in her lap, comforting her as if she was an upset child. The Captain and the scarred-face man stood together on the far side of the room by a row of narrow, thinly curtained windows. The Captain had six leather-bound notebooks in his hands. Jason moved closer so he could hear what they were saying.

'It's all in there,' the man said, 'Rohine, the senior engineer, kept a record of every experiment.'

The Captain opened the cover of the top notebook. 'And the pestilence,' he said, 'when did that start?'

The man shook his head. 'They didn't realise until it was too late – it spread so quickly.'

'And you?' the Captain asked, 'you've been with her all this time.' He raised his eyebrows. 'Yet you've never got ill?'

The man opened the collar of his shirt. His neck was free of the purple rash. He banged his chest with his fist and coughed. 'Miners' lung will kill me first,' he said.

Jason went to the creature on the floor. The man called her Vellen. Aja had a bowl of warm water. She sprinkled some pungent herb into it and washed Vellen's face and hands, her neck and shoulders, and wrapped blankets tightly around the rest of her body, reminding him of pictures he'd seen of Indian papooses. Aja removed the cloth from Vellen's eyes. Vellen turned her face to the darkest part of the room while Aja sponged her eyes.

He squatted beside her. 'Why do you haunt me?'

Her eyes blinked when he spoke but she said nothing. He sat beside her, forcing himself to look at her clawed hands resting on the outside of the blankets, at her almost bald head and at the weeping sore on the side of her neck. A strong, musky smell came from her body, so strong it was hard to be close to her. Her breathing slowed and she seemed to sleep. He reached out and put his hand gently on her shoulder the way he used to when Helene was little. Each night before he went to sleep he'd go into her room to check she was all right and to say goodnight. He knew, without understanding how or why, she was in some kind of danger and he needed to protect her. Beneath his hand Vellen's skin was cold and slightly clammy. Her shoulder was all bone and sinew, the muscle wasted away.

'Little sister,' he said, 'the world has torn you apart.'

URSULA-VELLEN

When they first brought me here I was never alone. The surface men worked in shifts, guarding me. A bitter-tasting gruel was forced down my throat and they milked my glands, greedy for the jewels that belong to Grandfather. My permission was never asked for, or given, and I couldn't speak their language to tell them of the dangers. I could never produce what they wanted. I needed to be in the caves with my sisters, singing to the crystals, carving out downward tunnels so Grandfather could find us, clearing the upwards ones so we could return to the surface for the festivals of longest and shortest night.

Their leader came at the end of every shift to check how much I'd produced. If there was none he shouted at the guards. They stood to attention, their bodies rigid. I could smell their fear; hear their hearts beating wildly behind their ribs. His skin radiated harsh white light. His voice snarled like an animal. It raced ahead of him through the corridors, searching for something to attack. His hands were thin and sharp, and cold.

The more they tried to force me to make the jewels the more my body rebelled. I became feverish, developed a cough, a rash broke out over my arms and legs. I vomited any food they gave me. I was overcome with bouts of shivering and sweating. One by one the guards got sick and left me.

When he realised I could produce nothing, he left me alone to die. The door was shut and, at last, the lights turned off. I lay abandoned on the floor like the rest of their rubbish. The embrace of darkness was welcome but without my cloak or blankets the cold ate into my bones.

I lay for a long time thinking of my lost sisters, wishing I could return to them. Once I woke and felt the pull of the new moon. I heard someone cry out to Grandfather, but it was only me, waking from a dream. How would Grandfather find the jewels he needed to renew him and remake the world now we were all gone?

Soon my body became numb and the coldness ceased. I chanted softly to myself in the darkness and chose that moment to slip into hibernation.

Time passed.

Uzra returned. He shook me awake from my death sleep; picked me up from the floor and wrapped me in blankets. He spoke to me and gave me water. It's the only word we share from my tongue. 'Vellen,' he said, repeating it again and again.

I pointed to my belly. I tried to tell him that during hibernation the growing had started but he didn't understand. I sipped water and swallowed the honey he gave me. How could I explain to him my final cycle had begun, and now it couldn't stop. In a short time, I will be the old shell and a new sister will be born of me.

She will need to be taken back to the caves so she can work with Grandfather. I fear she will be small, fragile, weakened by what they've done to me. And she will be damaged by my exposure to so much light. Her jewels will not be pure or strong like mine once were. But what else can I do? She is all I have left to give.

Who will sing to the crystals when I'm gone? Who will summon Grandfather? Who will organise the festivals? There will be no one to tell my sister the stories of her ancestors, no one to guide and support her. Where will she find the strength to carry on alone?

My sister grows within me. Her body lies curled beneath my ribcage. Her heart beats, a new pulse beneath my skin. So she may grow stronger, I drink what Uzra gives me: teas made with honey or molasses mixed with the bitterness of herbs, soups from sorrel and asparagus that grow wild on the outskirts of the city.

Today Uzra and the Captain have gone to the lake for fresh water. While they are away, Aja, the woman from Aretis, washes me and dresses my wounds. Her hands are gentle as she turns me on my side to wash my legs and back. She binds my head in a clean white cloth. Afterwards, we sit together in the half-light of the room at the back of the laboratory where she has made me a bed of blankets piled one on top of the other. The bed is thick and soft and eases the pain in my hips and the bruises on my arms and legs. We have some words in common, not many but enough to share, enough for me to tell her my name and rank. When we run out of words she gestures, her hands mapping snatches of the old language, and when I sign back she smiles.

'Grandfather,' I sign and point in the direction of the lake. I place my hands on my belly then make an arch. 'Sister,' I sign.

Her face looks puzzled. She reaches out and touches my belly with her fingertips.

I sign again, 'New sister.'

We sit in silence for a while. She leans against the wall with her legs stretched out in front of her. I lean against the blankets, folded now into two piles to support me. Her eyes are closed and her breathing slows. Her hand closes over my hand and wrist. I feel my sister's pulse beating beneath my own and wonder if Aja can feel it too.

When the moon is full it will be time to go to the lake and deliver my sister. Grandfather will know what to do next. Even in this room, many steps away from the water, I can smell him in the air and taste him in the water Uzra gives me to drink. His scent grows stronger by the hour. The river snakes will arrive first. They'll wait at the water's edge until my sister is placed in the water, ready for Grandfather to receive.

Aja's hand is still on mine. I grasp her fingers and squeeze tight. She opens her eyes. I move my fingers against the palm of her hand, making the sign for water. I click my tongue twice against the roof of my mouth and point in the direction of the lake so she knows what I mean.

She releases my hand and signs back, 'You want to go to the lake?'

'Yes,' I say, pleased she has understood me. 'Take me to the lake.'

JASON

Southern port

Aja had fashioned a pile of blankets into a seat for Vellen. The two of them sat side by side against the wall, gesturing to each other, and occasionally talking. Long silences developed. Aja untied her dark hair and let it fall loose on her shoulders. She scratched the front of her scalp with her fingertips the way Anastasia and Helene used to do when they had a headache. With a large, bone-handled comb she worked out the dust and tangles from her hair.

He remembered sunlight catching the sheen of Anastasia's blonde hair as she'd bent over him in the cot – her hair smelt of apples and cinnamon. She had an ivory and bone-handled brush and comb set which had been a wedding present and with which he'd liked to play. Sometimes she let him brush her hair, as long as he counted out loud and managed at least a hundred strokes. Her hair was thick and straight, each strand strong and glossy. Helene's was a mass of fine, red curls highlighting her pale skin and freckles. Anastasia never had time to brush it before she went to school so he did, turning it into a game and tickling Helene so she squirmed and giggled. In the morgue her hair had been faded and lank, drawn back unflatteringly from her face. It smelt of mud. After he'd confirmed her identity he kissed her forehead, resting his hand on the top of her head. His fingers brushed against her hair disturbing a fragment of leaf that crumpled when he tried to pick it up.

Anastasia was vain about her hair and always wore a bright yellow bathing cap to protect it from the sun and salt when she swam in the sea. It made it easy to spot her when she crested a wave or bodysurfed her way back to the shallows – a flash of brightness moving between the black, seal-like bodies of surfers, a little sun bobbing against the blue and white of the ocean. But she didn't wear it the last time she stepped into the ocean. He'd found it on a wooden hook in her laundry, on top of a blue swimsuit, both turned inside out to dry. One of her beach towels was thrown over the edge of the white plastic washing basket. Had she simply forgotten her bathing cap? Or was the actual day and time of her last swim unplanned? It was late autumn, the temperature no more than 14 degrees, and a southerly was blowing – cold even for Anastasia's stoicism.

A local surfer had noticed her car in the almost empty car park as he packed up his wetsuit and board. He knew her to talk to and recognised the personalised number plate on her car, *Miletus*. He'd dried himself off, changed into shorts and a sweatshirt, taken his binoculars and gone back down through the sand dunes to the beach. He spent an hour walking the black sand, searching through his binoculars for the yellow bathing cap until it became too dark to see. When he'd finally tracked down Jason he said the only thing he saw was a flash of white against the darkening silver of the ocean but it was dusk and the light was fading. And it was so far out he thought it must have been a bird or the last of the light catching the tip of a swell.

When Jason went to see Helene the next day to tell her Anastasia was presumed drowned she'd stared at him, her face completely blank. She was standing by the kitchen bench holding a bowl of homemade muffins. She stood motionless, captured forever in his mind as a still life painting: woman in a blue dress holding a green bowl, the dull light from the overcast sky behind her, the bench beside her a slab of brown out of which grew a glass vase of deep yellow chrysanthemums. He'd waited for her to say something, or to move, but she stood holding the bowl, staring at him until he walked over and touched her elbow.

'Helene,' he said. 'Are you okay?'

She blinked twice then slowly handed him the bowl of muffins.

'Do you want tea or coffee?' she said.

'Why don't you sit down,' he said, 'I'll make it.'

He filled the kettle, found teabags, two mugs and took milk from the fridge. Helene sat at the kitchen table with her eyes closed rubbing her temples with her fingertips. He put her mug on the table in front of her. 'When does David get home?'

She dropped her hands and folded them in her lap. When she opened her eyes, she seemed surprised to see him. 'Not till after seven. He's got a couple of late meetings.'

He sat opposite her and sipped tea. Outside the open window a tūī landed on the puriri tree. He listened to it moving through the branches, heard the short wooden clicks that began its call, saw the glossy flash of its black and green feathers and the flash of white as it turned its head and arched its throat.

'Your tea's getting cold,' he said.

'She did it on purpose, didn't she?' Helene said. 'Just one more thing she had to be in charge of.'

'I don't know.'

Helene took her cup to the sink and poured the cold tea out. She rinsed the cup and banged it down on the bench. 'Don't lie to me Jason. And don't make excuses for her. She always did exactly what she wanted – too bad about anybody else.'

'She wasn't that bad,' he said.

'Really?' Helene's hands began to shake. She folded her arms across her chest then tucked her hands under her armpits as if she was suddenly very cold. 'She wasn't *that* bad – how bad was she then?'

His lungs expelled all the air out of his body and he felt unable to take another breath. He thought he might faint. He closed his eyes and remembered the rush of anger he'd felt as he watched his mother walk back out of the surf, pulling off her yellow bathing cap and shaking out her shoulder-length white hair.

'Okay, Helene,' he said, 'okay.'

The following day David drove him out to Muriwai. Anastasia's dark green hatchback had been cordoned off with police tape but the wind had broken the seal and the tape dragged across the ground. Jason used his spare key to open the boot, expecting to see her clothes and shoes arranged in a neat pile but there was nothing except her usual travel rug and pillow, an empty canvas shopping bag, a pair of old sneakers, her favourite shawl, and a half-full plastic water bottle. He searched the front and back seats and the glove box hoping to find a note or some indication of her state of mind but the car was clean and empty. The gas tank was half full. He turned the key in the ignition and music from the compact disc she'd been playing filled the car. He sat in the driver's seat and listened to a couple of tracks. It was a compilation he'd made for her a few years ago: Glenn Miller, Count Basie, and Louis Armstrong. Music Samuel liked. He got out of her car and walked over to David who was leaning against his own car looking at the breeze rippling the surface of the sand dunes.

'It's okay,' he said. 'You go – I'll be fine. I just want to sit out here for a while.'

David pulled his sunglasses out of his jacket pocket. 'I'll go for a walk. I could do with some fresh air.'

He went back to Anastasia's car and played the CD from the beginning, listening to each track, allowing memories of his parents dancing together to rise. His father's favourite, 'Moonlight Serenade', was the final track. He turned the sound up. Tears ran down his cheeks and neck and onto his chest. He saw his mother supporting his father's frail body in her arms as they danced barefoot in the kitchen together, and the gold band of her wedding ring shining as she held his head under the bath water. He felt the warmth of her skin against his as she carried him from his cot into their big bed and laid him against a pillow that smelt of his father. In this earliest of memories, he'd curled up against her and fallen asleep as she read and took notes.

The music ended.

He hit the steering wheel with his fist.

'Why did you love the two of us so much and Helene so little?'

—Auckland—

Now I hovered between my study, where Jenny read in the armchair at the foot of the bed, and the southern laboratory – and I dreamed of Anastasia. She lay in a simple wooden boat. Her face was smooth, her hair loose about her shoulders, her favourite yellow and green dress draped gracefully around her strong body. Her wedding ring shone on her left hand. The tide was out and I had to drag the boat from the high tide line down to the waves. Helene stood on top of the sand dunes looking out to the horizon. I called out to her to help me pull the boat across the sand but she just pointed out to sea. I turned and saw a dark swell building, one that would turn into a huge wave as it came closer to the shore. In the boat by Anastasia's feet I found a thick coil of rope. I knotted one end to the prow of the boat and looped the other around my chest. I pulled the boat across the thick black sand and into the water, heaving forward with each step like a team of oxen. When I was knee deep I untied the rope and coiled it back into the bottom of the boat. Out at sea the wave was building. I needed to manoeuvre the boat through the wall of the wave before it crashed to the shore and smashed the boat to pieces. I got behind the boat and started to push. Once the water was at shoulder level I dived and, under water, gave the boat a final shove. It shot through the bottom of the wave leaving me behind. I closed my eyes and held my breath as the weight of water crashed over me.

JENNY

Jason still seemed to sleep most of the time but more often now there were moments when he was almost awake, although so far, he'd never been fully present in the room with her. She could feel him drifting in and out of consciousness; and there were times, usually late at night or very early in the morning, when his eyes were open and they followed her as she moved about the room. Occasionally tears seeped from his eyes and rolled down his cheeks.

She'd had every possible test done, as well as brain scans. She'd paid for the ambulance to come and take him to and from hospital. She'd paid for specialists, and for the nurses who helped her care for him at home. All the results said he was physically fine: there was nothing wrong with his brain, his heart, lungs, liver, kidneys or pancreas. He hadn't had a stroke. One of the neurologists she'd consulted said it was as if he's gone to sleep and got stuck in the fifth, REM, stage for long periods of time, much longer than normal; but really, they didn't know.

She worked half-days and learnt to delegate. She still met with her most important clients and oversaw their briefs. And although she didn't have many staff, they were competent, and reliable; business was ticking over. Life continued: she walked the dogs, had coffee with friends. David and the boys came over for lunch most weekends. Liam liked to come over more often and stay the night and neither she nor David had the heart to stop him. His company seemed to comfort Jason, lessening his agitation, calming those twitching eyelids and limbs. Last week after he'd curled up besides Jason and slept for a couple of hours, Liam said to her, don't worry Aunty Jenny, Uncle Jason will be all right; he'll come back soon. And she thought, well, he might only be a child but he seems to know as much as anyone about this.

UZRA

Uzra led the Captain through deserted streets to the outskirts of the city. They each carried two large, scoured kerosene tins to which they'd attached wire handles. Inside the tins were empty glass bottles. Once they got to the lake they would wade out, fill them with ice-cold water and carry them back to the laboratory. Before they filled the bottles Uzra led Damian to the lookout. They left their tins and bottles on the ground and walked up the thousand steps to the top deck. The air grew colder as they climbed. Uzra felt a familiar heaviness settle in his chest. By the time they reached the top he was short of breath and lightheaded. He staggered as he walked towards the railing. Damian put out a hand to steady him.

'I'll be alright,' Uzra said, 'I just need to rest for a minute.'

He sat with his back against wooden slats that supported the railing that ran the length of the viewing deck. The mountains and the lake stretched out behind him.

'These Southerners,' Damian said, standing in the centre of the platform and turning a slow 360 degrees so he could appreciate the view, 'they're good at building.'

Uzra pulled the brim of his hat down to shade his eyes from the glare. His arms and legs felt as heavy as his lungs. He could have easily closed his eyes and slept. The Captain admired the landscape and the blue-domed buildings. Uzra was grateful he wasn't alone, that there was someone to help him carry water and search for wild herbs. He'd managed so far to keep Vellen alive but soon they'd run out of food.

'I have to take her home,' he said, 'back to the caves of Aretis.'

Damian eased himself down beside Uzra. 'It's a long way.'

'If I can get her across the lake and onto one of the locos, I might have a chance.'

'These locos, how fast do they travel?'

Uzra took off his hat and waved it in front of his face to bat away an insect. 'Faster than a sailing ship with a good tailwind,' he said.

'Impressive,' Damian said. He stood up and smoothed down his quilted cotton jacket. As well as braid, a deep border of red and black stars decorated the hem and the cuffs of his sleeves.

Uzra wondered if it was just decoration or whether it signalled his authority or rank.

Damian stood up. 'I don't see any boats.' He held out his hand and pulled Uzra to his feet. 'How will you get her across the lake?'

They walked back down the steps, picked up their tins and bottles and walked towards the edge of the lake. The tightness in Uzra's lungs eased the closer he got to the ground.

He pointed to a stand of trees on their right. 'There's a jetty,' he said. 'Before they built the locos the lake was filled with hundreds of small boats. You could sail or row yourself or pay someone to take you across.'

'And after the locos?'

'There were barges to bring food and coal across, and ferries to take people. The small boats just got in the way.'

They walked towards the trees. Pebbles crunched beneath their boots. It was close to noon, the sun almost directly overhead. High above them a hawk circled. In the distance gulls squawked and scavenged for food. Uzra remembered the jetty full of men waiting for ferries to take them across to the locos so they could speed through the countryside to work in the northern mines. He'd made that journey many times. Barges piled high with coal had docked at the jetty, waiting their turn to be unloaded.

The jetty was still standing although in places some of the wooden planks were missing. Beneath the trees a dozen or so rowboats were overturned, their hulls facing the sky.

'If we can bring her down here,' Uzra said, 'we'll be able to get her across.'

Damian upturned one of the boats, searching for workable oars. A large brown spider scuttled past his foot. He stepped back and let the boat fall.

'And the locos are still running?' he said.

'I came down here on one three weeks ago,' Uzra said. He didn't mention it was the only one still running and coal had already been hard to purchase. But the engine driver still owed him a number of favours and, if necessary, he would commandeer coal and shovel it himself.

He and Damian walked to the end of the jetty and looked across the water to the base of the mountains. In the centre of the lake was a darker patch of water. They stood side by side watching as the surface water swirled and churned.

Uzra took off his hat and slapped it against his thigh. He began to laugh, then started to cough.

'What is it?' Damian said. 'What's happening?'

'River snakes,' Uzra said. 'Thousands of them.'

He reached inside his jacket pocket and took out a small wooden flute. He blew three soft, reedy notes, coughed again and started to play a series of six notes, repeating them many times to guide the snakes to the shore.

Damian stood quietly beside him, his hands tucked inside the wide sleeves of his jacket, watching the snakes as they began to move through the water to the edge of the lake.

As Uzra played they pooled in the shallows, their skin glinting in the light. He had never seen so many in one place.

He changed his sequence of notes. Why have you come here, he asked, but they just continued to swim through the lake to the shore, more and more of them until the edges of the lake closest to them were a moving carpet of brown and gold.

JASON

Auckland

Pale light shone through the yellow curtains in the study. I had returned. The drip remained connected to my left arm and the catheter still ran into a bag at the side of the bed. In the far corner of the ceiling there was a discoloured patch where the paint had started to peel. A dusty tendril of an old spider's web hung down and swayed a little. I blinked. Nothing changed. The peeling paint and the spider's web were still there. I was home again but for how long? I tried to move my right hand but only my forefinger twitched. My head felt too heavy to turn or lift. I'd shifted back but wasn't anchored yet.

Humming came from the foot of the bed; Liam's curly red hair appeared. He was playing with a model car, running it over the blanket, down one of my legs then up the other, pretending he was on a racing circuit. He was talking to himself, the way small boys did, giving directions to the car, making all the sound effects, crashing it off the blanket and onto the floor. I watched him, wishing I could reach out and ruffle that flame of hair, so like Helene's at that age.

Between my feet at the end of the bed there was a light brown shape, the size of a small cat. I stared, afraid it was the ginger apparition from my childhood come back to haunt me, but then saw it was Helene's old teddy bear. Liam must have brought it. My right arm jerked. My hand twitched with the desire to touch it, to see if there was any trace of Helene left.

I spun out again, shifted again, but this time not too far. I was on the space ship again, circling the planet, waiting for a glimpse of the great southern lake, the largest body of water left. The clouds parted and as the lake came into view the surface of the water moved in troughs and swells like an ocean. I magnified the view on the screen in front of me. The movement was coming from the centre of the lake; waves were forming, rearing up and crashing on the shore. I pointed the camera towards a section of the shoreline. A run-down wooden pier jutted out of a pile of rocks, forty or so metres into the lake. I magnified the view again. Thin brown water snakes, thousands of them, were swimming in the waves as they broke against the sides of the pier and the shore. I angled the camera back to the centre of the lake. The striped brown and gold head of an enormous snake rose out of the water and filled the screen. Its yellow eyes opened and blinked. It yawned and flicked its forked tongue. I leapt back from the screen.

Once my heartbeat settled I re-adjusted the camera. Three small figures approached the pier. One of them was Aja, her blue shawl draped over her head and shoulders. She was carrying a bundle in her arms. The other two were grey-haired men: Uzra slightly stooped, the Captain limping a little, each carrying the end of a wooden pole on which were hung four kerosene cans.

I put my hand on the screen. 'Aja.'

When they reached the pier Uzra and the Captain stopped and put the cans and the pole on the ground. One more time I magnified the screen, to be as close as possible, to see the expressions on their faces. Wind ruffled the men's hair; white mist from the waves sprayed their faces. Aja handed the bundled shape of Vellen to Uzra then stretched her arms out and up above her head. Her shawl slipped from her head and settled in folds around her neck and shoulders. She climbed four steps and stood on the pier looking out to the other side of the lake. The Captain joined her and she pointed to the centre where the water was churning, where the giant snake waited, using the current in its tail to create a whirlpool of waves.

Aja and the Captain walked to the far end of the pier. Waves slapped against the cracked wooden posts that supported the walkway. She reached inside the pocket of her tunic, drew out four small pellets and handed them to the Captain. He bowed his head and held his palm out, as if making an offering to the elements. Out of the water rose the huge head of the snake. I cried out a warning but no one could hear me. The snake swam towards them, covering the distance from the centre to the pier in a couple of heartbeats. Its body was vast and shining, glinting with thick stripes of gold as it moved beneath the surface of the water.

Aja turned and gestured to Uzra to join them. He walked carefully along the slippery wooden slats carrying Vellen in his arms. She was so wrapped up in blankets Jason couldn't see her face. Only the top of her head was visible, wound in white scarves. Uzra stood between Aja and the Captain, trying to protect Vellen from the wind and the waves.

I touched the screen again. 'Little sister.'

The snake raised its head out of the water and pushed through the rotting wood at the end of the pier.

Uzra stepped back. Aja grabbed his arm to stop him retreating down the pier to the shore. The snake leaned in and nuzzled Vellen, knocking Uzra to the ground. Aja and the Captain linked their arms through his and pulled him upright. Waves slopped against the jetty and it started to rock. Uzra held on to Vellen even though she was struggling to free herself from the blankets. Aja said something to him but he shook his head.

Once more the snake came close and rubbed his head against Vellen, this time knocking both of them over. Vellen rolled out of Uzra's arms, out of the blankets and onto the wet planks of the undulating pier.

She arched her back. Her abdomen split open.

The snake flicked out his tongue, caressing the length of her body.

A wave of electric blue light rolled over her skin and hovered in the air above her.

I moved closer to the screen.

A fit of shivering overtook Vellen. She convulsed once and then lay still. Uzra crawled towards her. Aja and the Captain pulled him back. Out of the cavity of her collapsed body, another, miniature Vellen emerged. Thick dark hair covered her head. Her eyes were closed against the light. The skin on her arms, shoulders and chest was smooth and dark and shiny, and her hands were curled into small, loose fists.

I pressed my face against the screen. 'Little sister.' I wiped tears away with my sleeve.

When I shifted back to my bed in the study I was lying on my side facing the wall, my face wet with tears. Curled behind me was Liam. His little body snuggled into my lower back. Liam patted me between my shoulder blades.

'It's alright, Uncle Jason,' he said. 'Don't cry. Don't cry.'

UZRA

Vellen's body was on the wooden slats of the pier, discarded where it had fallen as if she had shrugged off an old, worn-out coat. Uzra wanted to reach her, to prove to himself she was really dead, but Aja and the Captain pinned him down.

'Don't interfere,' Aja shouted in his ear, just as she had a few minutes earlier when the largest snake he had ever seen reared out of the lake and pushed them over, trying to take Vellen out of his arms.

What he was aware of now, as this new creature emerged from Vellen's remains, were the sudden flashes of blue lightning above their heads. The stench of sulphur rose in the air and beneath that was the duller, metallic smell of blood and the ripeness of Vellen's damaged and decaying organs. A rough trembling seized Uzra's limbs; he heard himself howl then he was shouting and gulping and crying and couldn't seem to stop. The Captain released his grip on his left arm and leg. Aja sat him upright. She knelt behind him and put both hands on his shoulders to steady him.

The snake's enormous head lay on the walkway, dwarfing the tiny dark-skinned body as she uncurled her arms and legs and crawled out of Vellen's abdomen. Thick black hair was matted against her head and shoulders. Claw-like nails spread out from her fingers and toes. She shivered in the cool damp air and attempted to sit up. The wooden slats rocked as the snake flicked its tongue out again, this time spraying a net of gossamer spit over the creature. Her muscles rippled as it touched her. She curled over on herself, exposing her skin to the cold wet planks. The silky strands of the net stuck to her and began to thicken, and as they thickened they formed a cocoon and changed to the colour of polished gold.

Uzra cried out the only words he knew from the old language, taught to him by his grandfather when he first dreamed of gold as a boy on the banks of the Otmas river: Ureure-lazuera – Golden one: saviour of the land and waters.

He rolled onto his knees and stood, shaking, his legs and feet wet from the waves and his face, arms and shoulders saturated from heavy spray. His chest was heavy, weighted with years of gold and coal dust. He staggered back a few paces, spread his feet wide and steadied himself on the pier. Below him in the water the river snakes gathered.

Out of his jacket pocket he took his wooden flute; he shook it, raised it to his lips and began to play. He couldn't hear himself through the sounds of the wind and the waves lapping and smacking against the posts.

Aja and the Captain pushed themselves up from the walkway and came and stood beside him. The Captain put his arm through Aja's and they stood close together, holding on to each other, their hair and faces glistening from the spray.

As Uzra played, the river snakes began to weave themselves into a raft, thousands linking themselves head to tail, forming the warp and weft so tightly they created a waterproof platform. They moved as one being, close to the head of the giant snake and hovered there, waiting.

The snake's tongue flicked out again, scooped up the golden cocoon and nudged it onto the centre of the raft. Uzra's breath faltered for a moment but he continued to play, his eyes never leaving the cocoon. The raft of river snakes turned a full circle and began to vibrate. It rose an inch in the air then shook itself and resettled on top of the water. The cocoon had not moved.

The snake turned back to Vellen's body and laid its head beside her. While Uzra had been playing to the river snakes the gash of her opened abdomen had collapsed back in on itself and closed. Aja and the Captain, still linked arm in arm, walked a few steps forward. Aja placed four pellets on top of Vellen's body. They stepped back. Once more the snake flicked its tongue over Vellen's body, this time drawing her and the pellets into its enormous mouth.

Uzra stopped playing and sank to his knees. He bent over and banged his forehead on the wet planks. 'No!' he said.

Aja came and squatted beside him. She put her hand on the base of his neck. 'She told me this would happen,' she said. 'This way she's never left behind.' She helped Uzra to stand and pointed to the raft. 'Her sister lives.'

Uzra wiped his face with the sleeve of his jacket. 'Ureure-lazuera,' he said. 'In the old stories the golden cocoon is called saviour of land and water.' He started to cough and searched in his pockets for his handkerchief. He spat and blew his nose. 'I never thought to see it.'

The three of them stood together on the pier and watched as the snake swam back to the centre of the lake. Its body rippled with newly garnered energy; its skin glowed as if lit from within. The raft followed, the precious cargo stable and dry.

The waves retreated. The lake settled. The wind dropped.

Uzra, Aja and the Captain helped each other down the steps, left the pier and retreated to a group of scrubby bushes twenty feet from the shoreline. They sat on the ground facing the water. Aja leant her head on the Captain's shoulder. He rubbed his hands over the sandy soil and pebbles; picked up broken shells and small pieces of pumice and let them trickle through his fingers. Uzra watched gulls swoop across the lake, heard them squawk as they landed on the far edge of the pier.

He closed his eyes and weighed Vellen's grief in his mind, tattooing it on his memory.

'What will happen now?' he said.

'They'll carry her back to the caves of Aretis,' Aja said. 'Vellen told me Grandfather Anisth sleeps and renews himself beneath the Northern Gate.'

Uzra saw the smashed and broken tunnels, the dead bodies of the Gardeners floating between chunks of coal, and the moment his frightened men found Vellen, the only Gardener left alive. She had screamed and shut her huge dark eyes when he raised his lantern to look at her face.

'She'll be alone in the caves,' he said. 'There's no-one to help her.'

Aja reached out and touched his wrist. 'I'll go back,' she said. 'A new village can be built.'

Uzra imagined returning to his own village. The only person he wanted to see was Erika. Would she leave the plains of Otmas and go north with him to Aretis?

'I need to repay my debt to Vellen,' he said.

'Come with me then,' Aja said.

The Captain stood up. 'Let's see if we can find a boat that doesn't leak. Then we can cross the lake and find that loco you were talking about.'

CAPTAIN DAMIAN

The rocking of the loco lulled Damian into a dream-like state. He and Uzra had been taking turns shovelling coal into the engine but he was now too tired to do anything but stretch out on the black leather seat in the carriage and rest. Aja sat cross-legged on the seat opposite him. Her eyes were closed, but he knew she wasn't asleep. She had retreated into herself and would stay like that for hours, until some point had been reached when she felt renewed, or when some external demand brought her back from the world of her ancestors to the present. He watched as the tension and tiredness faded from her face and a mask of stillness settled over her. Her breathing was slow and deep and as he listened to its steady rise and fall he felt the tightness in his own chest ease a little.

Outside the carriage window roughly ploughed but unplanted fields rushed by, with clusters of grey rocks creating a regular boundary line between the loco tracks and farmland. In the distance he saw a patchwork of white and black figures – sheep and goats grazing on the scratchy hillsides. He had not been in this part of the country before and wondered if it was always this barren or whether these remote villages and farms had been decimated by the southern sickness too.

He'd found the cause of the sickness and could report it to Saraz but there was little more they could do now to stop it spreading further except to enforce the existing quarantine. So many of the infected Southerners were dead he doubted any more damage could be done by them and the few left in the south weren't going anywhere. Of greater immediate concern to him was finding enough food and fuel to get everyone who had survived in Rona through autumn and another winter.

Towards evening the loco slowed and shunted into a small village midway between the mountains and lakes of the south and the flat plains and shingled rivers of the middle country. The station was a simple affair, an unpainted wooden platform in front of an old stone building that consisted of a single room. A thin plume of smoke rose from a crooked chimney into the darkening sky. Through the un-shuttered window Damian could see the shapes of four men clustered around a large fireplace. He watched as Uzra and the loco driver walked across the platform and stood by the doorway. Two of the men left the hearth, came outside and greeted them. Uzra shook hands with each of the men. He reached into his pocket and handed their driver a handful of the small round pellets that Aja called firelighters. They had great currency in the south even though outwardly they resembled nothing more than dried sheep droppings. A few more words were said before the driver went inside and stood by the fire. Uzra and the two locals, both small dark men with veins knotted like rope along their forearms, walked back across the platform and boarded the train. Damian understood the value of these firelighters and why Uzra used them to pay for their passage home but he had no personal wish to trade them for food or fuel or transport. He'd seen what they'd cost Vellen and Aja, and what they did to Grandfather Anisth. That was something he still found hard to believe even though he'd witnessed it with his own eyes. When he told Saraz of that transformation she might well think he'd taken leave of his senses.

He scratched his unshaven jaw and massaged his aching calf muscles. His arms, shoulders and back ached as well; his clothes were stiff with mud and sand. He was tired to his bones, and knew beyond any doubt he was too old for this kind of life. He wanted to sleep in his own bed and wake in the morning to the sound of Challis' chattering as he brought him his first cup of tea. And while there was plenty he could report to Saraz on his own he had decided it would be better to take Aja with him. While it was his responsibility to pass on what he'd learnt in the south, Aja knew more about Vellen and Grandfather Anisth, the caves of Aretis and the power of the firelighters. If anyone could convince Saraz of the need for further support it would be her.

The loco began to move again. Their previous driver came outside and stood on the platform. He touched the brim of his woollen cap as they left the station. As they picked up speed Damian looked over at Aja again. She sat just as motionless, her breathing still slow and steady. Her hair was unplaited, her clothes were stained and stiff with mud too, yet she appeared serene, her blue shawl draped around her neck and shoulders, somehow miraculously free of dirt, although her heavy leather sandals were caked with it. She had placed them neatly on the floor beneath her seat when they entered the carriage. Before she withdrew into herself to rest and recover she had sat cross-legged on the shiny black seat, shaken the dust and sand out her shawl and said, 'The ghost-visitor has left now.'

Damian felt the hair on the back of his neck stir as if a breeze had suddenly entered the room. The skin on his arms tingled. He waited for Aja to continue.

'He followed me from Aretis to Rona,' she said, 'and from Rona to the south. He stayed with us in the laboratory but now he's gone.'

'Was he someone from your village?'

Aja began combing her unwound hair with her fingers. 'He came to the village once. I found him on the bridge lying in the snow, frozen almost to death. I took him to my hut to keep him warm and fed him goat stew. He stayed for two days and nights then he left.'

'But he came back?' Damian asked.

'Later, after the village had been burned. But he was hollowed out by then, a shadow, drifting between worlds.'

Damian shook his jacket to remove the surface dirt and rolled up his shirtsleeves. 'What did he want?'

'I'm not sure,' Aja said. 'Perhaps he wandered too far and got lost.'

She folded the corners of her shawl across her chest and smiled at Damian. 'I'll miss him,' she said.

It was dark now and the black loco pulling the green-painted carriage in which they sat moved swiftly through the night. Occasionally Damian saw lights in the distance, perhaps from a farmhouse where a woman was kneading and setting bread to rise for the morning, or from someone checking on animals in a barn, or from a beacon lit in a village hall to guide travellers to safety. Clouds obscured a waning moon and the noise of the engine blocked out any other sounds. He couldn't tell if there were animals sleeping in the fields, whether wild creatures were out hunting or if dogs had been let loose to roam. He was encased in a wooden and leather carriage pulled by a steam engine fuelled by coal that was so scarce he knew Uzra was supplementing it with firelighters. He had the sensation of flying through an endless tunnel – a long straight tunnel dug beneath the earth that would eventually bring him to the surface and allow him to watch the sun rise in the morning. Then he could return to Saraz and Challis and his old friend Rico.

He rolled his jacket beneath his head and stretched out on the carriage seat. He closed his eyes hoping to slip into a deep and restful sleep but a vivid image of Vellen's body lying on the pier and the huge head of Grandfather Anisth resting beside it startled him and he sat up again. He wished he could withdraw into himself like Aja and avoid replaying everything that had happened since they'd arrived in the south, but every time he closed his eyes memories from each extraordinary day returned. In spite of overwhelming tiredness, he was unable to stop or control them. His stomach rumbled, his muscles twitched or went into spasms and in his mind there was a constant loop of repeating images and sounds. He rubbed the palms of his hands together and massaged the stiff joints in each finger and thumb. He'd experienced this kind of fatigue before, as a young soldier after a campaign and again when he was older and working with Rico on cases assigned to them by Saraz, when he'd had to witness the intense grief of the bereaved or the helpless rage of the victim.

In an attempt to stop the images battering him he went back over what Aja had said about the ghost-visitor, the shadow drifting between the worlds. At times he had felt something too, although it wasn't as clear or precise as Aja's description. He hadn't seen anything, but twice – once in his own home and then in the laboratory – he'd felt the presence of someone close to him, someone watching what he was doing.

The first time he'd shrugged it off, explained it as the strange intensity that emanated from Aja, the sense she gave of being surrounded by ancestors. She was never on her own, never just an individual. The second time was when Uzra had taken them to the laboratory and he and Aja had encountered Vellen for the first time. Aja had simply folded to the floor. She'd cradled Vellen and crooned an ancient lullaby. He felt the air pressure around him shift, the way it did when a storm was building. The room had been full of electric energy, making his hair crackle and his clothes stick to his skin. He heard the sharp intake of a breath behind him and felt something touch his shoulder. He turned to see who it was, but no one was there. The skin on the back of his neck and shoulders had been alive with nerve ends and he'd rubbed his neck and rolled his shoulders to relieve the sensation of being touched. He had turned back to Aja and Vellen and watched in silence as Aja presented her with a gift of firelighters and a few scraps of snakeskin. After that he had been plunged into the world of his own ancestors and saw again the stone man standing guardian by the entrance to the black river.

Now, in the darkness of the carriage with his muscles and nerves twitching with exhaustion and his vision filled with flickering images, he let go of any attempt to control his mind and allowed himself to move outside his body. For a couple of heartbeats he hovered above himself, seeing with a sudden stab of pity his plait of coarse grey hair, the deep lines on his face, the rough and reddened skin on his hands, the swollen joints in his fingers; then he was looking down at someone else, a man, middle-aged and grey-haired like himself, although his hair was cropped short against his scalp and the skin on his hands was smooth and his fingers were long and elegant. The man was lying on a narrow bed in a room with lightly polished wooden walls and a darker wooden floor. Two oblong windows above the bed let in early morning light. There was an armchair in one corner and a desk and bookshelves along the opposite wall. The man was asleep but his body was restless, his legs twitching beneath a soft blanket, his eyelids flickering. Every now and then he muttered something and attempted to turn over on to his side. Damian felt drawn to the man. Something about him was familiar even though he didn't recognise his face.

A woman with short, dark hair and large brown eyes came into the room and stood beside the bed. She was wearing an ankle-length blue robe. Her feet were bare. She picked up the man's wrist and took his pulse. The light caught a section of her robe as she bent over the man and kissed his forehead and the material shimmered and changed colour like water. Later, a boy appeared. He was smaller and younger than Challis and carried a cloth bag full of toys with him. These he spread out at the foot of the bed. Damian smiled when he saw a miniature loco and carriage, painted in green and black, just like the one he and Uzra and Aja were travelling in. The boy pulled out two other small toys, compact carriages with four wheels each but without animals or engines to pull them. He chose the sleekest one, painted red with a silver trim, and moved it up and down the man's legs, humming to himself. After a while the boy tired of his game and curled up on the bed beside the man and slept, one arm curved outside the blanket, his hand still holding the small red and silver carriage.

When Damian came back into himself the loco had stopped. Aja had opened the shutters to let in the early morning light. He was stretched out on the seat with his jacket draped over his chest and she was standing by his feet, her face slightly blurred in the dim light.

'You've returned,' she said.

Damian rubbed his eyes and sat up. 'How long have I been asleep?'

She moved to the window. 'We've reached the end of the track – now we walk.'

After they uncoupled the carriage and watched the loco shunt its way back down the track, Uzra led them across a field dotted with tree stumps and pieces of dark machinery that lay abandoned like the carcasses of deformed animals. As he walked past them Damian stared at each one, wondering at its use. Uzra pointed to a low stone building at the far edge of the field.

'There's a well behind there, with fresh water,' he said. 'We can wash and drink and fill our flasks.'

When they reached the building Uzra took a brass key from his jacket pocket and unlocked the heavy padlock that secured the door. He leaned against it and pushed it open. Inside, wooden barrels, tins, boxes, baskets and pottery jars were stacked against the back and side walls. The floor was dusty and the air smelt of straw, sacking and spices. The open doorway let in a shaft of pale-yellow light. The only windows were two small squares beneath the ceiling on the end wall. The walls were lined with wood and covered from floor to ceiling with thick brown hessian.

Damian walked over to a barrel and read the label, *Apple Wine*. 'What is this place?'

'The last southern outpost,' Uzra said.

'It's a long way from the south.'

'Before the sickness the Southerners believed they could build a loco track that ran from the south right to the north, connecting them straight to the caves and the firelighters. This is as far as they got.'

Uzra lifted a canvas coversheet from a pile of boxes and tightly woven baskets and handed a tin bucket, a long-handled ladle and a bar of yellow soap to Aja. 'For the well,' he said.

He pointed to a large wicker basket fastened with leather straps and silver buckles that was balanced on the top of three boxes. 'There are spare clothes in there, trousers and tunics and woollen shawls, if you want to change. Damian and I will sort out provisions while you wash.'

Damian watched Aja undo the buckles and open the basket. Inside there were three piles of neatly folded garments: dark-blue trousers, collarless light-blue tunics, and shawls, some light fawn in colour, some a deeper shade of brown that reminded him of wet sand.

Aja reached in and touched the rough weave of the top shawl. 'Thank you,' she said, 'I'm sure something will fit.'

Uzra led Damian to the middle section of the back wall. Large cream-coloured pottery jars were stacked in rows three deep and four high. 'Dried fruit, seeds and nuts,' he said. He lifted the smallest jar from the top of a row. 'And dried goat meat mixed with figs, grated orange rind and spices. A southern delicacy.'

Damian had seen it on sale in the market in Rona before the sickness came, but it was so expensive he'd never bought or eaten it. There were at least a dozen jars of it, sitting out there in the middle of nowhere.

He picked up a jar. It was surprisingly heavy. 'What do you eat it with?' he said.

'Rice or bread or sweet potato,' Uzra said. 'A small amount goes a long way.' He took the jar from Damian and tucked it under his arm. 'One should be enough.'

Damian stood beside Uzra as he pointed out barrels of wine and beer, jars of flour, barley, oats and rice, tins of honey, boxes of dried mushrooms packed in straw and, in a screened-off section in the darkest corner, glass containers of dried and ground herbs and small bottles of spices.

'Mainly medicinal,' Uzra said, 'I don't know the use of half of them. The Southerners were always experimenting.'

Damian picked up a glass bottle that was the height and width of the palm of his hand. The label had no legible name just a series of letters and numbers: *BL6351a.* 'What will happen to all of this?'

Uzra searched through the herbs and spices, unscrewing lids and sniffing. Occasionally he sprinkled powder on his finger and tasted it, screwing up his nose in distaste at the bitterness. The ones he recognised he put to one side.

'We'll take what we can carry, anything that reduces pain or fever, or,' he tapped his chest, 'congestion of the lungs.'

Aja stood in the doorway, dressed in clean blue trousers and tunic, her damp hair spread out on her shoulders. She carried the bucket and ladle in one hand and her wet, washed clothes in the other. 'Do we have time to dry these?' she said.

Uzra found her a wooden sawhorse left behind by the carpenters who had lined the walls of the building. He brushed it down and carried it outside the door into the sunshine. Aja draped her wet clothes over it and stood behind it with her face turned to the sun. She began to lift her hair off her shoulders, letting it fan out to help it dry.

Damian stood in the doorway and studied her, observing her strong hands lifting up her hair then letting it fall, and even though her feet and legs weren't moving he felt he was watching her dance, or, more precisely, he was seeing the moment before her dancing began, the moment when impulse and energy coalesced and the desire for movement rose and began to flow through her legs and hips. It was the first time he had seen her this relaxed, with her body and mind focused entirely in the present. It was also the first time he'd seen her without her blue shawl either draped across her shoulders or wrapped around her face and head to protect her from the sun and wind. She looked younger, more vulnerable.

He took a step back and half closed the door, wanting to remain shadowed, to observe without being noticed. There was something about the rising and falling of her hair, her moment of simple pleasure in the warmth of the sun on her clean hair and skin, the graceful movement of her arms and hands as if she was offering her hair and her spirit to the sun. It disturbed him and reminded him of someone else. He sat on one of the heavy wicker baskets behind the door and put his head in his hands. When he closed his eyes he saw another tall, strong-limbed woman. She was wearing a knee-length green linen tunic with yellow flowers around the hem and her thick, straight blonde hair was loose on her shoulders; her arms were around a thin, grey-haired man whose eyes were covered by opaque dark glasses. They were swaying gently together as if they were the only two people left in the world. Damian knew he didn't know this couple yet they were familiar to him, like distant relatives, recognisable by family traits rather than by their individual personalities. Light from a long narrow window caught the woman's hair and burnished it white gold.

He stayed behind the door replaying the image of the man and woman dancing together in a room with filtered light until he felt a hand touch his shoulder.

'Your turn,' Uzra said, handing him the bucket, ladle and soap.

Damian removed his jacket and went to the wicker basket to find a change of clothes. Outside he stood barefoot on the damp wooden boards beside the lichen-covered stones of the well and poured cold water over his head and shoulders until his clothes were soaked. He rubbed the hard, yellow soap against as much of his shirt and trousers as he could reach then poured more water over himself. He stripped and draped his clothes over the edge of the well, letting them drip onto the boards. The breeze goose-bumped his skin and he shivered in spite of the warmth of the sun. Once he was clean and dry he dressed in the same plain, dark-blue trousers and light-blue tunic as Aja and Uzra. The uniform of southern workers, he supposed, similar to those he'd seen sailors wear when they came into the port of Rona to unload their cargoes of fish, fruit and vegetables. Only the Captains and rich traders had worn bright colours and finely woven silks and wools.

When he returned to the front of the building he saw Uzra had built a small fire to boil water and was busy making tea. Aja had piled dried fruit and nuts onto a wooden tray and spread a calico covering on the ground. Another wicker basket was open beside her and she removed three pottery mugs. Her hair was still loose and half dry. He sat beside her and when she passed him a mug his hand brushed against hers.

She looked at him, the corners of her mouth twitching into a smile. 'Be careful, too many visions and you'll become a ghost-visitor too.'

He sipped his tea and ate a handful of almonds and dates. What worlds did she have entry to that she knew of his dreams and visions? He looked away, pretending to study the shape of the clouds and flocks of birds that were specks of grey wheeling in the distance. Uzra broke more twigs onto the fire to keep it going and sat down, forming a triangle on the coversheet, the tray of food in the centre between them.

'A day's walk from here to Otmas, then two, perhaps three, from there to Rona,' he said, mapping out the rest of their journey. 'Six or seven days to Aretis, depending on the weather, or less if we sail up the coast and then walk inland.' He scratched his chin and took some dried figs and raisins from the tray, jiggling them in the palm of his hand. 'Will you come with us Captain?'

Part 4: Vines and Bees

Father Anselmo – Silver-Jean – Ruth

DEVIL VINES

Spain 1462

Father Anselmo led the donkey up the dusty path towards the monastery of San Pedro. Another half hour and he would be home, ready for the comfort of his garden and his hives. The late afternoon sun was hot on his back and shoulders and sweat ran between his skin and coarse brown robe. He wiped his face with one of his wide sleeves and stopped to drink from the gourd in the basket tied to the donkey's back. He rinsed his mouth then drank deeply, letting some of the water trickle down his chin.

Once he was home, had unloaded the donkey and taken it to the stables to be washed and fed, he would fill two buckets of cool water from the well, take off his sweat and dust-stained clothes and bathe before he went to the refectory to join his brothers for their simple evening meal of bread and bean stew.

He put the gourd back in the basket, wiped his chin, patted the donkey on the rump and walked on.

The sky had been cloudless all day but as he reached the top of the rise allowing him a first view of the outer walls of the monastery, he saw thick, black smoke billowing into the air. He stood with his hand clutching the wooden crucifix he wore round his neck, trying to locate the origin of the smoke. After a moment he realized it was not coming from the monastery but from the untidy cluster of low wooden buildings further along the river that housed the tanner, his family and his business. Father Anselmo started to run, pulling the donkey behind him. Hurry, he said to himself and the donkey, hurry in case we're needed.

By the time he reached the tannery the monastery bells were ringing and all the buildings were ablaze. Monks were spread out in a line from the river, passing leather buckets full of water to others who threw them on the fire. He tied the donkey to a large oleander bush well away from the flames and rushed to help.

They worked for an hour, dousing the flames with water and soil until all that was left were sodden piles of burnt leather, ash and mud. Father Anselmo and the monks waded into the river to wash the worst of the smoke, ash and dust from themselves. Only then did he think to ask where the tanner, his wife and children were. He'd somehow assumed they must have run to the monastery to get help or been taken inside the walls to keep them safe, but no one had seen them. Nor had the alarm been raised until the monks had seen and smelt the smoke, and by then the fire was well ablaze.

While the others returned to the monastery to change their wet robes, Father Anselmo and Brother Marcus searched for human remains, sifting through the cooling debris with shovels and sticks. Finding nothing, they walked further south along the riverbank.

'I saw him yesterday,' Brother Marcus said, 'when I was walking back from the village. He said he was working from dawn 'til dusk. He wanted to be ready for the fair next month.'

Father Anselmo nodded at Brother Marcus. Something didn't feel right. He kept his eyes on the ground searching for anything that might give a clue to what had happened to the tanner's wife and children.

'How many children did he have?'

'Two young ones and a new-born.'

They walked as far as the wooden bridge that served as a gateway to the village and the grazing fields on the other side of the river.

'Let's circle back,' he said. 'We might as well check he didn't have a day off or take his family foraging.'

They left the bridge and the river and walked in a wide arc towards a grove of cork oaks that grew at the base of the gently sloping hills where he liked to collect wild herbs. By the time they reached the trees their robes were almost dry.

Father Anselmo stood in the shade for a moment then put his hand on Brother Marcus' arm. 'Look,' he said. He pointed to the ground a few metres in front of them. 'There's something caught in the roots of that tree.'

They moved closer and saw the edge of a yellow and black shawl. Brother Marcus bent down and picked it up, shaking dust and a few dried leaves from it. 'Hard to say how long it's been here,' he said, 'but it's not stained or damaged.'

They found them on the far side of the grove. Killer vines had trapped the tanner's wife and two children, squeezing their chests, throats and faces, suffocating them. The tanner, being taller and stronger, stood holding the baby above his head as if offering his last child to the heavens. The vines were climbing past his elbows searching for his wrists and fingertips. Father Anselmo unsheathed the knife he always wore attached to the rope around his waist and began hacking at the vines on the tanner's chest and arms. The vines hissed as his knife sliced through them. A thick milky substance bled out and stung his fingers and the palm of his hand.

'Help me,' he shouted to Brother Marcus, 'it's too late for the others but we might just save the baby.'

Brother Marcus dropped the black and yellow shawl. He leapt forward, knocked the tanner to the ground and grabbed the baby a second before the tip of the vine touched the baby's cheek.

Father Anselmo continued to slash at the vines, inadvertently cutting the surface of the tanner's skin as he did so. As soon as blood touched the vines they shrank back.

'Holy mother, forgive me,' he said, and sliced a cut down the length of the tanner's arm.

Blood ran out. The vines shrank further back and began to wither. The tanner moaned. His eyelids fluttered. Father Anselmo lifted him into a sitting position.

'Bebita,' the tanner whispered. 'Bebita.'

'She's safe,' Father Anselmo said.

The tanner coughed and tried to spit. Blood ran from his nose onto his lip. Father Anselmo made the sign of the cross on his forehead and began to pray. The tanner's breath rattled in his chest.

Brother Marcus brought the baby girl, wrapped tightly in the shawl, over to him and knelt on the ground so the tanner could see her. He reached out and touched her cheek, smearing it slightly with his blood. She whimpered a little but didn't cry. Her eyes closed, opened, then closed again. Brother Marcus held her against his chest and she went to sleep.

The tanner sighed. A shudder ran through his body. Father Anselmo laid him on the ground and whispered absolution in his ear. The tanner moaned and clutched his arm. Father Anselmo took off his crucifix and placed it on the dying man's chest sitting with him until he drew his final breath.

'Brother Marcus, take the baby back to the monastery and let them know what's happened,' he said. 'I'll stay with the bodies. Tell them to come as quickly as they can. Make sure they bring shrouds, holy water and shovels so we can bury them decently.' He made the sign of the cross on the forehead of the sleeping baby. 'And bring me a tinder box so I can make a fire.'

He laid the bodies in the shade; the two children nestled between the tanner and his wife. The vines had withered and died, the only sign of them now a few dried stems and leaves and the stain of their milky sap on the ground.

Brother Anselmo had seen vines like this once before when he was a boy, working on the outskirts of the forest with his father. They'd been collecting firewood and mushrooms, and tending the beehives his father and uncle kept. His uncle was getting frail and his father had been training him to blow smoke into the hives so the bees wouldn't sting him and to check the honeycombs, a job he liked.

He loved the order and busyness of the hive, its self-contained nature and common purpose, each insect working for the good of the whole. And as long as he remained calm, the bees seemed to trust him and not sting, even though he took their honey, the fruit of all their labour.

His father had left him for a few minutes and had gone back into the forest to see if he could find some more mushrooms. He was just about to remove a honeycomb when he heard his father shouting for help. Still holding his bundle of smoking reeds in his hand, he ran towards the trees.

His father was kneeling on the ground. Vines were twisted around his legs and were beginning to wind themselves around his hips.

'Burn them off me, boy,' he shouted. 'Don't worry if you hurt me.'

He blew on the reeds to make them burn faster and rushed at his father's legs. They were lucky. The vines fell away and his father escaped with bruises, scratches and a few surface burns.

'Devil vines,' his father said, once they were back at the hives. 'They come out of nowhere and attack when your back is turned.' He emptied his bag of mushrooms and threw them away, then washed his hands with some of the drinking water they carried with them in an old wine bottle. 'Don't eat anything from the entrance of that forest, son,' he said, 'the place has an evil spell on it.'

After that, each time he tended the hives he remembered his father's warning and avoided the forest, even though many useful plants grew there. Once he entered the monastery and had access to the library he searched for information about the devil vines but found nothing. And ten years later, when he decided being a monk wasn't enough and he wanted to study for the priesthood, he went to the seminary in Madrid and while there he sought out the leading apothecary of the day who said he hadn't seen the vines himself but had seen sketches and read about them in ancient botanical scrolls he kept locked in his attic.

Father Anselmo remembered his excitement when he went back to the apothecary's home a week later to read the scrolls. The parchment was thin and stained in places. The sketches were faded but still clear enough to see. The words were written in Greek not Latin. He was only beginning to wrestle with that language and struggled to make sense of it. He spent the morning carefully copying down all the information about the plant so he could get Father Philippos to translate it for him but Philippos shook his head when he read the words. He crossed himself and refused to put them into Latin for him. 'The Devil's work,' he said, 'a plant used by the ancients to cast spells – mixed with other herbs it can make someone see things in the past or the future.' He'd shaken his head and told him to destroy the writing and wash his hands with holy water.

Father Anselmo fanned the bodies with a large piece of bark to keep the flies at bay. He hoped the burial party would make good time so they could dig the graves before dark. He gathered bark, twigs, sticks and some larger branches and piled them together in readiness for the arrival of the tinderbox. He needed ash to sprinkle on the ground so the vines would never come back. He no longer believed in evil spells, but the Devil, like God, moved in mysterious ways. And if ash destroyed the killer vines – as the information in one of the ancient scrolls had said it did – it was his duty to use it to do so. He was sure a loving God would not condemn him for trying to protect the lives of others.

Brother Marcus and three other monks arrived just before sunset. Father Anselmo lit the fire immediately. They took turns digging the family's grave, blessed and shrouded the bodies and lowered them into the earth. Father Anselmo led the funeral prayers and when they were finished the monks picked up their shovels and filled the grave with the freshly dug soil. A rough wooden cross was roped together and planted at the head of the grave.

Brother Marcus had brought bread, cheese, apples and wine from the monastery and, after they had washed their hands and said grace, the four of them sat together sharing a simple meal and waiting for the fire to burn down. The sky was clear and the stars bright. A luminous half-moon rose in the sky. In the distance they heard the occasional howling of wolves.

Once the fire died down Father Anselmo shovelled hot ash in a wide circle around the grave. When it had cooled a little he dug it into the top soil and smoothed it down with the back of the shovel. Finally, he and the monks sprinkled holy water over the grave and around the circle of ash.

As they walked back towards the monastery Father Anselmo asked Brother Marcus about the baby girl.

'Oh, she's fine, Father,' he said. 'I took her to the infirmary. Brother Gregory is looking after her. He's feeding her watered goat's milk mixed with a little honey until he finds a wet nurse from the village.'

After he checked on his donkey, bathed and changed his clothes, Father Anselmo went to the infirmary. The baby was sleeping peacefully in a makeshift crib close to the hearth. In the glow from the fire the soft down of her hair was red-gold and her cheeks were rosy pink. He reached out and touched her little fist and her hand opened and clutched his finger.

'Rosa,' he said, 'that's what we'll call you.' And he put his hand very gently on her head and blessed her then bent and kissed her on the cheek.

SILVER-JEAN AND RUTH

Auckland 2026

Silver-Jean curled onto her side and pushed her cheek further into the pillow. From the edge of sleep came the image of a wolf, running fast, a bloodied pup in its mouth. It stopped and shook its wet fur. The limp body of the pup flopped from side to side. The wolf raised its head, glanced at the gathering clouds and howled at the snow then turned east and loped towards a stand of pines, leaving behind a thin trail of blood. Later, soldiers in torn greatcoats marched across the freshly fallen snow, singing dirges that swelled until they filled the sky – the surface world was cracked, its seams jagged with morphine, its holes patched with sackcloth. In her crooked hands Silver-Jean cradled the wolf's shadow.

When she woke the dawn had the paper-thin greyness of a moth's wing. Her mouth and lips were dry, the back of her neck damp with sweat. The wind rose; puriri branches scraped against the side of the cottage and shadows flickered across her bedroom wall.

She switched on the radio, turning the dial till she found the world service and listened to a programme on the growing number of refugee camps in Kenya, her mind drifting from and returning to the images of the wolf and the dead pup. Pins and needles prickled her hands. At 6.45 she put on her padded cotton kimono and made jasmine tea.

Outside the kitchen window her neighbour's lawn and vegetable garden were dew-covered in the early morning light. She waved at Jason. He was pottering about in his dressing gown and gumboots inspecting newly planted bushes of lavender and rosemary. Like her, he woke early, often disturbed by dreams. She would visit him later and tell him about the wolf and the soldiers singing. She nursed her cup between her breasts, feeling the warmth of the tea seep into the hollow place around her heart. Beyond Jason's backyard and the suburban streets, cell phone towers and satellite dishes stitched the edge of the blue, bush-covered hills.

Joel was out there.

He'd been gone ten days.

They'd argued when he decided to re-join the volunteer medical search team.

He'd sat at the kitchen table scanning old Department of Conservation maps.

She washed ochre-coloured paint off the bristles of her favourite brush at the kitchen sink. 'You've done enough for other people.' She squeezed the water out of the bristles with an old tea towel. 'We need to look after ourselves.'

He folded the maps and stacked them in the middle of the table. 'What if people are still out there? What if they're sick or crazy?'

She stood behind him and put her hands on his shoulders. 'You don't have to be dropped by helicopter into the bush to find sick people.'

He reached up and gently squeezed one of her hands. 'You used to admire the work I did.'

The joints in her fingers were swollen, her skin stained with paint. She took her hand away and stood by the bench. 'Why is it so hard to stay?'

That night they lay with their backs to each other, silence carving space between their bodies. In her sleep she and Uncle Jack went searching for seals, for a glimpse of their coats, wet and grey against the blackness of the rocks.

The following morning Joel had packed his clothes, phone and camera, rolled medical supplies into his sleeping bag and pulled on his hiking boots. She'd stood like this at the window, clutching her cup, her long silver hair still bound in the plait she wore at night. At the last moment, when she'd almost given up, he turned and touched her, brushing his fingers against her hair and the back of her neck. He kissed the top of her head.

'You smell like nutmeg,' he said.

She knelt and reached into the cupboard below the sink.

He accepted the tiny jar of honey. 'I'll phone.'

He walked down the path. At the sea wall he turned and raised his hand in a mock salute. The sky was pale lemon above unlit houses and empty streets.

Ruth reached the clearing at the top of the track and surveyed her territory. Yesterday, for the first time in almost two years, she'd heard the thud, thud of helicopter blades in the distance, but today there were no signs of disturbance – her fences and traps were intact.

Rain clouds rolled in from the west. She breathed in the lush smell of the undergrowth. The bush and her patched green and brown clothing camouflaged her. She sat with her knees drawn up, her back against a tree trunk, and closed her eyes. Wolfe lay down beside her. In the canopy above her the hives were busy. The buzz of worker bees and the rustling of birds in the undergrowth reassured her. She reached over and rubbed the thick fur on Wolfe's back.

Joel had phoned. There'd been static and an echo on the line. His voice faded then surged. He'd spent two days tracking down and talking to retired helicopter pilots but he finally had a lead. Four years ago, eight infected women, along with some experimental beehives, had been dropped by helicopter into dense bush just below the mountains.

Silver-Jean had been leaning against the kitchen bench, facing the window. It had been early morning and her neighbour Jason was in his vegetable garden turning over freshly dug soil with a fork. Rainclouds were massing in sky.

'What good will it do if you find them?' she said.

'You're better than that.'

'Joel, I didn't mean…'

The line crackled then died.

When Silver-Jean was five the operations to straighten her hands and feet began. Every summer she lay on the couch in the kitchen with her hands and feet in casts and filled the long afternoons reading or listening to the radio. Three times a day her mother administered the sticky pink medicine that took away the pain. After each dose images swooped like magpies, diving through the ceiling to land inside her head. Sometimes they erupted out of the earth beneath the floorboards, shouting and jangling like puppets.

One summer Uncle Jack gave her a picture book on seals. He told her stories about them and about other animals that had magical powers and whose coats shone silver in the moonlight. When visions and nightmares overtook her, she looked for the seals, watching them sunning themselves on the clusters of rocks that rose out of the surf. Their long whiskers twitched as they lifted their heads to the sunlight, their grey pelts glistened against the white foam and shiny wetness of the black rocks. Monsters with grinning faces and deformed limbs shrieked and cackled, but the seals remained untouched and unharmed on their island of rocks, their barking calls somehow peaceful in the sun-filled ocean air.

When the casts came off at the end of each summer she used the crayons and coloured pencils Uncle Jack bought her to draw seals. At sixteen, it was her watercolours of seals that gained her a place in art school.

Five years ago, a few days before he died, she'd wheeled Jack out to sit in the garden so he could feel the sun on his skin and watch the birds.

'I'm worried,' he said.

She adjusted his straw hat so it shaded his eyes better. 'I'll look after you.'

'No,' he said, his arm quivering as he pointed to their hives nestled among the manuka bushes at the far end of the garden. 'The bees – there's something wrong with the bees.'

Silver-Jean took off her kimono and put Joel's old raincoat over her nightdress. She pulled on gumboots. Between the shed and clothesline clumps of silverbeet shone dark green beside comfrey plants and borage; the comfrey was being attacked by slugs. She ground her heel on a snail. The shell scrunched. Insecticides were still banned – it was either soapy water or killing them like this, one by one. At the far end of the garden their empty beehives still sat encircled by manuka bushes.

A few weeks after Jack died, worker bees started abandoning their queens and drones. They flew out of hives to forage for nectar and never returned. At first the dying hives were isolated in pockets along the east coast, but within a few months it had spread. With other local beekeepers, she and Joel had gone to public meetings. No one agreed on the cause: pathogens or parasites, environmental pollution, insecticides, cell phone transmitters and satellite dishes. All, some, or none of them –take your pick. They were given a week to consider options. The vote was 69 to 53 for mass aerial spraying.

Eighteen months later, only eight per cent of the country's hives had survived. The asthma rate doubled, fruit and vegetable production dived, and half the population developed skin rashes. An emergency government instituted food rationing and, in an about face, banned all insecticides. Gangs of hand pollinators were conscripted from the unemployed. Soldiers walked door-to-door, inspecting cellars and garden sheds, collecting insecticides in green plastic buckets. Silver-Jean hid their remaining jars of honey in shoeboxes at the back of the wardrobe in case they were confiscated too.

She imagined great piles of chemicals in sealed containers, sitting outside the gates of Horticultural Security Headquarters. 'How will they destroy them?'

'They'll bury them,' Joel said, 'pour concrete over the top.'

Each night as she entered sleep she waded through underground bunkers searching for honey. Phosphorescent poison rose from the surface of the bunkers and burned holes in her skin. Giant bees swarmed above her trying to find a way out.

New regulations were announced. Anyone suffering from recurring skin rashes had to report to their local health centre for registration and treatment. Neither she nor Joel, nor Jason's wife Jenny, reported theirs, or the bouts of fever that followed. Silver-Jean made her own ointment from comfrey and lavender. Whenever the rash appeared she covered their hands, arms and back with ointment and when the fever flared they retreated to bed with cold compresses and manuka tea sweetened with honey.

Silver-Jean wiped the squashed snail from the sole of her gumboot onto the damp grass and went back inside. In the bathroom she filled the basin with warm water and washed her face and hands. She checked the clock. At 10:00 the power would go off for six hours so she cooked eggs, boiled rice and filled her thermos with hot water. From her dwindling supply of honey she scooped a teaspoonful and stirred it into her tea.

The image of the wolf running with the dead pup in its mouth refused to fade. She reached above the sink to the row of hooks that held their cups and chose Joel's favourite pottery mug. The rough green glaze was lumpy against her arthritic fingers. She closed her eyes and rubbed it against her cheek. His voice returned: you're better than that.

She threw the cup against the wall.

When she picked up the broken shards of pottery, she cut herself. A drop of blood blossomed on her fingertip, perfect as a single pearl, and fell onto the wooden floor.

Wolfe leapt into the creek hoping to play but Ruth gave a low growl and continued down the track. The weather was closing in. She whistled and he followed, shaking water from his coat. She veered off the track to check her hives and traps and harvested a small comb of honey and three plump wood pigeons. She wrapped the honeycomb in a clean rag, snapped the pigeons' necks and threw them in the bag she carried around her waist. Wolfe barked at the smell of blood and circled her, wanting breakfast. Ruth growled again and walked on.

In the clearing in front of the caves she boiled water, plucked, gutted and washed the birds. She threw scraps to Wolfe, chopped the birds into quarters and put them in her only pot.

Rain came down across the hills. She retreated to the sheltered entrance of her cave. Memories of Marta nudged at her as she sat on a wooden log and stitched together a pile of rabbit skins.

Silver-Jean peeled a hardboiled egg and cut two thin slices of bread. At the kitchen table she chewed each mouthful slowly, feeling the muscles in her jaw stretch, her teeth tear and grind the bread.

A dead pup, its neck broken, carried away in the wolf's jaw.

A polished wooden box sat open on the table beside the empty fruit bowl. Inside were alcohol swabs and syringes. When she finished eating she wiped a patch of skin on her arm and injected her daily dose of morphine. In the distance she heard dogs barking. She closed her eyes and saw the wolf, running across an open plain. Feathers fell from the sky like coloured rain.

Ruth woke before sunrise and listened for the thrumming of helicopter blades. She pulled aside the heavy sacking that curtained the entrance to her cave. Outside a faint, almost full moon was setting.

Each month, when the moon grew full, she remembered the smell of soldiers' sweat as they herded her and the other women into helicopters. The blades beat above their heads. She and Marta had huddled together in the bowl of the machine, hugging their backpacks and bedrolls. Inside her waterproof jacket she'd hidden the tiny brown and white pup she'd rescued after its mother had been drowned the day before.

The soldiers released them in four pairs. She and Marta were last.

They were given tents, blankets, flour, tinned food, hunting knives, seeds, and a double ration of syrup that looked like watered-down honey. It smelt faintly of mud and even though it was sweet it had a bitter aftertaste. She hated it but, in the end, it was all Marta could keep down.

When the moon was as round and white as Marta's face Ruth heard a voice in the air above her head. She knew Marta talked to her because she needed to, not because she expected her to reply.

Full moon. Time to bleed.

Marta's voice called to her, disturbing the sanctuary of the bush.

Joel took three days to find the last campsite. The final helicopter pilot he'd interviewed had agreed to drop him close to the first campsite. He gave Joel a map and shook his hand. 'I'll be back in a week,' he said. 'Be careful. There've been rumours about one of the women in the last camp.'

Joel hitched his pack on to his shoulders. 'How long since someone's been up there?'

The pilot shrugged. 'A couple of years – we just used to fly in low, drop rations and get the hell out.'

On the first day Joel hiked past the deserted first camp and the remains of five empty hives. A shallow grave and picked over bones presented a clear enough story. The second day he found another grave covered with soil and rocks. He took photos and sketched a better map. Further inland he discovered more hives. They looked in better shape. He could hear the faint buzz of bees in the distance. He imagined the smile on Silver-Jean's face when he told her there were healthy bees producing honey again.

Ruth lay down with Wolfe close beside her. She closed her eyes and saw a line of women being inspected by army doctors, the tell-tale purple rash covering their arms and necks. She tossed, feverish, on her bed of rabbit fur. Infected men approached the women's tents with knives. Whenever she woke Wolfe's eyes glinted back at her, a comforting glow in the darkness.

In the morning she heated water, stripped and washed. She scooped warm water into a tin and poured it over her thighs to remove the first stains of blood. She dried herself with a piece of worn blanket, pressed her lips together and hummed a tune her Russian grandmother had taught her. It was a song conscripted soldiers sang when they'd marched across snow-covered steppes.

Words buzzed, swarming in her jaw and throat.

At sunset she cut branches and formed them into a rough circle. She sat cross-legged in the centre, facing the opening of Marta's cave. Beating on a tin with a broken branch, she built a pattern of sound to help her ride the onslaught of words and images.

The full circle of the moon rose in the sky. Ruth howled. Wolfe arched his back and retreated. Voices marched out of Marta's cave. Ruth sprang to meet them, teeth bared, tin and branch raised. Words formed in her mouth:

Ruth is wolf
Ruth is tree
Ruth is fire and stone.

She stamped her feet; beat the tin against her thigh. Blood flowed, seeping down her legs to stain the ground. Moonlight streamed through the entrance of the cave. She turned towards Marta. Her body was wrapped in blankets the soldiers had given them. A fence of stones encircled her. Her journal lay on her chest.

Ruth approached Marta and her book of words. She picked up Marta's hunting knife and slashed the inside of her arms. Blood bloomed against her damaged skin. Drumbeats echoed in her head. She held her arms over the journal and let her blood drip. Marta contained the words – and her own blood still flowed.

Voices shuffled out of the cave, singing her grandmother's tune. Following them was the flash of knives above her head, the flicker of moonlight across her face as men held her down, the sound of soldiers laughing in the distance.

Light from the full moon kept Joel awake. He lay in his sleeping bag breathing the peppery smell of the bush. He listened for wild pigs and thought of Silver-Jean, asleep in their bed back home, her silvery hair braided, her twisted fingers curled into loose fists. When she slept her body twitched and jumped, her nervous system damaged from all the operations and the morphine she'd been prescribed since she was a child.

They'd met when she was an art student in Japan. He was on holiday after working in refugee camps in Africa. He'd spent the first week in an exhausted haze, avoiding conversation, absorbing the simplicity of the white gravel and green moss of the Kasui-En Annex, the hotel's private stone and gravel garden. During the second week he noticed a small woman with silvery hair sketching the garden. He saw her again when he visited Murin-An, one of the famous stroll gardens in Kyoto. She was standing on her own, admiring the trajectory of the stream.

'They say it's best in autumn,' he said.

The next day they travelled to the northern outskirts of Kyoto to see Shoden-Ji. She took photos of azaleas among a river of white gravel.

'One day,' he said, 'I'd like a garden.'

He returned to Africa; she finished her last year of study in Japan. They wrote. Sometimes he phoned. His tiredness seeped down the telephone lines and she took it and held it safely in her scarred hands. She sent him miniature watercolours: Zen gardens, men fishing off rocks, seals sunning themselves on southern coastlines.

When clouds covered the moon and the bush retreated into shadow Joel fell asleep and dreamed of Silver-Jean dancing to the sound of drumming. Her hair was luminous, spread out over her thin shoulders. The bones in her hands and feet were smooth and straight. The deep lines around her mouth had vanished. She swirled past him, laughing, but a trace of tears still glistened on her cheeks. She called his name and beckoned him to follow, inviting him to dance. Her hands moved in front of her body, as delicate as falling willow leaves.

They sat together on a simple wooden bench in Shoden-Ji garden. Across the river of gravel, a gardener wearing a wide-brimmed hat was pruning azaleas. Silver-Jean laid her hands in his and said, 'Uncle Jack was right. There's something wrong with the bees.'

Ruth stood outside the cave. The wind was cool on her damp skin. Her mind was empty. She dragged the circle of branches inside and laid them behind the stones that surrounded Marta. She lay down to sleep.

Joel woke at first light with a crick in his neck and his mouth in the dirt. A mist of fine rain cobwebbed the bush. He rubbed his neck and shoulder, rinsed his mouth with water, shouldered his pack, zipped his jacket and pulled down the brim of his hat. Ferns flanked him on either side, spattering drops of water on his face and shoulders as he climbed to the final campsite. Two fantails followed him, darting in and out of the bush, playing hide and seek then returning to swoop around his face and shoulders. When he reached the ridge above the clearing the mist lifted. Through his binoculars he saw a large vegetable garden, a fireplace made from a circle of stones, and sacking and skins sewn together and stretched over wooden poles in front of two caves. A large brown and white dog chewed on a bone.

He didn't see the woman at first. Her clothing, patched together with fur and feathers, camouflaged her, making her look like an enormous bird as she moved across the open space between the shelter of the caves and her garden.

From the safety of the ridge he watched the woman and the dog move in and out of the caves and around the camp. She worked in the garden for a couple of hours. Her only tools were a short-handled spade and a hunting knife. He could see how strong and fit she was. When she'd finished gardening she retreated with the dog to the awning stretched out in front of the caves. The dog was a complication. There was no way he could get close to the camp without alerting it.

Joel thought of Silver-Jean, alone and frail in the cottage, painting her watercolours, waiting for him to return. He put down the binoculars and scratched the three-day-old stubble on his chin. From the outside pocket of his pack he took a plastic bag and scooped out a handful of nuts. The tiny jar of honey Silver-Jean had given him was nestled in the corner of the pocket. A teaspoonful of honey would give him the energy to decide how to approach the camp. He unscrewed the lid and balanced the jar on top of his pack. In the distance he heard the dog bark.

He turned back to the camp and raised his binoculars. The woman was squatting by the fireplace skinning rabbits and the dog was circling her, excited by the smell of blood. Joel caught a glimpse of her face. The skin on one cheek was red and puckered like it had been cut and burnt. Her arms were crisscrossed with scars. She looked up towards the ridge, as if she sensed someone was there. Instinctively, he dropped the binoculars and took a step back.

He closed his eyes and rubbed his temples. For a moment, the buzzing behind him didn't register.

The first bee landed on his wrist. It was the size of his forefinger. The sting went deep and he shouted in surprise as much as pain. He brushed his arm against his leg. The second bee attacked the inch of exposed neck above his jacket collar. The sting burned into his flesh. His skin began to swell. He swung around. Dozens of giant bees swarmed around the open jar of honey. 'Shit,' he said. 'You idiot!'

He staggered over to his pack and tried to kick the jar of honey onto the ground. His hat fell off. Bees flew at his face, stinging his eyelids, his checks, his lips. He screamed. One entered his mouth. He dropped onto the ground; rolled over and over. Bees covered his head. They burrowed into his ears. Above the buzzing, the pain, and the sound of his own cries, he heard the barking of the dog.

Ruth stood in the bush and let the bees crawl over her. They settled on her arms and shoulders covering her like a cloak. Wolfe sat a few feet away, guarding the body. It was face down in the dirt.

When the bees left her and returned to their hives Ruth tied Wolfe to a tree and rolled the man over. His face was a pulp of swollen flesh.

She removed his binoculars and hung them around her own neck, took his compass and army knife from his jacket pocket and put them in her pouch. Into his sleeping bag she rolled the ground sheet, the spare tee-shirt and socks, antibiotic tablets, antiseptic cream, painkillers and packets of freeze-dried food she found in his pack. The cell phone, notebook, camera and hand drawn map were no use to her. She untied Wolfe and together they walked back down the track, leaving his body to the bees.

The power came back on just before sunset. Silver-Jean washed her paintbrushes and turned on the radio. In the garden she picked silverbeet and watched the light leave the sky.

That night her sleep was disturbed by dreams of giant bees swarming through the bush. She searched for her colony of seals but, for the first time, the rocks were bare. The sound of barking dogs woke her.

At the kitchen window waiting for the kettle to boil, she looked out across the vegetable garden and empty beehives. Next door, Jason was in the backyard with his two labradors, throwing soft rubber balls across the grass for them to chase and retrieve. They'd been tiny puppies when Jenny died of the fever four years ago. Silver-Jean waved then gazed past him to the bush covered hills.

Joel was out there.

In the afternoon Jason came over. They sat at the table drinking the tea he'd brought her. 'You look tired,' he said. 'You've been working too hard.' He reached over and patted her hand.

Tears rolled down her cheeks. 'He's not coming back.'

'How do you know that?'

'The seals have gone.'

Part Five: Time

Past – Present – Future
Jason – Griffin – Jesse –Liam

JASON

Auckland 2036

On my desk are sheets of paper torn from an old exercise book, the
pages written in pencil and difficult to read. They were delivered
yesterday while Liam was out foraging, firstly at the government
sanctioned market and then, once it was finished, at the unofficial co-
op. The young woman must have waited until she saw I was alone in
the house. She stood on the backdoor step with the sun directly behind
her. Her head was lowered and she was looking at the concrete step as
if it was something worth studying. 'Can I help you?' I said.

She thrust the pages at me. 'Joseph,' she said. 'He gave me this
address. He said you might be able to help.'

She looked at me carefully then, a thin, anxious face, her eyes a
sudden flash of deep blue, giving me a glimpse of ocean.

'You know,' she said, 'to stop me going crazy.'

Her blunt awkwardness was somehow appealing and, without
meaning to, I agreed to read them. She smiled and I saw she was
much younger than I'd first thought, just out of girlhood and, if she
was prepared to seek me out, already troubled by visions. My seventy-
four years descended like a weight on the back of my neck. I almost

stumbled as I took a step towards her. The skin on my hand looked reptilian as I held it out. 'What's your name?'

'Griffin,' she said. Her hand shot out and brushed mine briefly before darting back to her side. 'I meet with others. Sometimes. At Joseph's.'

'Does it help?'

She shrugged. 'What else is there?'

'Only me, I'm afraid.'

At my desk I turned the lamp directly on the pages, wrote her name on the top of each one and arranged them in the best order I could, given Griffin had only dated some of them. I refilled my cup with precious and, no doubt illegal, green tea, cleaned my glasses and struggled through the first three passages, making notes as I went.

Sheep... steep, windswept hills... Rain clouds come down from the north. Drumbeats march up the beach, rata tat tat, rata tat tat, rata tat tat...

... dragged by my hair. Pushed... falling... flung out of a horse-drawn cart onto cobblestones... smell of boiled wool and mutton fat.

...Cold... Walking on a beach... winds blowing spray into the air. On the hills...ewes call out to their lambs...

...Pulled backwards. Falling ... unwashed wool, lanolin on cracked skin. A butcher steps up behind a sheep... Skin stripped back ... Flesh, flecked with veins. The severing of the head, brains poached in milk, presented to the old one...

I took off my glasses and closed my eyes. Even with the lamp I was straining to read the faint, untidy script. Liam would have to read the rest to me in the morning. I now regretted agreeing to do this without looking at it first – it was too much for me to read, analyse, make notes and comments, and return it all to her in three days' time. Why had I agreed so readily?

I took stock: the entries had plenty of detail, something in their favour, but they were jumbled. Over the years I'd figured out working with visions like this was always about separating everything out: the current situation, no doubt bad enough; the fear of the visions as well as the fear contained within them; the layers of time, their complex geography and archaeology. Once everything was separated, it was possible to go back and search for threads, work out connections. If she was strong enough she could choose to stop or carry on – but it was a vocation I had no right to recommend. Perhaps, like me, this girl felt she didn't have a choice. I imagined there'd always been others, more sensible than me, more grounded, ones who'd just said no thanks to dreams and visions and simply walked away.

And, of course, there was Liam, in a class of his own. Able to say yes or no, depending on his judgement of, or interest in, the situation. He'd learnt to pick his archaeological journeys and, so far, touch wood, he'd returned unharmed. I believed Helene walked with Liam. She stole over his shoulder, came to rest in his fingers when he was playing the piano, guided his energy. And Liam held her within himself like a lotus flower, she blossomed at his call, steadying and directing him. Twenty years after her death she still walked into the room every time Liam opened a door; a pleasure mixed with pain of such needle-like precision that it came and went in a single breath.

Liam knocked on the study door, looking for the tray and empty teapot.

'The tea was okay then?'

'Wonderful – I won't ask how you managed to get it.'

Liam grinned and looked down at the desk. 'Still working – the girl from yesterday?'

'I'm going to need your help.'

'Just reading?'

'So far.' I organised the pages into a single pile. 'She's a friend of Joseph's.'

Liam put the tray back on the desk, took the top page and scanned it. 'What've you got so far?'

'Sheep and fear.'

'Something to do with The Flock then.'

A rush of recognition. I removed my glasses, loosened my collar and rolled my shirtsleeves to my elbows to steady myself. 'I'm getting too old for this. It's so obvious. I should've picked it up immediately.'

Liam squeezed my shoulder. 'Nobody's the right age – anyway, when I was at the market yesterday I saw a bunch of new recruits. They were all hyped, singing 'Blood of the Lamb' like their lives depended on it, passing out pamphlets, their faces washed clean of individuality.' He picked up the tray and teapot again. 'Don't worry. We'll work on it in the morning. I saw her waiting outside the house until I was gone – there's something about her...'

I closed the curtains and lay down the narrow daybed under the windows. My feet and legs were cold so I pulled the faded tartan rug over them. The mattress was a bit hard, a little lumpy, but I refused to throw it away. It was an old friend. Over the years I'd spent many months lying on it, guarded by Liam, learning how to enter into the heart of my own and others' dreams and visions and to return – most especially how to return. Never completely unharmed but, in the main, safely.

I wanted to rest now, go to sleep early, like the old man I was, and rise early, so I'd be fresh for work in the morning.

In the kitchen Liam was chopping and stirring herbs into the stew he was cooking for tomorrow. I heard him washing and drying dishes and pots, putting them away in the cupboard. I drifted on the borders of sleep. Familiar faces rose, not visitations, not ghosts crossing borders, just memories from the past when I first went to Aretis, transported there by Helene's death, unprepared and unprotected.

After breakfast Liam cleared and wiped down the kitchen table. I brought Griffin's pages from the study and spread them out. Liam sat beside me and read the next section aloud:

Cottage doors swing open, banging cast-iron handles against stonewalls in the wind. Foam drenches the air above the shore and sprays her face and hair. Her hands and feet are cold. She hunches her shoulders, pulls up the collar of her coat and walks alone on the pebbled beach under an almost full moon. The hills above the beach are bare, the shepherd and his sheep nowhere to be seen. The sound of drumming fills her head, rata tat tat, rata tat tat. Out of the darkness a face looms. She thinks it is a spec-tre rising out of the sea and cries out but it is a young woman, pale as the moon, her face surrounded by wet dark curls.

'We're hiding in the caves,' she says.

'She's writing in third person now,' I said, making a note. 'The earlier sections were in first.'

Liam nodded. 'Trying to find her feet – trying to work out if she's participant or recorder.'

'The landscape,' I said, 'is it familiar?'

'Yes and no.'

'Memory or vision?'

'Too early to tell.'

'Connection?'

Liam laughed. 'Let's read some more – I don't want to jump to any more conclusions than I have to.'

…The women…form a single line and walk towards the dark-ness at the back of the cave.

She waits with the women, listening to the sound of her own breathing and to the waves pushing pebbles up and down on the beach. Above the waves she hears a low whistle and the baaing of sheep. One of the women whistles back, lights her lamp and holds it above her head.

She blinks in the dull light. Barefoot men, trousers rolled up to their knees, are guiding sheep along the beach and into the mouth of the cave. In the distance she hears the rata tat tat, rata tat tat of a drum. The men shepherd the last of the sheep inside. They pile driftwood and drag bull kelp in front of the entrance. Two more women light lamps, hook them onto poles and hold them high above their heads.

…They herd the sheep along the channel, moving them as fast as they can, men and women with their arms out, running, whistling to guide them up and through to the hills on the other side as soldiers march along the beach making so much noise with their beating drums they can't hear them escape.

Half an hour later they're on the other side and the sheep scramble up the hill. The woman beside her stops to catch her breath. 'They'd take every last one,' she says, 'They'd starve us out if they could.'

'Why? What do they want?'

The woman looks at her as if she's gone simple. 'What they always want,' she says, 'someone else's land and livelihood.' She sits down, gathers up the hem of her petticoat and squeezes the moisture out. She starts to laugh. 'Sheep is what they want alright, and not just the ones with wool on their backs.'

Liam put the pages down. He rolled his shoulders and stretched. 'Okay,' he said, 'She's good. If she wants to, and has the stamina, she'll make a good journeywoman.' He went to the bench, filled a pot with water and placed it on the gas ring to boil. 'Your thoughts?'

I smoothed the pages with my fingertips. 'You're right about the sheep –there's a clear reference: *'Sheep is what they want alright, and not just the ones with wool on their backs.'*

Liam spooned tea leaves into the teapot. 'Wonder how much she's figured out. Did she say anything?'

'Only that she meets sometimes with a group of others at Joseph's – I assume they're all afflicted.'

'Hmmm...' Liam poured boiling water over the tea leaves. 'Interesting.' He put the lid on the teapot and carried it to the table.

We let the tea draw then I poured two cups and passed one to Liam. 'Let's read one more passage then I'll take the dogs for a walk.'

Deserted cobblestone streets, empty cottages, doors swinging and banging in the wind. Out on the burnt-off hills two skinny sheep graze on a crop of thistles. She walks along the beach, her coat collar turned up, eyes watering in the stinging breeze. On the shelf in the cave are the remains of boots, woollen stockings and jackets. At the back of the cave where the floor slopes up above the high tide line are scraps of sheepskin and bones. She climbs through the passageway and walks over the hills, ash and soil clinging to her stout leather boots. Further inland a stand of oaks that has provided shelter and shade for generations has been chopped down, their stumps exposed and raw in the weak winter sunlight. She sits down, leans against the rough skin of a stump and runs her hand across the roots. Her fingers find the smooth brown skin of an acorn. She rubs it clean and puts it in her pocket. She curls herself among the roots of the butchered trees and sleeps.

I wrapped an old blue scarf of Jenny's around my neck and buttoned my coat. Although the day was sunny, the wind was brisk, a south-easterly, and I didn't want to catch a chill taking the dogs out past the mangrove swamps and along the coastal walkway. Even though I'd survived every journey, I was weakened by the strain of them. Liam looked after me but we both knew I could be felled by something as simple as a cold or chest infection. I whistled for the dogs, the last descendants of Jenny's original labradors, and when they appeared, running from the old laundry where they slept like kings on sheepskin mats, I clipped their leads onto their collars. It was over ten years since Jenny's death, twenty since Helene's, even more since Anastasia's. Each year on Helene's anniversary Liam played her favourite pieces on the piano, and on Jenny's he gently asked me if I wanted to bury her ashes. And each year I thanked him and said, no, I think I'll keep them with me one more year.

As I walked over the wooden bridge at the entrance to the park, the dogs pulled on their leads and barked with excitement so I unclipped them and let them run. I wound their leads around my wrist and followed them more slowly, stopping every ten metres or so to look at the view. The tide was in, covering all but the tops of the mangroves and the water was brown and shining. A lone kayaker paddled through the wetlands, weaving in and out of the trees, sometimes retreating when his way was blocked. I walked here to remind myself that not everything had changed. The park, the mangroves and the coastal walk remained in spite of everything else: my waning strength, the end of visiting Aretis, the spreading sickness, Jenny's sudden death, and the growth of the Flock. Soon enough I, too, will be gone. Liam will carry on, and if this young woman, Griffin, was good enough perhaps she'd join him in their work.

I stood on a section of the walkway and gazed at the harbour. The day was overcast, the water grey-green, the breeze just beginning to strengthen. Two windsurfers assembled their gear on the stretch of sand to my left. The dogs were nowhere to be seen. I whistled twice and waited until they came running back along the path. 'Come on you two,' I said. 'There's still plenty to do.'

GRIFFIN

The water from the hot tap in the kitchen was running cold and had been for weeks. It pooled in the tarnished aluminium sink and had an oily sheen. Griffin screwed up her eyes and splashed water on her face. She pulled on yesterday's sweatshirt and jeans and heated the last of the milk on the gas ring. When the milk was almost boiling, she added the end of her supplies of brown sugar and cinnamon. She stirred the milk, let it bubble for a few seconds, poured it into a chipped mug and took it over to the window of her upstairs flat. The smell of the heated spice filled her nostrils, pushing to the background the sharp brine of the sea and the smoke of peat fires lingering from her dreams.

On the street below three men rode past on bicycles, khaki-coloured packs on their backs, brown armbands sewn onto the sleeves of their black jackets, brown cloth caps pulled low on their foreheads, each with an image of a white lamb printed on the crown. They were on their way to the shopping centre to attend the first prayer service of the day.

Griffin finished her milk in two quick gulps. She grabbed her coat and daypack, unchained the door of the flat, locked it behind her and ran downstairs. At the bottom of the stairs she unlocked another door, pulled it shut and walked along the narrow corridor that led to the street-level shop. Flame, the tattoo artist she sub-let the shop to, was fast asleep on a mattress behind the counter, lying on his back with his mouth open, snoring, his left arm flung out on the floor, the fingers of his right hand curled round a tankard of home-brew. His stained black tee-shirt had ridden up over his tattooed belly. Griffin stopped for a moment and watched the rise and fall of dragon's wings as he breathed. She smiled as she opened the back door of the shop, re-locked it, and walked to the shopping centre. Her pack was hooked over one shoulder, the books inside smacking against her back.

The first squall of rain, a sudden rata tat tat, hit the roof of the book exchange while she squatted between the shelves. She ran her fingers across the spines of well-thumbed paperbacks, searching for stories she hadn't read.

Images from her dream of sheep grazing on wind-swept hills returned as she exchanged books and listened to Joseph complain about fresh graffiti splattered across his windows, and another attempt by members of The Flock to close his business. At the counter, waiting while Joseph checked her books, her mind was full of shearing sheds – the springy, greasy feel of wool, lanolin seeping into the pores of her skin, the tang of sheep pellets, shearers' sweat and the heavy sacking of wool bales heating up in the sun.

Joseph clicked his fingers in front of her nose. 'Feeling alright?'

Griffin rubbed her cheekbones. Her skin was cold, the tips of her fingers slightly numb. 'I'm going to the council meeting,' she said. 'You should come.'

Joseph shook his head. 'They'll trash the place if I leave it.'

Outside the book exchange a group of men, fresh from the prayer service, surrounded her, shoving handwritten leaflets in her face, shouting against the evils of fantasy and fictional sin – only the Shepherd's word needed to be listened to or read.

Griffin protected her chest and stomach with her pack. She put her head down and pushed through them. 'Excuse me,' she said. 'You're blocking the path.'

She hurried towards the bakery. The wind whipped the panels of her coat open, twisting them around her legs. She pulled them straight and stepped around a puddle. Her boots were old, the leather and stitching worn. They wouldn't last another winter.

On the footpath in front of the bakery an old man in dirty grey trousers and matching jacket clutched a hot meat pie in one hand and a bread roll in the other. The door to the bakery was open. The smell of fresh bread made her stomach grumble but she had no cash this morning and nothing to trade with. She followed the old man. He took small stiff steps, doing a slow shuffle towards the bus shelter. The rain started to fall again, wetting his straggly white hair and beard.

She sat at one end of the wooden seat, her pack resting on her lap. He sat at the other and began to eat his pie, flakes of greasy pastry falling into his beard and down the front of his jacket. Steam rose from the pie each time he took a bite and the smell of mutton fat wafted towards her. Griffin stared at the food, her grandmother's voice echoing in her head. Ah girlie, your stomach thinks your throat's been cut.

Rain drummed on the plastic roof of the bus shelter. Water dripped from a gap in the roof down the back of the wooden seat. She sat further forward to avoid her shoulders getting soaked. The main road was filling with cyclists. Government officials rode past on motorbikes, beeping their horns to clear a path for themselves through the maze of bicycles. Rain ran in the gutters drenching the grey rubbish bags piled on the footpath. The Federation of Local Collectors and Recyclers was on strike again, refusing to go back to work until their wages for the last three months were paid. People huddled under shop awnings, waiting for a break in the traffic so they could cross the road to the bus stop or the bakery. The road was slick with rain and littered with rubbish; so easy to slip, to fall. Pigeons gathered by overflowing rubbish bins, pecking in rough circles around them, squabbling over soggy crusts and crumbs. It was all grab and gobble, no sharing when it came to food. Griffin watched the pigeons in front of the bin closest to her. She leaned forward to see which bird would grab the last crust.

Her stomach grumbled again. Even though she didn't trust what the baker put in them, she wanted a pie. This one looked as if it was mainly mutton fat. The old man had just taken the last bite. She looked away, glancing instead at the shiny black puddles on the footpath in front of her. A pair of splayed feet in torn sheepskin slippers skirted the puddles. A flurry of pigeons' wings rose a few inches off the pavement. An elderly woman heaved herself onto the bench between Griffin and the old man. She had the musty, fungal smell of stale clothes, dirty feet and unwashed hair. Her ankles were swollen. Her big toes stuck out of holes cut in her slippers. The skin on her bare legs was bruised reddish-purple and streaked with broken veins. Griffin shuffled further to the edge.

From her cloth shopping-bag the old woman took slices of stale bread. She broke off a crust and threw it on the footpath. Two pigeons scuttled over. One gobbled up the offering, the other, a spongy pink growth on one of its claws, waddled over and stood in front of the woman's foot. She tore a piece of soft bread from the middle of a thick slice and rolled it between her fingertips, turning it into a pellet, and held it out to the bird. It pecked straight from her hand. She threw more pieces of bread just beyond her feet. More pigeons arrived. Sparrows darted between them, swooping between the larger birds to scoop up crumbs. The pigeon with the deformed claw stayed close to the woman, waiting to be hand fed.

Griffin's eyes began to itch; the way they did when a gust of wind blew pollen-filled dust across her face. She rubbed her eyelids with her knuckles. The itching spread to her nose and throat. She sneezed. The sounds of the street echoed and warped. She was falling, pulled away from the solidness of her body, her eyes transformed into a camera, recording image after image:

bag-lady, bus-stop, raindrops, birds' wings, wet crumbs, wet pavement, old lady's hands, dry scabs, purple bruises tattooed on wrinkled skin, old man's flapping eyelid, bird's claw.

The camera moved closer and closer until the spongy pink growth on the bird's claw filled her vision. Then the shutter snapped and she was back on the slat seat, inhabiting her body right down to her fingertips, lungs gasping like a diver resurfacing, stomach aching and grumbling, street noise suddenly roaring in her ears.

When the bus came she shouldered her pack and stood back to

give the two old people time to move in front of her but they sat side by side, not moving, merely exchanging a look, waiting for the bus to leave so they could continue with their real occupation, sitting together in the only sheltered bus stop, feeding pigeons.

People shuffled on board and complained about how late the bus was. The driver shrugged his shoulders, held his hands up in a gesture of surrender then tapped the steering wheel with his fingers. 'Don't blame me. I've been queuing for biofuel since six am.'

As the bus pulled away Griffin turned back and stared at the old people: two ancients sitting in a bus shelter throwing crumbs to pigeons and sparrows, watching, unconcerned, as the only bus going into town that day left. There was something sacred about them, two wings of an unkempt, crumbling cathedral squatting in the rain, encircled by birds.

Below the surface of her mind, cottage doors swung open in the chill breeze, sheep grazed, ewes called to lambs so they wouldn't run too close to the edge of the hills and plunge onto the beach below. The rata tat tat, rata tat tat of drumbeats echoed in her ears.

At the council meeting she sat at the back on the aisle, her feet resting on her pack. The second speaker's megaphone wasn't working properly; his voice boomed then faded. She gave up trying to make sense of his speech. Not that it mattered. He was wearing a brown armband and a cap with a white lamb sewn on the crown. She knew he'd be against book exchanges, internet access, cell phones, work collectives, and the increasing number of underground markets.

The third speaker declined the megaphone and projected her voice. Griffin had seen her before, in the shopping centre talking to Joseph, knocking on the doors of the bakery and recycle centre, even waiting behind the derelict supermarket at night to canvass the butcher. She was middle-aged with tight curly grey hair that reminded Griffin of unwashed wool. She wore a loose black and white tunic over grey trousers and stout walking shoes. A large blue and red Citizens' Coalition badge was pinned above her left breast. The Coalition refused to use bicycles and walked everywhere, in protest at the unfair distribution of transport and rationing of biofuel.

'Wolves are out there,' the woman said.

The audience clapped.

'Unless we organize ourselves into collectives we'll be lambs alright – lambs to the slaughter.'

Griffin's face grew hot. The corners of the room crinkled and began to pulse and flash with colour. She closed her eyes. She was being dragged backwards by her hair. A few moments later her head was released and she fell forward, a ragdoll flung out of a horse-drawn cart onto cobblestones. The streets smelt of boiled wool and mutton fat.

Cold and hungry, she walked on a beach covered in grey and white pebbles. An arctic wind blew spray into the air. On the grassy slope above the beach an ancient shepherd watched over a flock of sheep. Ewes called to their lambs across the field.

Griffin forced her eyes open. The Citizen's Coalition speaker had finished. People stood up, clapping and whistling. The candidate from The Flock left the stage and re-joined his supporters. They marched out of the hall together, faces blank with righteousness as they sang the first lines of their signature hymn; *Blood of the lamb, wash over me…*

After she ticked the box for Citizens' Coalition on her voting paper and slid it into the cardboard box in the lobby, she went to the Council cafeteria behind the hall. A group of volunteers were handing out cups of something that resembled coffee and passing round trays of homemade sandwiches and fruit. She accepted a thick sandwich filled with some kind of jam and put two small apples in her pack for later. She retreated to a corner table to watch the crowd.

Directly in front of her a group of thin young women gobbled sandwiches. Other youths hovered beside them, skinny and hunched, nondescript in baggy trousers and op-shop jerseys, the lines of their faces angular, their eyes shadowed by fringes of uncombed hair. The sound of their voices slid in and out of her hearing. Behind them she heard the baaing of sheep.

She scored another sandwich – plum jam, she decided – and wrote in her journal:

Pulled backwards. Falling forward. Birds' claws, lambs call-ing out to ewes. The smell of blood, the greasy feel of unwashed wool, lanolin on cracked skin. The butcher steps up behind the sheep, pulls it against his body, slits its throat, strings it up by its hind legs, a long slice down the middle, the gush of guts and blood, the smell of it, a sudden burning in her throat. Liver and kidneys – hot and slippery. A precious layer of yellow fat. The skin stripped back, taken by the women to be soaked and washed clean and cut to make jackets, strips sewn together for floor rugs or put on cots in winter to warm babies or arthritic bones. Flesh, flecked with veins. The severing of the head, brains poached in milk, presented to the old or toothless, as easy on the stomach as a plate of scrambled eggs.

Last night as she fell asleep the taste of dried apricots had settled in her mouth – rich, slightly metallic, rising through her oesophagus, colliding in her throat, settling on the back of her tongue. Her arms and legs had twitched as she curled on her side, her muscle fibres shortening, flicking with stored tension.

This morning when she woke there'd been a lingering aftertaste of shepherds' pie. Slices of cooked mutton ground by hand, mixed with tomato paste and rings of fried leeks, the top of the pie a thick layer of mashed potatoes mixed with salted butter, milk and grated cheese.

Everyone dreamt of food; it was a collective, subterranean longing, a reaching out for sustenance and comfort. Whenever she visited Joseph to swap books or wait for him to open the back room for meetings, they shared favourite dishes from childhood, swapping as much of the recipes as they could remember, imagining ways of tracking down missing ingredients. Last week he slipped a thin packet of nutmeg into the pages of one of her books. In return she gave him some of the dates Flame had traded with her for a bag of sugar.

Once the trays of sandwiches and apples were finished, people returned their empty cups and left the cafeteria. Griffin offered to help with the washing up in the hope of finding out where the apples had come from. She listened to the other women as she dried thick white cups and saucers and placed them on cleaned trays. She called over her shoulder, 'Shall I put the cups on the top shelf?'

The Citizen's Coalition candidate came and stood beside her. 'Anywhere will do.' She shook hands with Griffin and helped her unpack the trays. The name badge on her tunic said Drusilla Sullivan, Secretary, Western Districts. They stacked the cups on one long shelf and piled saucers below them.

'I've seen you before,' Drusilla said, 'outside Joseph's Book Exchange. He said you were alright.' She took one of the empty trays by the handle and let it swing between her fingers.

Griffin walked back to the kitchen with Drusilla and collected more cups.

'The Flock's gaining ground in your area,' Drusilla said.

'Hard to miss,' Griffin said. 'They meet every morning and evening in the old community centre.'

'There's a rumour people join up and then go missing.'

Griffin carried another tray into the pantry. 'They know I'm not interested.'

Drusilla glanced at the doorway. It was empty. She passed over a ration card. 'You don't have to join, just keep an eye out. Report anything interesting to me.'

Joseph unlocked the small room at the back of the shop where he recycled computer, cell-phone and bicycle parts. Griffin opened the curtains and pushed the old sash window up to let cold air into the stale room. The rain had stopped and the footpaths and backyard gardens glistened in the weak sunshine. She stood at the window in her bare feet, breathing fresh air and drinking a cup of strong, black-market coffee. Her coat, socks and boots were in Joseph's kitchen, drying out in front of the fireplace after she'd walked back from the council meeting in the rain.

Joseph stood behind her. 'I'm not sure it's good for you, meeting with these people,' he said. 'They're almost as crazy as The Flock.' He tapped one finger on her shoulder. 'Don't take what they say too seriously.'

She moved away from the window and started clearing a space for six or seven folding chairs. 'Why do you let us meet here then, if you think we're all nutcases?'

He stroked his beard and grinned at her. 'Freedom of expression – even for loonies.'

She sat on one of the chairs and rubbed her feet. 'I don't know what else to do.'

He unfolded another chair and sat beside her. 'I know someone – an old man. I went to school with his nephew, Liam. He might be able to help.' He took a pencil out of his pocket, wrote a name and address on a piece of paper, folded it over and handed it to her. 'He's a bit strange but he's not crazy.'

Griffin put the paper in her pocket. 'Thanks.'

'Don't tell the others,' he said.

At the end of the meeting opinion was as divided as usual. Dallas and Emalani thought the abandoned cottages signified a further downturn – less food and fuel, more unpaid work, the rata tat tat of the drums heralding increasing conscription into agricultural and pollination gangs.

Griffin jotted down their interpretations in her journal. She smiled but said nothing – you didn't need to be having visions to predict the possibility of increasing conscription.

Bev and Pita concentrated on the slaughtering of the sheep and the cooking of its brains, talking about their childhood experiences of living on a mixed sheep and dairy farm sixty years ago. It was a warning, they said, to return to the wisdom of their grandparents: use everything, waste nothing.

Rowena, at fifteen the youngest member, wrote squiggly notes in her own exercise book but said nothing. The dreams and visions she'd shared with the group at previous meetings were full of fire and pestilence, a leftover, Griffin believed, of being taken to some of the first Flock meetings by her parents when she was a child.

After the meeting she sat with Joseph in the kitchen eating baked potatoes and roast pumpkin. When she was finished she rubbed her fingers across the greasy plate and licked her fingers.

'Glad you liked it,' Joseph said.

'Drusilla Sullivan from the Coalition asked me to spy on the Flock meetings.'

'Spy?'

She put her empty plate on the bench and washed her hands. 'What would you call it?'

'Keeping an eye out?'

'She gave me an extra ration card – I owe you.'

'Get yourself some new boots,' Joseph said.

After she said goodbye to Joseph, Griffin walked across the open square that led to the community centre. The clouds had almost cleared but puddles of water remained in the depressions and cracks of the uneven and broken concrete.

The evening prayer meeting had already started. She stood shadowed by the trunk and branches of a plane tree, listening to the singing. Usually she paid no attention to the words, concentrating only on the sound of the four-part harmonies, but tonight she listened more carefully: *Blood of the lamb, wash over me… we are sheep that have lost our way… sacrifice your life to the shepherd…*

She closed her eyes. Cottage doors swung open and banged their cast-iron handles against stone walls in the increasing wind. White foam from the waves drenched the air above the shore and sprayed her face and hair. Her hands and feet were cold. She hunched her shoulders, pulled up the collar of her thin coat and walked along the pebbled beach under an almost full moon. The hills above the beach were bare, the lone shepherd and his sheep nowhere to be seen. The sound of drumming filled her head, rata tat tat, rata tat tat. Out of the darkness a face loomed. She thought it was a spectre rising out of the sea and cried out in fright but it was a young woman, pale as the moon, her face surrounded by wet dark curls. 'We're hiding in the caves,' she said.

Griffin opened her eyes as members of the prayer meeting filed out into the square. The lights in the hall were turned off and the door was locked. The square emptied but she remained hidden behind the tree. Clouds were moving in again obscuring the sliver of new moon, rain coming through on the rising south-westerly. She wondered how long her extra ration card would last if she found nothing to report.

She stepped away from the tree and crept towards the darkened hall; slipped round the back of the building and saw a feral cat with a rat in its mouth springing away from her into the darkness. She returned to the front of the building.

Glass smashed above her. She leapt behind the tree again. A man fell out the first-floor window and rolled onto the grass verge. His hands and feet were roughly bound with rope. His face was scratched and bleeding, his breath rasping in his throat as he struggled to breathe.

Griffin scanned the square. She stepped out from the tree's shadow.

'Are you alright?'

His body jerked then curled to protect itself.

'It's okay,' she said.

She bent over, put her hands under his armpits and hauled him behind the tree. He lay on the ground while she untied the rope from his wrists and ankles. With the end of her scarf she wiped blood from his face.

He rolled over and sat up. She propped him against the tree trunk. He coughed and spat blood and phlegm onto the grass. She was falling again, following the moon-faced woman along the beach and into the entrance of a cave made accessible by the low tide. 'Hurry,' the woman said, 'we've only got a couple of hours before the tide turns.'

Griffin shook her head and put the man's arm over her shoulder. He leaned on her as they walked the three streets to the tattoo shop. Through the small window by the back door she could see Flame measuring sugar, getting ready to brew beer. She knocked on the windowpane.

He unlocked the back door. 'Trouble?' he said.

'Beaten up by The Flock.'

He helped her lift him up the stairs.

'Thanks,' she said.

Flame scratched at the dragon's head on his hairy belly then wiped his nose with the back of his hand. 'I'll get back to me beer.'

Griffin sat the man on a chair beside the sink. She wet the edge of a tea towel and dabbed at the dried blood on his face. He closed his eyes and bit his lip when she used tweezers to pick fragments of glass from his forehead and chin.

'What's your name?'

He opened his eyes and blinked a couple of times as if he had just woken up. 'Scott,' he said, 'What's yours?'

She rinsed the tweezers under the kitchen tap and patted his face with the dry end of the towel. 'Griffin.'

He stood up, still shaky on his feet but able to limp over to the window. Beneath the cuts and scratches his skin was pale. Tomorrow there would be swelling and bruises. He leaned on the windowsill. 'I've been following my daughter to the prayer meetings,' he said. 'She's only fourteen. I pretended to go along with things, but they're not stupid.'

Griffin touched the extra ration card in her pocket. The edge was smooth and slipped between her thumb and forefinger.

Scott moved away from the window and sat on the stool she used to reach the top cupboards. 'They go on and on about making sacrifices now so you can be rewarded later. They have meetings where they ask you to hand over your ration card and trust in the bounty of the Shepherd.'

'People do that?'

'The young ones.'

She fitted a fresh gas canister and boiled water over the portable gas ring. 'What happened to your daughter?'

Scott rubbed his forehead then winced as his fingers touched cuts and bruises. 'There was a big meeting last week. She and her friends handed over their cards. There was singing and dancing and extra food laid on in the hall.' He sighed. 'Haven't seen so much meat in years. People gorged themselves. Then the young ones were taken away to attend some special ceremony – I haven't seen her since.'

In a large mug Griffin mixed a paste of powdered milk, water, cocoa and sugar. She added another splash of water to thin it then poured it into a pot of simmering milk. Once it had been brought to the boil she turned the gas off and tipped it into two clean cups. She handed one to Scott. 'What happened to you?'

'I kept going to meetings, trying to find out where they'd gone but I wouldn't hand my ration card over.'

'So, they beat you up?'

Scott held his cup with both hands. 'Not right away. A group of us, parents mainly, were taken into the back room after the meeting last night.' He lifted the cocoa to his mouth. After a few sips his cheeks and throat flushed with warmth. 'The Pastor went on about making sacrifices in hard times.'

He drained the cup, stood up and put it on the kitchen bench. 'After an hour he brought the heavies in. They stood around the walls with their hands behind their backs, just waiting for the Pastor's word. The others handed over their cards and were allowed to go home.'

'They'll starve.'

Scott shrugged. 'Not if they work for The Flock.'

Griffin swirled the dregs of her cocoa round the bottom of her mug. 'What kind of work?'

'Farm work, I guess,' Scott said. 'That's what they do, isn't it? Raise sheep and goats; grow vegetables. There's rumours they've leased more land out past Waimauku.'

'That's a fair hike,' Griffin said. 'How do they get them out there?'

Scott limped back over to the stool and lowered himself onto it. 'I've seen trucks pull up at the end of meetings.'

Griffin went back downstairs and borrowed the cleanest spare blanket she could find from Flame. It smelt of smoke and burnt sugar. When she came back Scott had removed his boots and stood by the sink in bare feet. The skin around his eyes was starting to swell. His bottom lip was split, his chin cut, both cheeks puffy and dark with bruises.

She insisted he take the bed, spread the blanket on the floor and laid her sleeping bag on top. She wondered what would be useful to tell Drusilla. Kids stripped of their ration cards and transported to farms to be used as cheap or unpaid labour?

She closed her eyes.

Inside the cave, steps had been cut into the rock and pale skinned, dark-haired women stood on them, removing their shoes and stockings, their skirts and jackets, passing them over their heads to a girl who squatted on a stone shelf that jutted above the high tide line along the wall of the cave. She folded their clothes and shoes into tidy piles and sat down beside a candle lamp to keep guard. The women tucked up their petticoats to prevent them getting wet and she saw the whiteness of their feet, ankles and calves as they went down the steps. They formed a single line and walked towards the darkness at the back of the cave.

She waited with the women, listening to the sound of her own breathing and to the waves pushing pebbles back and forth on the beach. Above the waves she heard a low whistle and the baaing of sheep. One of the women whistled back, lit her lamp and held it above her head.

Griffin blinked in the dull light. Barefoot men, trousers rolled up to their knees, were guiding sheep along the beach and into the mouth of the cave. In the distance she heard the rata tat tat, rata tat tat of a drum. The men herded the last of the sheep inside. They piled driftwood and dragged bull kelp in front of the entrance. Two more women lit lamps, hooked them onto poles and held them high above their heads.

A deep channel ran through the centre of the cave and rose to the west. They herded the sheep along the channel, moving them as fast as they could, men and women with their arms out, running, whistling to guide them up and through to the hills on the other side as soldiers in red coats marched along the beach making so much noise with their beating drums they couldn't hear them.

Half an hour later they were all on the other side and the sheep were scrambling up the hill. The woman walking beside her stopped to catch her breath. 'They'd take every last one,' she said, 'They'd starve us out if they could.'

'Why?' Griffin said. 'What do they want?'

The woman looked at her as if she'd gone simple. 'What they always want,' she said, 'someone else's land and livelihood.' She sat down, gathered up the hems of her petticoats and squeezed the moisture out. She started to laugh. 'Sheep is what they want alright, and not just the ones with wool on their backs.'

They spent the night out on the hills above the caves taking turns to watch the sheep. The women took off their top petticoats and wrapped them around their heads and shoulders like shawls to keep warm. The moon was high and clear, the sky embroidered with stars. Tricked again, the soldiers had returned along the beach, unable to work out how the sheep had disappeared.

She woke briefly and listened to Scott's breathing then drifted back to sleep again with the rata tat tat, rata tat tat of the drum in her ears. Soldiers marched through cobblestone streets, their red coats blazing in the early morning sun. Young boys were sent out as scouts to sleep each night among the branches of trees; woken by the approaching drumming, they dropped silently to the ground and ran back to the cottages to warn the old people. Their parents and older brothers and sisters were hiding up on the hills with the sheep.

She finally slept and woke an hour before dawn and lay on her back on the floor, her head resting on the torn lining of her rolled up coat, her mind awash with images: sheep spread out over grassy hills, soldiers marching woodenly up and down the beach to the sound of a drum, men and women running barefoot through caves, their shadows elongated in the flickering light of the pole lamps. They were agile, strong, but they were thin and increasingly hungry. Their gardens were going to seed as they tried to save their sheep from being taken by the army. The sheep needed shearing so the older women could wash, comb and spin the wool, knit stockings and jackets, and weave blankets and shawls to keep their families warm in the coming winter.

She dozed and dreamed of peaches and apricots, of the deep purple plums that used to grow in her parents' orchard and of the dark, sweet cherries she and her mother had loved. She remembered her Aunt Lizzy's apple and black-currant pie served with ice-cream or custard. Her mouth filled with saliva. Tears wet her cheeks. All she had left in the kitchen cupboard were a few handfuls of rice. She dressed and slid her extra ration card into her trouser pocket. She left Scott a note, took her pack and walked to the shopping centre.

Government stallholders were unloading trestle tables from two khaki-coloured army trucks. When the food stalls opened she queued for cooking oil, rice, flour, oats, sugar, milk and gas canisters. Brown and red lentils were available for the first time in months. The fruit and vegetable stall consisted of a large bin of green and yellow-skinned pumpkins. There were no eggs, cheese or apples. The bakery opened its door at eight-thirty and she queued again for fresh bread. Each time the sliding door between the front and back of the shop was opened there was the smell of boiled mutton. The meat pies, she was told by the grubby looking baker's assistant, would be ready in an hour.

When she came out of the bakery she saw a group of young people standing together in the far corner of the centre. They wore heavy boots, woollen coats, brown hats and scarves. Their faces were flushed from walking. They put their backpacks on the ground and formed a circle. Some of them began to sing, *Safe with the shepherd, safe in the flock, safe from the sins of the world...* Their clothes and boots were in good condition, almost new, their hair and skin shiny and clean. How healthy they looked compared to the rest of the people in the square. She watched them handing out leaflets to the thinning crowd, sharing water and apples amongst themselves, singing and clapping. She moved closer. Their packs were full of handwritten leaflets, water bottles and fresh food: apples, hard cheese wrapped in pieces of soft muslin, slabs of heavy, dark bread, thick slices of preserved meat. Whatever else had happened to them, they were now well fed.

When she returned to the flat Scott was rinsing the dirt and blood out of his shirt in the sink. His eyes were so swollen they were almost shut.

'There's a group of teenagers in the shopping centre,' she said, 'singing and handing out leaflets.'

She unpacked her supplies and stacked them in the cupboard, attached the new canister to the gas ring and boiled water.

Scott squeezed the water out of his shirt, hung it over the back of the chair and smoothed the creases out with his fingers. He put his jacket on over his tee-shirt and buttoned it up.

'I can't go like this,' he said, waving his hand in front of his face. 'I'll wait till it gets dark.'

Griffin cut half a pumpkin into chunks and dropped pieces into the pot. 'What will you do?'

Scott shrugged his shoulders. 'Try and find her.' He took a photo out of the inside pocket of his jacket. 'This is Jesse,' he said.

Griffin studied the photo: curly brown hair framing a heart-shaped face, the hint of a smile for the camera, a slight gap in her front teeth. The same light brown skin and dark eyes as her father. It was a recent identity photo, the date and government number stamped across the top left-hand corner.

'There's about twenty of them. She might be there.'

She drained most of the hot vegetable water from the pot into a glass jug, mashed the pumpkin, added salt and nutmeg and some fresh milk to make a thick soup. She cut two slices of bread and spooned the soup into bowls.

Scott put the photo back into his pocket. He looked at the bowls steaming on the bench. 'I've nothing to trade with.'

Griffin passed him a bowl of soup and a spoon. 'The cupboard's okay at the moment.' She indicated the chair for him, pulled up the stool and sat at the table she'd made by balancing an old door on a couple of wooden boxes. The soup was hot and salty. She sprinkled more nutmeg on top and dipped the crust of her bread into the bowl. 'But I could do with a new pair of boots. Once you're better we've got some walking to do.'

The cobblestone streets were deserted, the cottages empty, their doors swinging and banging in the wind. Out on the scarred and burnt-off hills two scraggy goats grazed on a crop of thistles. She walked along the beach, her coat collar turned up, her eyes watering in the stinging breeze. On the shelf in the cave were the remains of boots, woollen stockings and jackets. At the back of the cave where the floor sloped up above the high tide line were scraps of sheepskin and bones. She climbed through the passageway and walked over the hills, ash and soil clinging to her stout leather boots. Further inland a stand of oaks that had provided shelter and shade for generations had been chopped down, their stumps exposed and raw in the weak winter sunlight. She sat down, leaned against the rough surface of a stump and ran her hand across the roots. Her fingers found the smooth brown skin of an acorn. She rubbed it clean and put it in her pocket. She curled herself among the roots of the butchered trees and slept.

Drusilla Sullivan sat in Joseph's kitchen, bare feet soaking in a bucket of warm water, her thick socks and heavy boots by the door. Griffin told her about Scott and Jesse.

'As soon as Scott's recovered we'll hike out to the farm,' Griffin said. 'It's a couple of days each way but he's hopeful Jesse's out there.'

Drusilla pushed a handful of curls behind one ear. 'We need to find out if these kids are being held against their will.'

'The group in the shopping centre last week seemed happy enough – they had plenty of food.'

'Might just be advertising – part of their recruitment drive.'

Griffin shrugged. 'Their hair and skin looked healthy – that takes more than a couple of decent feeds.'

'We need to know how they're using their ration cards,' Drusilla said. 'Where they bulk buy.'

Griffin wriggled her toes in her new boots. 'I thought you were in favour of food collectives.'

Drusilla dried her feet on an old towel. 'I am – our whole campaign's based on it. But the government's still strongly opposed.' She looked out the window. 'Yet they turn a blind eye when it's The Flock.'

They walked; the women and older children carrying the extra clothing and blankets they'd hidden, the men with the smaller children tied to their backs in case they fell when they slept. They walked inland, away from the coast, to the high country, following old mustering trails but driving no sheep before them. The caves had been discovered and raided by the Redcoats, the sheep slaughtered, the old people rounded up and executed. They'd heard the shots ring out as they scrambled up the hills, knowing they'd gained precious time because of that sacrifice. Clouds of dark smoke rose in the sky. They watched from the shelter of tors that dotted the next range as the soldiers torched the dry grasses of the lowlands. They climbed, the young ones too tired to complain, the women holding on to each other, their faces cemented with dust and tears. The men walked ahead, silent, their minds empty of everything but survival. There would be time later for revenge.

They reached the upland valley dotted with ancient cairns just before the snows came. The women repaired the shepherds' huts, collected wood and dung for fuel while the men and boys searched the valley for wild sheep and goats.

The mountain winds blew snowdrifts around the huts. Three babies died. The ground was frozen hard so they wrapped the tiny bodies together in a blanket, covered them with snow and piled rocks on top. In spring, when the snow thawed, they would bury them properly.

On the days when the winds dropped and the sun shone, the men dug pathways through the snow and scavenged for meat: birds, rabbits, wolves, a stray deer if they were lucky. It was so cold their beards and eyebrows froze. The sun was so bright on the white snow when they dragged a carcass back their eyes burned and they were blinded by the glare.

Griffin re-read the name and address on the piece of paper Joseph had given her. It was only two suburbs further west, less than an hour's walk each way. She left early in the morning with her notes tied in a neat bundle inside her backpack. The visions were getting more intense, invading her senses when what she most needed was to pay attention to what was happening around her, especially now she'd agreed to help Scott – and she didn't want to lose her extra ration card.

She stood behind a cluster of birch trees watching the house. After half an hour a tall auburn-haired man opened the front door, called out goodbye then walked down the street with an empty pack on his back. Easy enough to work out he was going to the market and would be gone for a while. She gave it another ten minutes then slipped round to the back door and knocked.

An elderly man with short, white hair opened the door. He wore thick sheepskin slippers, dark blue trousers and a hand-knitted, pale blue sweater. He stared at her. 'Can I help you?'

'Joseph,' she said. 'He gave me this address. He said you might be able to help.' She pressed two fingers against her left temple. 'You know, to stop me going crazy.'

He almost stumbled as he took a step towards her. When he held out his hand she noticed he had a slight tremor.

'What's your name?'

'Griffin.' She shook his hand; his skin was dry, and thin as paper. 'I meet with others. Sometimes. At Joseph's.'

'Does it help?'

She shrugged. 'What else is there?'

'Only me, I'm afraid,' the old man said.

She took off her pack, unzipped it and handed him her notes bundled together with string. 'I've written it down. As much as I can. When it started. What I see.'

He smiled at her then and she noticed he still had all his teeth.

'That's very well organised of you,' he said, 'I appreciate it.'

She adjusted the straps on her pack then slid it back on. 'What happens next?'

He held her notes against his chest, this thumb rubbing against the rough string knot in the middle. 'I'll read these and write down what

I think and, in a few days, I'll get my nephew to take them to Joseph's. Then, if you want to, you can come back and we can talk.'

She left him standing on the step watching her as she walked down the street. She turned around when she reached the corner and waved to him as if he was someone she knew well and would miss. He stood at the back door, an old man in his slippers clutching her notes. He raised his hand, more a salute than a wave, then went inside and closed the door.

Griffin and Scott walked along the edge of the western motorway. The mountain women fed gruel made from bones and gristle mixed with the last of the dried oats to their children. They rubbed animal fat on their hands and feet to prevent chilblains and cracked skin, and tied woollen scarves around their heads to protect their ears from the wind.

On the motorway, a few bicycles and motorbikes sped past but most of the early morning traffic was people like them, individuals or groups on foot. The biggest contingent was the twenty or so teenagers up ahead from The Flock. The girls sang as they walked and when the group rested for a couple of hours at midday two of the boys kept watch. Towards evening three army trucks drove slowly past them to the checkpoint and waited for the walkers to arrive.

Griffin described the village, the caves, the soldiers and the sheep, and the flight of the villagers to the mountain valley to Scott as they walked at a discreet distance from The Flock. Scott listened in silence.

'What do you think?'

He squeezed her shoulder. 'I don't know much about this kind of stuff,' he said, 'but I think the old fella's right. There's got to be a reason for it happening to you.'

At the checkpoint they showed their identity papers and gave their reasons for leaving the city boundaries: sick friends, not long for this world, needing care and support.

A soldier stamped their permission to travel for two weeks on the back page of their papers. 'You're not with The Flock then?'

'No,' Scott said, 'Just going in the same general direction.'

He waved them through the turnstile. They tucked their identity papers back into their coat pockets, adjusted their backpacks and walked on until the group from The Flock turned off down a side road. A hand-painted sign with a large yellow and brown arrow pointing further inland announced: *Harvest Home Collective Farm and Gardens.* In smaller letters on the bottom of the sign were the words: *The Flock welcomes all those who labour.*

They sat on the grass verge close to the sign and drank from their water bottles. The road was deserted but, in the distance, Griffin could hear sheep being rounded up, shepherds shouting and whistling to their dogs.

She glanced at Scott. 'Can you hear sheep?'

He grinned and pointed left. 'Don't worry, it's coming from the fields over there.'

Snow melted. The rivers and streams filled. The ground began to thaw. Sun warmed the shepherds' huts; green shoots were seen in the meadows. On the morning Old Mary died of pneumonia the women gathered outside the huts and dismantled the stone cairns that had protected their babies' bodies all winter. Two of the men stayed behind from the hunt and dug a grave in the cold earth. They laid the babies in Mary's emaciated arms and buried them together. Later in the afternoon the men and boys carried the skinned and cleaned carcasses of a goat and a sheep into the largest hut. They handed the freshly washed skins to the eldest woman and laid the meat on the hearth.

That night, after they'd feasted and were resting, one of the senior men, his hair and beard streaked with grey, stood up, his back to the warmth of the hearth. 'When the thaw's over and the streams have settled, four men will return,' he said.

The women shifted children in their laps. The boys stopped arm wrestling on the floor.

He looked past their faces, his gaze resting on the rough-hewn carving of a fox above the door. 'We need to decide who should be sent.'

Griffin walked behind Scott. The paddocks on either side of the road were dotted with sheep. Most had dusty black wool but one or two were a dirty white. If they weren't shorn soon the spring rains would saturate them, making them too heavy to stand. She hadn't seen so many animals in years, not since she was a small child. She tapped Scott on the shoulder. 'They must have a breeding programme.'

He ground the toe of his boot into the dirt. 'The Flock seems to have a lot of things.'

JESSE

The smell of roast mutton and boiled onions filled the main kitchen. Jesse stood at the wooden table in the centre of the room washing potatoes in a large plastic basin. The water in the basin was cold and her fingers ached. Once she'd washed the dirt off she passed them to Ngaire who wiped them and chopped them in half.

When the water was dark and clotted with mud she lifted the basin off the table and carried it out of the kitchen and down the hallway to the back door. It was heavy and she balanced it against her hip, trying not to slosh dirty water on the floor or down her clothes. She'd already scrubbed the floors earlier that morning and didn't want to do it again.

The door was unlocked so she pushed the handle down with her elbow. Outside, she was surprised by the brightness of the sunlight. The lower sections of the windows in the kitchen had been painted over and those on kitchen duty always worked in a muted half-light.

She walked across the concrete path and poured water and clots of dirt onto the grass. In the distance, across the kitchen paddocks, she saw four windmills turning in the southerly breeze. The arms of the windmills fluttered with faded rags. Shepherds whistled to their dogs and the smell of sheep and horse manure was in the air.

She rinsed the basin at the outside tap, refilled it and hurried back inside. They needed to finish the potatoes and start peeling the sack of apples that had been delivered by a benefactor last night.

Ngaire was sprinkling salt over the trays of potatoes. 'Thought you'd got lost,' she said.

Jesse slid the basin back onto the table. 'How come there's only two of us on the roster today?'

'No idea,' Ngaire said. She handed Jesse a tray. 'Put these in the bottom of the oven.'

Jesse slid the tray in and shut the oven door, her cheeks flushed from the sudden heat. 'Have you seen Donal or Petra?'

Ngaire sliced an apple in half and then into quarters. She glanced at the door. 'There's no point wondering, Jesse. People come and go all the time.'

Jesse bent over the sack and filled a bowl with apples. Their skins were firm and streaked with red. She lifted one to her nose and smelt it. 'Slightly under-ripe,' she said. 'We'll need to add dates or raisins – we're short on sugar.'

They stood side by side slicing and peeling apples, dropping the skins, cores and pips into a slop bucket for the pigs.

'Why didn't they come and say goodbye?' Jesse said.

Ngaire looked towards the door again. 'Maybe they've been sent somewhere else – this isn't the only farm.' She put her knife on the table and scooped the pile of sliced apples into a baking dish.

'Maybe they – ' Jesse stopped as the door opened.

Les, the farm's main butcher, carried a fresh lamb carcass across his shoulder. His large white apron was smeared with blood. He laid the meat on the table.

'Visitors for dinner,' he said. He went to the sink, unsheathed the large knife swinging from his belt and washed it under the tap.

'How many?' Ngaire asked.

Les looked around the kitchen. 'Only the two of you?'

'Who's coming?' Jesse said.

'Never you mind – just get cracking.' He stood in the doorway and winked at them. 'I'll find you a couple of helpers.' He swung the door shut behind him then opened it again. 'Six,' he said, 'Bigwigs from town – that's all I know.'

GRIFFIN

Griffin and Scott squatted behind the hedge and peered through a small gap in the foliage. An army truck drove up and stopped at the front gate of the farm. The driver got out and pushed opened the gate. He walked to the back of the truck and untied the heavy green canvas flap. A soldier jumped down. 'Right you lot, out you come,' he said.

Two middle-aged men, wearing faded denim overalls and handcuffed to each other, came off first, ducking their heads as their bare feet hit the ground. The soldier prodded them with the butt of his rifle. 'Over there,' he said, pushing them through the gate to the guardhouse thirty metres or so up the narrow gravel drive.

Half a dozen skinny teenagers followed, squinting in the sunlight. They bunched together, shoulders hunched, hands in their pockets.

'Off you go,' the driver said, 'sooner you go through, sooner you'll get a decent feed.'

Three kids, somewhere between eight and ten, with dirty faces, matted hair and no jackets or coats, slid off the truck and slouched through the gates behind the teenagers.

'Where the hell are their parents?' Griffin whispered.

'Looks like they haven't seen a bath in while,' Scott said.

'What do they do, drive round the streets picking up homeless kids?'

Scott moved back from the gap in the hedge and sat on the grass. 'Looks like it.'

'That's some kind of recruitment drive,' Griffin said.

Scott lay back down and pulled the peak of his cap over his eyes, 'More important is how we get inside.'

Towards sunset two motorbikes escorted an army jeep through the gates, past the guard on duty and up the drive.

Griffin woke Scott. 'Someone else's arrived.'

They crept along the hedge until it intersected with a barbed wire fence. It was almost dark and the front of the main farmhouse was hidden from view. They were looking at the eastern side of the building. Griffin could just make out a large vegetable garden. Shafts of light shone from the top half of four large windows. Even with the doors and windows shut she could smell lamb roasting. And someone was frying onions. The back door opened and a young woman came out carrying a large bucket. She swapped the bucket from hand to hand as she passed the garden and walked over to a long shed. She pushed the door open with her shoulder and the smell of pigs rose on the dampening air. After a few minutes she came back out, swinging the empty bucket in her hand. She pulled the door behind her and walked back across the garden towards the kitchen, singing softly to herself.

Scott gripped Griffin's arm. 'It's Ngaire, Jesse's friend.'

They crept back along the hedge and lay down in the long grass again. 'What do you want to do?' Griffin said.

'See if she's alright.'

'You'll need to get inside to do that – or get her to come out here.'

Scott sat up and put his head in his hands. 'Maybe we could leave her a message?'

'How?'

'In the barn. With the pigs. When it's dark, I'll find a way in. I'll leave her a note.'

'What if someone else finds it? Then we'll all be in trouble.' Griffin rolled onto her stomach and propped herself up on her elbows. 'We need to find a way in, *and* a way back out.'

They waited on the overgrown berm until it got completely dark, sheltering by a section of macrocarpa hedge closest to the main gate. The smell of food coming from the kitchen reminded Griffin they hadn't eaten anything since breakfast. She shared the last of their bread and apples. 'And we need to get our hands on some of that food.'

The kitchen and dining room in the main building were lit up. Through the uncurtained windows of the dining room they watched two young women setting tables and carrying trays.

'It's Jesse,' Scott whispered. 'I'd recognise her anywhere.'

'We'll go when they're all eating,' Griffin said.

Once people were seated around the tables they scouted the perimeter of the hedge and fences, keeping low and quiet, sometimes crawling on their hands and knees.

'Hope the dogs are locked up for the night,' Scott said.

Griffin could smell the rich mix of the animals in the paddocks closest to the main house – sheep and goats mainly, but one paddock had three horses that stopped grazing and stared at them. The pigs were obviously so valuable they were kept inside the barn to protect them from the elements. As they crept further round she saw there were more outbuildings and another large empty paddock. In it, framed against the night sky, and with the light of the rising moon illuminating them like paintings, she saw four large windmills, their pale-coloured sails resting in the breezeless evening. For a moment she thought she saw something flutter down one of the sails, a flash of darker colour that hung motionless for a second before it crumpled like a dropped sheet. Then it was gone.

Scott tugged her arm. 'Come on, we need to find a way into the kitchen.'

'Better to make for the barn,' she said. 'Look for a section of fence we can crawl under.'

She crawled along the fence line behind Scott for another five minutes, stopping when he checked the barbed wire for weak spots. The temperature was starting to drop and dew was forming on the grass. The knees of her jeans were cold and damp. A shaft of light sliced the ground in front of them then circled the paddock in front of the windmills.

Scott turned and pushed her face down onto the wet grass. 'Another foot and they would've seen us.'

Griffin wiped dirt off her face. 'Another inch and my nose would've been stuck on that barbed wire.'

She watched the light sweep past them again and noticed there was a patch of cleared earth under the fence in front of them. 'Look,' she said. 'Someone's been here before.'

Scott dug into the crumbly soil with his hands, pushing it into a mound inside the paddock until a shallow trench had been cleared. 'If I hold the bottom of the fence up you can wriggle under here.'

Griffin lay on her stomach, put her forehead on the ground and used her elbows to push herself through. On the other side she wiped her face on her sleeve.

Scott took off his jacket and handed it to her. 'Wrap it around your hands so you can lift up the wire.'

Griffin needed both hands to lift the wire. The light swept past them again as Scott wriggled under. 'At least we've both got dirt on our faces,' she said.

They pushed the soil back to cover the trench and patted it down then waited, counting the seconds between each sweep of light, preparing to run in the moments of darkness, but after two more circuits the light vanished as mysteriously as it came.

She grabbed his hand. 'Okay. Let's go.'

JESSE

Jesse woke before dawn and dressed in the darkness, careful not to wake Ngaire. It was cold and her fingers were clumsy as she tried to button her loose white blouse and thick black cardigan. Thankfully, she was still able to wear trousers although there was a new rumour the women and girls would have to start wearing long skirts all the time now, not just at choir and prayers. Not that anyone ever directly ordered anything. An edict from the Pastors wasn't even necessary – that's what was so irritating: a rumour would start and within a week everyone had conformed. Two weeks ago, she'd watched the older women rush to cut a bolt of soft, navy-coloured cotton into large squares so they could all wear headscarves. Pastor Rhys had been leading prayers when they all filed in and knelt on the wooden floor behind the men. He nodded at them and smiled at Jocelyn and Noelle, the two eldest women, but never said a word. Now they wore headscarves all the time, except when they were in their own quarters. Not that she was complaining. She was warm and well fed, she still had friends here – although some of them had been sent off to other farms – and while she didn't love working in the kitchen it was better than being outside in the rain and wind minding the sheep and goats.

She bent down and picked up her shoes and crept out of the bedroom she shared with Ngaire. In the beginning there had been two other girls in with them, Maggie and Claire-Louise, but they'd moved on too.

In the kitchen she swapped the empty gas canister for a full one, lit the stove, filled the largest kettle with water and set it to boil. The pig bucket was by the door, full of scraps from last night's feast. She pushed away the thought that plenty of people in town would be grateful for those scraps and decided she might as well empty it now rather than trip over it until Ngaire got around to doing it later in the morning. Anyway, they would need to refill it by the look of two more sacks of potatoes leaning against the side of the kitchen table, not to mention the boxes of pumpkins stacked underneath it.

Outside, the sky was just beginning to lighten and, although there was only the gentlest of breezes near the house and outbuildings, in the furthest paddock she could see the sails of the windmills turning. Thin strips of colour fluttered like ribbons on the sides of the sails. It gave the windmills a slightly festive air and reminded Jesse of pictures she'd seen in old children's books of English families going to the village fair.

The scrap bucket was heavy. She needed to concentrate and use both hands to carry it across the garden to the barn. She staggered a little as she approached the sliding door and was grateful to put it down. The piece of bent wire used to secure the door was missing but the door itself was closed. Ngaire must have been in a rush last night. She pushed it open and the ripe smell of pigs and rotting fruit and vegetables hit her. Once she heaved the bucket up to the lip of the wooden fence that enclosed the pigs in the centre of the barn, she tipped the scraps out as widely as she could. 'Best fed pigs in the whole darn country,' she said, watching two huge sows waddle towards the fresh food.

'Hello Jesse.'

She dropped the bucket on her foot. 'Shit!' She kicked it away and spun around. 'Dad?'

He walked towards her out of the shadows at the back of the barn, his eyes on the open door. 'Hello love.'

'What are you doing here?' she said.

'Just wanted to see you're alright.' He smiled. 'Aren't you going to give your old man a hug?'

His arms went around her. She heard him sigh. For a moment she allowed her head to rest on his shoulder. There wasn't much to him beneath the thin shirt and torn, stained jacket.

'You've lost weight,' she said. 'When was the last time you had a decent meal?'

He held her away from him and studied her face. 'You look well.'

'I'm fine,' she said.

'I saw Ngaire yesterday,' he said, 'coming to the barn to feed the pigs.'

Jesse picked up the bucket. 'I've got to get back,' she said, 'I've left water boiling on the stove.'

Scott squeezed her hand. 'Can you get us some food?'

'Us?'

A young woman stepped out from behind a bale of hay and walked towards her. She held out her hand. 'Hi Jesse, I'm Griffin.'

Jesse swapped the bucket from her left to her right hand. 'Dad, the water, I've got to get back, they'll be wondering where I am.'

He reached out and stroked her hair. 'Okay love, we'll wait here till tonight.'

When she got back to the kitchen Ngaire was pouring the hot water into two large teapots.

'You took your time,' she said.

Jesse washed her hands then arranged milk jugs and cups on a large wooden tray. 'Are the higher-ups staying for breakfast?'

Ngaire grinned. 'What do you think?'

Jesse carried the tray into the dining room, placed the jugs and cups on the table and returned for the teapots. Ngaire sliced and buttered bread and piled it onto two plates. She began frying left over potatoes.

'I'm starving,' Jesse said. 'Can you leave some of those for me?'

Ngaire nodded and pointed to the safe. 'There's plenty of lamb left. Get yourself a couple of slices.'

After they served breakfast and cleaned up Ngaire went to the pantry to check their supplies of flour, sugar, barley and dried fruit. Jesse quickly cut thick pieces of lamb, mixed it with the bowl of left-over potatoes and layered four slices of bread on top. She put the bowl in the clean scrap bucket and covered it with a hand towel. 'Just going to pick some herbs,' she said as she passed the pantry.

The sun had burnt off the dew and the path from the kitchen to the barn was now dry. The garden was divided into four sections with the herbs closest to the barn. She carried the bucket as though it was heavy and walked straight to the barn, hoping no one had seen her first trip to the pigs earlier this morning. Mint, thyme and sage she would pick on the way back.

The barn door was slightly ajar. It slid open when she pulled it. Dust motes in the air and shadows on the back wall.

'Dad?'

Scott appeared from behind a wooden post. 'Here love.'

She lifted the food out of the bucket and gave it to him. 'I'll come back later for the bowl.'

'We need to talk,' he said.

Jesse shook her head. 'There's no point, Dad, I'm not leaving.'

'I'm not asking you to, sweetheart.'

'We work and they feed us, Dad.' She swung the bucket from one hand to the other. 'And I like the singing. That's all.'

Griffin stepped out from behind her hay bale, brushing dust and straw from her coat. 'Thanks for the food,' she said.

Scott handed her the bowl. She broke off a piece of bread.

Jesse turned to go. 'Be careful, she said, 'and keep the door closed.'

Scott grinned and pinched his nostrils. 'The pigs – it takes a bit of getting used to.'

Griffin reached into the bowl for a piece of meat. 'The windmills in the back paddock,' she said. 'What are they for?'

Jesse shrugged. 'We're assigned to the kitchen. Only the beekeepers go there.'

'The Flock has hives. I thought they were banned?'

Jesse started to walk away. 'Best not to ask too many questions,' she said.

GRIFFIN

Griffin sat on the ground with her back against the hay bale and the bowl between her knees. She made a lamb and potato sandwich then gave the bowl back to Scott. She made herself chew slowly so it lasted longer, hoping that might trick her stomach into feeling full.

All the previous night she'd lain awake on the dirt floor of the barn, her head resting against her backpack, following the four highland men who'd been chosen to return to their old village on the coast. Wrapped in plaid blankets, they left the huts an hour before dawn. All of them carried knives tucked into the leather belts that secured their breeches and three of them had stout shepherd's crooks. Each of them carried a small sheepskin bag over his shoulder filled with strips of dried meat. They walked through lush grass and across streams filled with water warming itself as it flowed against rocks and stones. Occasionally, as they travelled further down the valley and into the beginning of the low country, they saw wild sheep. The whole of the first day no one spoke. The men knew each so well a single gesture was enough to communicate the need to stop and rest or eat. When dusk fell they made a shelter behind a windbreak of gorse and thistle bushes. They took turns sleeping and watching, two of them sitting back to back with their knives drawn across their knees while the other two slept.

In the morning, they washed their faces with fresh water from the closest stream, rinsed their mouths and drank their fill. They walked until noon. Stretched out before them lay the field that had once been graced with hundred-year-old oaks. Now, gouged and burned-out tree stumps rose out of the lush spring grass.

One of the men bent down, picked up an acorn and wiped it clean against the fold of his blanket. He spat on the ground. 'They didn't even put it to good use,' he said. 'Burning oak as if it was firewood.'

They made their way through the field, keeping low to the ground, circling stumps and the remains of charred logs until they reached the back entrance of the cave. Branches had been roughly woven together to form a gate. On it were tied scraps of material, fluttering in the breeze like faded ribbons. The men squatted before it, the oldest man touching the largest strip of material. It had faded to a washed out grey. He shook his head. 'Whose colours were these?'

Two of them lifted the gate away from the entrance and laid it gently in the grass. The other two gathered dried twigs and branches and bound them together to make torches. As they entered the cave they saw in the flickering torchlight human bones and smashed skulls, mostly picked clean of flesh. The men walked in single file with their knives drawn. Most of the bones were clustered towards the back of the cave but some had been dragged towards the middle. The sea entrance had been left open to the weather, allowing scavengers to enter at will. The rock shelf where they used to place their shoes and jackets and outer skirts to protect them from the high tide was empty. On either side of the cave entrance someone had piled stones from the beach to form cairns; a sign not to enter the cave because the dead lay inside.

They waited by the entrance to the cave watching the tide recede and the gulls swoop and scream. In the late afternoon the wind picked up and they wrapped their blankets around their shoulders and chests and tucked the corners into their belts. No one walked on the beach or approached the caves. No bells could be heard ringing the hour. When it was almost dark and the tide was turning they walked across the stones and pebbles onto the coarse sand and headed towards the village.

On the outskirts, a few feet from the low stone wall that had once encircled their cottages and marked the village boundary, they saw a windmill, its wooden paddles and sails moving in the rising breeze. They crouched in the darkness behind an overgrown hedge of rowan bushes and waited.

The wind dropped and the windmill stilled.

In the distance a single shaft of light from a lantern swept back and forward. It moved closer to them. Boots scrunched loudly on the cobblestones then softened as they met the hardened earth in front of the windmill. Two Redcoats stood facing the slowly moving sails, their backs to the men. The smaller, younger soldier held the lantern above his head. The men held their breath and unsheathed their knives.

'Time to cut another one down Sir?'

'Looks like he might have saved us the bother,' the older soldier said. 'Remove the body at first light.'

'Yes, sir.'

Two of the men sprang from their hiding place. Their knives sliced the soldiers' throats before they knew anyone was behind them. They doused the lantern and dragged the bodies behind the bushes.

In silence they stripped them of their jackets, trousers and boots and took their muskets and bayonets. One of the men took off his blanket and put on the largest jacket. He spread out his blanket and wrapped up the rest of their booty.

While the older two kept watch, the younger two crept towards the windmill scanning the ground left and right for the body the soldiers had spoken of.

A cold fog moved in from the sea. It spread across the beach towards the village, softening the sharpness of the night air, hiding the northern stars, limiting their vision to a foot in front of them. Steam from their breaths mingled with the fog while they searched.

When they were almost close enough to touch the stone base of the windmill a bundle of bloodied rags tripped them up. They swore in unison and crouched beside it. The body was emaciated; its arms and legs were broken, shards of bone jutting through starved and beaten flesh. Strands of rope had eaten into the skin covering wrists and ankles. They turned the body over to see the face but, in the darkness and with the rictus of death, it was unrecognisable. The top front teeth had bitten into the bottom lip. They wrapped it in one of their blankets and carried it back to the others.

Griffin waited until Scott had finished eating. She sat with her back against a hay bale, grateful no one but Jesse had entered the barn. In her head she went over everything she'd seen during the night, making sure she'd forgotten nothing so she could write it down and share it with the old man, Jason, and his nephew, Liam, when she got home.

Scott sat opposite her finishing his meat and potato sandwich. He wiped his hands on the knees of his trousers and put the empty bowl behind one of the hay bales. 'Haven't eaten lamb in years,' he said. 'Almost forgotten what it tasted like.'

Griffin stood up and brushed straw and dust from her legs and arms. In spite of not washing for days, crawling through mud and under fences, and sleeping in a barn next to pigs, Scott looked relaxed for the first time since she'd met him. 'Before we leave tonight I need to check out the windmills,' she said.

'I'd like to stay another day,' he said. 'Make sure Jess really is okay.'

Griffin offered him her hand and pulled him upright. 'Not a good idea.'

'I've hardly seen her.'

'She's here of her own free will. And doesn't want to leave.'

Scott closed his eyes and sighed. His shoulders sagged. 'She's all I've got.'

Griffin patted his arm. 'She's healthy. Well fed. She has her friend, Ngaire.'

'Maybe I should stay,' Scott said. 'Give in and join the bloody Flock. At least I'd see Jesse and get to eat properly.'

Griffin shrugged and walked over to the pig pen. The two enormous sows were lying on their sides down the far end, resting. She looked at the remains of vegetable scraps and curls of apple peel they'd been gorging on. They might be well-fed but they were only there to breed and be slaughtered. And if she and Scott weren't careful someone would soon come into the barn to check on the pigs or clean out their pen and they'd be caught.

'Stay if you need to,' she said. 'It's your choice, but if we don't get out of this barn by the end of the day we'll all be in trouble.'

Griffin heard the door slide open. She peeked between the hay bales and saw Jesse had brought Ngaire with her. They both carried slop buckets. Ngaire hoisted hers up onto the top rail of the pen and tipped the scraps out. The pigs snorted and wheezed like old men, heaved themselves up and trotted over. Jesse walked to the back of the barn. 'Dad?'

Scott stepped out from behind the bales. 'Over here.'

'I've got food for you.' She put the bucket down, took the lid off and handed him two brown paper parcels. 'Lamb sandwiches,' she said, 'and some dried fruit.'

Scott handed the parcels to Griffin and hugged Jesse. 'Thanks, love.' He held her tight.

Jesse rubbed her father's back, patted his shoulder a couple of times then stood back and looked at him. 'Once it gets dark you've got to go. They'll notice if I make any more trips to the barn or if any more food goes missing.'

Ngaire walked over to Scott. 'Working in the kitchens is the best place to be,' she said. 'We'll be okay.'

'What if they move you somewhere else?' Scott said. 'How will I know where you've gone?'

'We're allowed two letters a month,' Jesse said. 'If you write I can reply.'

Griffin watched as Scott hugged Jesse again. Ngaire picked up her bucket, slid the barn door open a few inches and peered out. 'Come on, Jess,' she said. 'Coast's clear.'

Griffin and Scott stayed resting in the barn until they heard the dinner gong strike. Fifteen minutes later they slipped out the barn door and slid it quietly behind them. Griffin took off in a crouching run towards the fence line. Scott was right behind her, his breath loud in her ear. She lay on the ground and wriggled forward until she found the right spot. The loosely packed soil only took a minute to scoop out.

Scott lifted the barbed wire. She crawled under and rolled clear, her face brushing the grass. The dew was just starting to settle.

Scott flung his jacket over the fence. 'Hurry up,' he said. 'No need to stop and smell the bloody roses.'

She knelt, wound his jacket around her right hand, used her left to support her right wrist and pulled up the bottom row of wire as high as she could. He was almost through when he caught the back of his shirt on a barb. She heard the fabric tear.

'Stop,' she said. 'You'll have to take it off or the whole thing will rip.'

The first sweep of the searchlight grazed the grass verge, missing them by a couple of inches.

'Get down,' Scott said.

'I can't let go of the wire,' Griffin said. 'You'll be punctured by the barbs.'

The light swept passed them again and, in the distance, dogs began to bark.

Scott fumbled with the buttons and wriggled out of his shirt, scraping his chest against the ground. As soon as he was through Griffin let the fence go. She unwound his jacket and threw it to him. He lay face down on the grass, breathing heavily. Just above his shoulder blades his skin was cut and there was a trickle of blood.

'Don't worry about the shirt,' he said.

Griffin pulled it free. It was ripped beneath the collar and across the shoulders. 'I'll mend it when we get back.'

The searchlight roamed past them once more and the barking of the dogs sounded louder.

Scott began to slither on his stomach then he crawled on the berm beside the fence line, heading towards the main entrance and the road. Griffin crouched by the fence holding his shirt in her hand. He stopped when he realized she wasn't behind him, turned around and crawled back.

'What are you doing?'

'I need to check out the windmills.'

'Why?'

Griffin shook her head. 'Wait for me behind the hedge by the main entrance. If I'm not back by dawn just go.'

Scott wiped the dirt off his mouth and cheeks with the sleeve of his jacket. He was shivering without his shirt. 'I'll come with you.'

'No, you're cut – if they let the dogs out they'll smell your blood. I won't be long.' She rolled up his shirt and gave it to him. 'I'll be fine.'

There were three windmills spaced evenly in the large paddock and, scattered between them, six large hives. The closer Griffin got to the windmills the more she could hear the whirring of paddles and the creaking of sails in the breeze. Sheep grazed in the paddock and a couple of horses, one white, the other dark brown, stood, ghost-like, a few feet in front of the largest windmill. All I need now, she thought, is Don Quixote and Sancho, and the picture will be complete. She stood completely still by the wooden fence looking at the horses and at the sails moving behind them.

Something didn't make sense. Moreporks hooted in the windbreak of pines on the western side of the paddock. She concentrated on the sails and let her mind go blank. After a minute she realized they were turning much faster than the light breeze could propel them. But there was no sound of machinery, no hum of electricity nor rumble of a generator. Someone must be inside turning them manually. While she stood in the dark and watched, the sails of the largest windmill began to speed up while those on the other two slowed and finally stopped. A cry rang out and the white horse raised its head and whinnied. She crouched down. There was another cry, more desperate than the first, then a low, muffled groan of pain. A door opened in the front of the largest windmill. The sails stopped, as if someone had applied a brake. Two men stood in the dimly lit doorway facing Griffin. One was bareheaded; the other wore a brown cap. Both were broad-shouldered, well-muscled, well fed. They stepped across the threshold and into the paddock. The horses stopped grazing and moved out of their way towards the fence line. Griffin lay on the ground, trying to make herself invisible. She held her breath. The men turned their backs, faced the windmill and looked up at the sails. She rolled over and squinted through the fence rail.

The bareheaded man shouted something and the sails moved a half turn then stopped again. The man in the cap walked back to the doorway and lifted a long wooden pole from a hook. A curved metal prong attached at one end glinted in the light. Bile rose in Griffin's throat. She put her hand to her mouth and bit hard on her thumb to stop herself crying out. The man with the cap carried the pole back, lifted it above his head and slashed at the closest sail. Griffin heard the soft thud of a body hitting the ground. He poked at it with the blunt end of his pole, turning it over till it lay a few feet from the door. The bareheaded man said something to him and laughed. They stepped over the body, went back inside and shut the door.

Griffin rubbed her hands up and down her arms to stop herself shaking. A strange mantra beat in her mind: all this way, all this way. She crouched on the ground and banged her fist on the dew-covered grass. Her vision rippled and shimmered. The earth seemed to tilt. She was colder than she had ever been, her bones turned to ice, her skin numb and mushed as melting snow. Time merged and separated, trapping her in an invisible dance. Windmills turned. The slap of canvas sails beat in her ears. Bees swarmed above her head.

Four men walked away from the village through thickening fog, along the beach to the caves, carrying two blankets between them, one cradling the broken body from the windmill, the other hiding clothes, boots, two muskets and two bayonets. They knew soldiers had taken their land and settled in their cottages. They didn't know who the dead man was but considered him a brother and would place his bones in the caves with the remains of the rest of their kin. Tomorrow night they would return and each night after that until, one by one, they had picked the soldiers off, cut out their hearts and thrown their butchered carcasses, piece by piece, to the screaming gulls.

Griffin saw the door open again. A shaft of yellow light lit up the bloodied clothes that covered broken flesh and bones. Two boys, no more than ten or eleven, came out and heaved the body onto a stretcher made from a strip of canvas supported by wooden poles. They carried it across the paddock to the windbreak of pines. Sheep scattered as they stumbled across the rough grass. The horses shook their manes and moved further into the shelter of trees. The boys took the lid off a shallow drinking trough and dumped the body in it. They stood for a minute holding the ends of the empty stretcher, sniffing and shivering in the cool night air. They were under-nourished, barefoot and even from the distance of the opposite fence line Griffin could smell their fear. The horses came out from beneath the trees. They nudged at the boys, rubbing their noses against their faces. The boys dropped the stretcher, put their arms around the horses and laid their heads against their necks.

Her mother's voice exploded in her head: Go! Go now! Before the men come to take the boys back inside. Before Scott weakens and endangers the girls. Before you're caught and strung up on the windmill.

She saw Jason standing in his doorway, his hand raised in salute as she walked away. She saw his nephew, Liam, his auburn hair shining under the lamplight as he sat at Joseph's kitchen table and went through the comments his uncle had made. You're good at this, he'd said. You can find the connection. Come back and we'll work with you. She'd been on her own since she was twelve years old she'd said, she didn't need anyone telling her what to do. But she hadn't understood until now how hard it was. How mixed up. How dangerous.

The horses snickered. The boys dropped their arms from around their necks. The door opened.

Griffin ran.

JASON

10 months later

It was dark; my chest hurt. The claws of a creature I couldn't identify gouged my belly.

'Liam,' I called. 'Liam.'

When I woke again I was still in the study but the pain had gone. My chest was bound tightly with crepe bandages. Liam was by my side, sitting on a kitchen chair; Griffin was at the foot of the bed, chewing her thumbnail.

'I was scared you weren't coming back,' she said.

I managed a shallow breath, not wanting to push too hard against the bandages. 'What's the time?'

Liam checked his watch. 'After three. I gave you something to ease the pain, to help you sleep.'

Drugs of any kind were scarce, especially morphine. I didn't care and wouldn't ask where Liam got it. There was nothing to be done except rest, and hope, if things got too bad, Liam would let me go.

Most of my time now was spent lying on the bed in my study, my mind drifting between the past and the present. I sifted through memories, trying to recapture the shape and taste of my visions and journeys. I slept on and off, and dreamed, and often woke confused, resurfacing on a familiar tide of anxiety. Liam or Griffin sat with me when my longing to return to Aretis and to see Aja and her companions overwhelmed me. Often, I woke to find my face wet with tears.

I was too frail now to fulfil my old role as archaeologist, even if I'd had the strength of mind to navigate the shift. And that mysterious coil that had once compressed and expanded behind my diaphragm had collapsed some time ago. All I could do was describe how it had been to Griffin, how I'd nurtured that springboard and used it to plot search-and-return journeys as if I were an ancient Polynesian navigator.

I dozed. Drifted. Images of giant water creatures rose and fell in my mind: whales surfacing for air off the coast of Kaikōura; the massive octopus I'd read about that Kupe was reported to have slain on his voyage to Aotearoa all those centuries ago; the elegant manta rays I'd seen swimming in Northland bays when I was a boy and, rising out of the darkness of the river, rising again out of the great southern lake, the huge brown and gold head of the largest snake I'd ever seen, a creature I'd never thought possible to imagine. Aja and Vellen had called him Anisth, Grandfather Anisth, Guardian of the Northern Gate – the one who stitched together the corners of the world. I could still see the waves washing against the broken-down pier, Aja and the Captain standing arm and arm, knees bent, feet wide apart, bracing themselves against the rising wind and water. Uzra on his knees on the wet wooden planks, trying to cradle Vellen in his arms; Anisth, his head rearing out of the water, flicking his electric tongue, knocking Vellen out of Uzra's arms. Nothing, before or since, had frightened me so much, or moved me more.

I'd returned to Aretis only once after seeing that, but I was the faintest presence, wraith-like, unable to do more than float like dust on the breeze, without strength to coalesce into something solid. I caught glimpses of Aja, herding goats on the scrubby hillside above her village, checking her beehives, a dark-haired baby strapped on her back. A teenage boy ran ahead of her; smoke from the communal oven rose in a white plume behind her. As I got closer she'd stopped walking and sniffed the air. She smiled and breathed deeply, pleased to sense a familiar scent on the breeze.

Vellen's home in the caves above the village was impenetrable, the air inside too moist, too dense to enter. I waited until the full moon rose in the sky, hoping she might come to the surface, but all I saw was Aja and a white-haired man – the Captain, aged but still vigorous – scattering sunflower seeds at the entrance. They left a small jar of dark honey and some flat bread baked that morning. I stayed until dawn, listening to the sounds of the river below the village, watching the moonlight touch the dun-coloured thatched roofs of their round huts and their vegetable gardens. I saw the small, steady glow from the kiln Aja used to fire her pots.

The memory of Aja standing on the hillside sniffing the air with such contentment was close to my heart. I returned to it in the small hours of the early morning when I couldn't sleep, noting the look of happiness on her face; and I remembered the effort it took for me not to disappear completely.

On that last visit to Aretis, as I struggled to direct my energy or hold an image steady in my mind, I thought of Stephen. Lying in the darkness by the river, I wasn't able to build the tension I needed to coil and spring, and I wondered if that was what had happened to Stephen. Perhaps the river had claimed him. It had almost claimed me. I'd already started to sink, to disappear into the water, until the Captain came down to the river and sat on the smooth, round stones close to the water's edge. His joints were stiffer, his hands no longer able to grip the curved sword of his office as tightly or wield it with his former strength. He'd eased himself onto the largest stone, stretched out his legs and rubbed his knees. He was my last chance. I nudged the circle of energy surrounding the Captain, testing its density. I only needed the smallest amount to gain enough momentum to hurl myself back across the border.

As I absorbed some of the Captain's energy, images ensnared me. An ancient stone carving of a man raised its head and stared at him; shafts of light sliced and shimmered across desert sands; the cold mountain waters of the river washed over him, numbing his head, arms and legs. The Captain stood in a hospital ward while a nurse pulled back the sheet from a woman's face, her shoulders and neck covered in a livid purple rash. He watched as Aja stood in the sun and fanned her wet hair across her shoulders; he gripped Aja's hand as she laboured to give birth; stood outside a round hut and held his daughter in his arms, raising her to catch the first light of her first day.

The Captain had shivered and pressed his hands to his temples. He pushed himself up from the riverbank. I coiled and sprang. The wooden bridge across the river was streaked with light. I merged with the light and landed on the other side, entered my physical body again, gasping for air, heart tearing in my chest, holding onto the Captain's memories of Aja. I should've let them go, released them before I crossed the border. I knew now they'd weakened me, drained my strength and, no doubt, the Captain's too. Ever since, something had been sucking my vital energies. It had been wrong of me to take what belonged to the Captain but, somehow, I just couldn't let them go.

GRIFFIN

Griffin sat in the kitchen with Liam drinking tea. 'That was close,' she said. 'I could feel him slipping. Something was pulling him down, sucking him into itself. His chest and back were bruised as if he'd been beaten up. It wasn't just his heart.'

Liam drained his cup. He looked so tired she wondered if he'd fall asleep at the table.

'Put your head down for a couple of hours,' she said. 'I can manage.'

Liam scratched his scalp. His faded auburn hair fell out of its ponytail. He let it fall across his face and shoulders and massaged the back of his neck. 'I'll get some fresh air,' he said. 'Take the dogs for a walk. See Joseph and Scott. Check if there's any news.'

Griffin reached into a cloth bag lying on the floor by her chair. She pulled out four sheets of paper, folded them over and gave them to him. 'Can you give these to Scott? I promised I'd get them to him last week.'

Liam stood up and stretched. 'More recipes?'

Griffin yawned. 'My grandmother's. He wants them for Jesse.'

Liam took the pages and put them in the inside pocket of his jacket. He filled a bottle with water, screwed the cap tight and wiped it down with a tea towel.

'Ask Flame what he wants in exchange for more ginger beer,' Griffin said.

Griffin slept and dreamed she was running barefoot across dusty fields at the end of summer. She wore a faded blue dress over a thin white shift. The sun was warm on her back and shoulders; the air full of the scent of wild thyme. Her hair was long and loose and swung behind her as she ran. Two others ran with her, friends from the village that lay outside the monastery walls. They were laughing and calling her name – Rosa. In her hand she carried a posy of wild herbs she'd gathered from the fields on the edge of the forest. When she reached the main gate of the monastery she turned and waved goodbye to her friends; then she slipped inside the walls, smoothed her hair, shook dust from her skirt and walked towards the apothecary's gardens.

'Father,' she called, 'Father Anselmo, I've got the herbs you wanted.'

When she woke, Griffin was left with the image of an old man with a white tonsure walking towards her through the last golden rays of evening light, and she thought, I've never in this world been as happy as that.

LIAM

Liam handed the recipes to Scott. 'Joseph tells me The Flock now have over a hundred beehives,' he said.

'Jesse hasn't mentioned anything,' Scott said. 'But she wouldn't, given all her letters are read before they're sent.'

'Do you think it's true?

Scott handed Liam a mug of Flame's homebrew. 'Two boys were rescued from the Helensville farm last week– half-starved and terrified. Both of them had arms covered in bee-stings.'

Liam gripped the mug of beer against his diaphragm. The last of his energy drained out of him and he swayed on his feet.

Scott grabbed the mug. 'Sit,' he said, pushing a chair towards him.

'Are the boys alright?'

'Touch and go.'

'Have they said anything?'

'Flame won't let anyone near them, not until they're stronger.'

Liam nodded. He yawned so hard his eyes watered. 'Sorry,' he said. 'I need to sleep for a couple of hours.'

Scott gathered a pillow and blanket from his mattress on the floor and pointed at the old sofa. 'More comfortable there,' he said.

Liam curled his body around the lumpy squabs of the sofa, pulled the blanket over his legs and slept, the sound of bees buzzing in his ears.

JASON

Outside the open window the sky began to lighten, changing from grey to pale blue. I watched the last quarter of the moon fade and clouds gather. The sound of the bees came long before I saw them. Once they appeared, they swarmed over the dilapidated hives in my neighbour's backyard. They circled the hives twice before rising above the roof of the old cottage, moving off across the street and disappearing towards the hills. Silver-Jean had left me the cottage in her will and it had been empty ever since her death. Liam wanted to pull down the house and hives and turn the property into a vegetable and herb garden. It was a good idea but, somehow, I'd always found an excuse to leave it just as it was. Sometimes I went over, unlocked the backdoor and stood in the kitchen, imagining Silver-Jean sitting at the table, drinking sweetened tea while she shows me her latest watercolour. What would she think of the bees coming back, huge and dangerous, unless, like me, you were somehow immune to their sting?

The bees had returned a few months ago, not long after Liam told me about the two boys Flame's cooperative had rescued. Last week, when they were more or less recovered, Scott had brought them over to visit. They were small and skinny, their arms still bandaged but the rest of their skin and their hair looked healthy, and Scott reported they'd both gained weight in the last few weeks. Griffin sat outside with them under the cabbage trees letting them pat the aging labradors.

'They say The Flock has over fifty hives at the Helensville farm,' Scott said.

I'd propped myself up higher on my pillows so I could look out the study windows into the garden. 'Are they making honey?'

'According to the boys, only ten of the hives have honey – that's how their arms were so badly stung. They were sent to get it, with only their faces covered.'

'Where have the bees come from? More importantly, why have they returned now?'

Scott walked over to the windows and squinted towards the western range. 'Rumours say they've come from the west coast, out of the densest areas of bush. Some of the stories are pretty wild – bees the size of your hand; huge swarms arriving to feast on manuka flowers; bees that attack some people but not others.'

I thought of Silver-Jean, sitting in her cottage, weeping because her husband Joel had never returned. He'd been warned how dangerous his trip was, and no one had been prepared to spend time or resources searching for his body. She'd been convinced a feral dog had killed him – she'd dreamt of wolves – but nobody really knew what had happened.

I looked at Scott. 'If The Flock can have beehives then I guess we can too.'

'Do you know any beekeepers?'

'No, but if we put word out through Joseph, we might find someone.'

I thought about the two boys, almost recovered, and now, I hoped, immune to bee stings. I could have the cottage and hives repaired, the backyard cleared, more manuka planted, a garden dug. If the boys were trained properly, supervised and given the right protective gear, they could take over the hives, earn a living as they got older, and survive away from The Flock. Silver-Jean would like that, her old home nurturing bees, making honey again. I would talk to Liam and Griffin.

LIAM

Liam removed the green and yellow shawl that covered the piano and opened the lid. He sat on the old wooden stool from his childhood, straightened his back and spread his hands across the keys: he chose his mother's arrangement of 'Moonlight Serenade', his grandfather's favourite piece of music. As he played, his mother's presence filled the room. He could feel the pressure of her hand on his shoulder, the way it had when he was a boy practising his scales and learning his first set pieces. She'd been a gentle teacher but surprisingly firm, and he'd learned quickly, at first wanting to please her, then enjoying being able to play for its own sake.

'He's dying, Mum,' he whispered, 'and there's nothing I can do.'

GRIFFIN

Griffin sat in the old armchair in her bedroom listening to Liam playing the piano. He'd played that piece of music a number of times in the last few weeks. She checked she had paper and pencils close by then closed her eyes and let herself sink. At first there was nothing, just darkness and the sound of her breathing, and in the distance, the faint sound of the piano. She waited. A pinprick of light appeared on the outer edge of her vision. She drew the light towards her. When it was close enough to touch she opened it and stepped inside. She was in a clearing, looking up into the foliage of a large oak tree. The sun was warm on her head and shoulders. Her feet were hot from walking in her new sandals. She bent down to loosen the stiff leather straps.

Vines sprang out of the ground. They reached out for her, their long sticky tendrils wrapping round her ankles and shins then shooting up to her knees. She tried to pull them off but they were stuck fast to her bare skin. She needed a knife to cut them before they could merge with her flesh and their spores enter her bloodstream. The vines had surrounded her so suddenly, they were everywhere now; there was nowhere to run. Her legs started to swell; her veins stung as the tiny spores invaded her body. She pushed her hands away from her sides and tore at the vines as they crept up her torso and chest. But they were faster and stronger. My throat, she thought, when they reach my throat they'll choke me and I'll die.

'Help, she shouted, 'Father Anselmo, help me.'

Through the gloom of fast-growing vine leaves she saw the flash of his brown robe and white hair.

'Rosie-girl, what are you doing?' He rushed towards her. 'Blessed mother! You've disturbed the devil's vine. Stay still. I'll have to cut you out.'

He opened the leather pouch attached to the plaited cord around his waist; scooped out a handful of charcoal ash and threw it on the vines writhing at her feet. They shrank like startled snakes and began to wither. Two steps closer and he was slashing at the vines around her ankles and rubbing handfuls of ash on her shins and calves. The vines loosened their grip and began to drop from her legs.

'Here,' he said, giving her the pouch, 'rub the ash on your skin, it will help the swelling go down.'

Her hands shook so much the first handful scattered across her knees and fell on the ground. Tears trickled down her face.

'Now, now, Rosie-girl,' Father Anselmo said. 'You're safe now. The stinging will stop once we get you home and bathed. I'll give you some poppy syrup to take the pain away and help you sleep.' He finished cutting the vines from her chest and shoulders, pulled them away from her clothes and threw the shrunken leaves and stems on the ground. 'We might have to cut an inch or two off your hair, sweetheart, just to make sure there are no stray spores.' He took the pouch back off her and sprinkled the last of the ash on the ground by their feet. His arm went around her shoulders. 'See, it's almost gone. Soon it will be like it never happened.'

Rosa watched as the vines shrivelled back into the earth. In less than two minutes all that was left were patches of charcoal ash. 'Father, why did they wake up? I've walked this way so many times and nothing's ever happened. I was just standing here watching the birds build their nests.'

Father Anselmo squeezed her shoulder. 'Never mind Rosie, just make sure you never come on your own again. If you're walking by yourself go the long way round.' He scratched the front of his tonsure then plucked at his hair with his fingers. A curled vine leaf fell to the ground. 'And just in case, even if you're with others, always carry a knife and some charcoal ash.'

Griffin opened her eyes and stretched out her hand for her pencil. She wrote everything down as quickly and accurately as she could, feelings of panic still fluttering in her chest and belly. The vines had appeared out of nowhere. If Father Anselmo hadn't turned up when he did, she – Rosa – would have suffocated. Griffin sensed that Father Anselmo kept a close eye on her, determined to protect her as long as he could. She made a note to herself: next time, enter through FA.

Liam had finished playing 'Moonlight Serenade' and the house was quiet. Griffin had left Jason resting in his study and hoped he'd fallen asleep. He slept so little these days, a few hours in the early morning, and a nap in the afternoon. She'd sat with him throughout the morning, reading and chatting to him, trying to tempt him to have some soup. He'd taken a few mouthfuls, declared it delicious but not eaten any more. His vertigo was getting worse; even lying down, he said, the room swirled and pulsated; sitting for any length of time made him feel as though someone was rocking his head in one direction and pulling the room in another. The bruises on his chest and abdomen hadn't faded either.

She read through her notes. She would go through them with him tonight if he wasn't too tired.

JASON

I pushed myself higher up on the pillows – far enough so I wasn't staring at the ceiling, but not so upright the room started to spin. Sweat broke out on my forehead. My hands trembled. No longer could I write more than a poor signature. My new will, drawn up with Liam and Griffin's agreement yesterday, sat on the desk. The house was to be shared equally between the two of them. Silver-Jean's property was to go to Flame and Scott's cooperative, for the development of gardens and hives to employ refugees from The Flock.

Griffin came in with another bowl of soup. My whole body shook. 'Rosie,' I said.

She put the bowl on the desk and ran to get Liam.

They held me upright while I had a few mouthfuls of the soup then let me sink back into the pillows.

Liam bent over me. 'Do you need morphine?'

'Not yet.'

They sat beside me, Liam by my head with a hand on my shoulder, Griffin by my side, her hand resting lightly on my chest.

I reached for her, clutched her fingers. 'Take me with you.'

Her eyes widened. She looked at Liam and raised her eyebrows.

'What would you like to do, Uncle?' he said.

'Take me to Father Anselmo.'

Liam lay on the bed beside me, something he hadn't done since he was a child. He cupped my back and legs with his body, wrapping his arms around me, resting my head against his shoulder.

Griffin held my hand.

'Don't cry, Rosie-girl,' I said.

We flew beneath mountain ranges, two hawks on a clear, late summer morning. The valley lay curled and sleeping, the only plume of smoke coming from the communal oven in the centre of the village. Aja was white-haired and a little stooped, standing outside her hut to greet the dawn, her shoulders wrapped in a blue woollen shawl. We flew past the captain's grave, high on the hillside overlooking the river. Four children climbed the hills, laughing and chasing each other, and goats climbed even higher, searching for the sweetest grasses. We entered the caves where Vellen laboured, singing to herself as she harvested crystals, producing just enough pellets to keep Grandfather Anisth alive. Even he was older now, his strength diminished. But while all the other gates were crumbling, the Northern remained intact. Only Vellen knew in which part of the caves Uzra's bones were buried. His son, Otmas, oversaw the extraction of coal from the caves and guarded the firelighters Uzra had saved by hiding them in caches all over the valley.

We flew south, following the trajectory of the river to the coast. The sea sparkled. Small boats with blue sails moved out across harbours to fish in the open sea; larger boats with white sails carried passengers, food and fuel between northern and southern ports. At the southernmost tip of the island we circled an abandoned city and a lake with deep turquoise water. The remains of a wooden pier jutted from the shore. Gulls squawked and shrieked. The shoreline was dotted with pumice stones. We hovered for a moment then flew out to sea leaving the island behind.

We travelled for a day and a night and came upon a land blessed with forests and many birds, with fields for grazing animals and fields furrowed for planting, and we flew on until we reached the monastery walls where we landed in the branches of a rowan tree that grew beside the apothecary's garden and dispensary. Father Anselmo was stretched out on his cot in his cell beside the dispensary, his breath laboured. Rosie sat beside him, sponging his face and chest with a rosemary-infused cloth. Prayers had been said; he'd been anointed with holy oil. Monks were singing in the chapel. In the garden the huge faces of sunflowers were heavy with seeds. Every two hours Rosie trickled a little more poppy syrup onto his tongue and gave him a sip of water.

We waited in the rowan tree until Father Anselmo slipped into unconsciousness and Rosie walked outside for a moment to get some air. She looked up at us, perched on the top branches of the tree.

'So, it's true then, you've come back, you strange pair.' She shook her head at the sight of us. 'Perhaps you're angels in disguise, for whoever saw two hawks sitting together?' She rolled her shoulders and arched her back, stiff after sitting for so long. 'He said you would, but I thought he was being fanciful, drifting on a dream from the poppy seed.'

We flew in through the open door and landed on his cot, one on either side of his head. Rosie waited by the door, head bowed, hands clasped together. We fanned our wings then settled beside him, blinked and closed our eyes.

In my study, Griffin squeezed my hand gently, then she let go. I entered

Father Anselmo's waning energy and settled in the space between his breaths. Anselmo stirred; muttered *requiescat in pace* – rest in peace. He drew another difficult breath and then another. I breathed with him, feeling the rattle growing in his lungs. I saw a stone man and the liquid darkness of a wide, deep river. Grandfather Anisth flicked his electric tongue; Aja spooned goat stew into my swollen mouth. My mother, Anastasia, danced barefoot in the kitchen and held my father in her arms. Helene sat at the piano, giving a public recital, the scars on her wrists covered with long white gloves. Jenny entered my study carrying a cup of tea, her body wrapped in a blue silk robe that shimmered like water when she moved. She touched the side of my face with the back of her finger. Liam curled into the small of my back, patting my shoulder with his small boy's hand. Griffin stood on the doorstep and thrust a bundle of papers at me. Rosie stood in the doorway, the light from the setting sun a halo illuminating her hair. Father Anselmo's breath faltered. She came to his side and reached for his hand. I felt myself begin to disassemble, my cells entering the final stages of their disintegration. I took a jagged breath. In what was left of my mind I returned to my mother's study and to the image of Blue Marble – that jewel shining in the darkness of space.

Words floated up and out, a final exhalation: *Sometimes I think I've spent my life learning how to change gear, to shift from one state to another. And sometimes I think I've fallen into a no-man's land, and I wander, ghost-like and grieving, unable to find my way home…*

My heart burst open to embrace the globe. A speck of stardust, I saw my life, my brief moment of being and knowing, reflected in time's reptilian eye.

Blue Marble glowed, waiting, as always, to welcome me home.

Acknowledgements

I'd like to thank all those generous souls who over the years read and gave feedback on earlier drafts and sections of this novel including Anne Kayes, Bronwen Hughes, Jane Scott and all those members of both writing groups I have belonged to. Most of all, thanks to my sister Erin, who has always given considered helpful feedback and support.

Many thanks to Sandra Morris Illustration Agency for putting me in contact with Amandine Riera who designed such a wonderful book cover and to David Lawson for allowing me to use his photo as part of the front cover. Thanks also to Chris Watton from Write Choice for line editing and proof-reading and to fellow writers Kirsten Warner and Leanne Radojkovich for their letters of support.

Finally, thanks to the team at Cloud Ink Press and in particular to Helen McNeil for believing in this book.

About the Author

Trisha Hanifin has lived most of her adult life in Auckland where she has worked in adult and community education, specialising in adult literacy. A graduate of the Masters of Creative Writing programme at AUT in 2010 (first class honours), her writing has won several awards and been published in a number of literary journals and anthologies including *Landfall, Bonsai: Best small stories in Aotearoa New Zealand, Flash Frontier, Headland* and *Turbine*.

In 2019 the unpublished manuscript of *The Time Lizard's Archaeologist* was awarded second place in the Ashton Wylie Mind Body Spirit awards. It is her first novel.

Find out more at trishahanifin.com